A TOUCH OF MADNESS IN
THEIR DANCE

"Take care what you're about—I might demand payment," Mycroft cautioned.

I was in no mood for caution. The night had gone beyond such tame stuff. "And what payment would you demand, sir?" I asked archly.

His eyes stared into mine unflinchingly. "Just what you think, Mrs. Audry."

Then the music swelled and we began a swirling dance, crinoline swaying as my feet moved on wings over the floor. Of course it was the champagne that lent that touch of madness to our dance. That feeling that nothing mattered but the music and the waltz and being in Mycroft's arms. Especially being in Mycroft's arms, where I felt safe. It was about the most treacherous place I could possibly be, but the solidity of his warm chest against mine, the strength of his arms holding me, his very presence was a bulwark against despair.

His black eyes were devouring me. We were back at the door where we had begun. He spun through the opening and pulled me hard against him. Before I knew what was happening, his head came down and his lips plundered mine in a ruthless kiss . . .

Other Leisure Books by Joan Smith:

DESTINY'S DREAM
SILVER WATER, GOLDEN SAND
EMERALD HAZARD

JOAN SMITH

A WHISPER ON THE WIND

LEISURE BOOKS ▌▌ NEW YORK CITY

A LEISURE BOOK®

April 1990

Published by

Dorchester Publishing Co., Inc.
276 Fifth Avenue
New York, NY 10001

CHAPTER ONE

WHEN I LOOK BACK ON IT, I THINK OF IT AS BEGINNING IN Paris, but actually Paris was just the bearing of the fruit. The roots run much deeper, their origin obscured by time and distance. But for practical purposes, the story began in Paris, on a bench by the Seine River.

Overhead and along the quai, stately chestnuts were in bloom, their white cones nestling among the green, like candles on a Christmas tree, so beautiful. Sunbeams sifted through the leaves, dappling the Seine with dancing circles of light. Two mud-colored ducklings bobbed so close to shore I was tempted to reach down and gather their soft fluff into my hands. Paris's sun was warmer than London's, its breezes more romantic, its people more interesting. And I knew that when I lifted my eyes, I would be enraptured by the image of Notre Dame.

I made myself wait a moment, savoring the thrill, before looking up and across the water. Then I slowly raised my eyes, and felt goosebumps lift the hair on my arms as I beheld the cathedral. Twin towers soared heavenward into the azure sky, while the stone bulk of medieval flying buttresses reached out to hold them to the ground. There it had stood, a fortress against the elements and revolution for hundreds of years, and there it would stand when I was dead and buried. I was actually in Paris. Any wonderful thing could happen. Something was bound to happen.

"Look at the filth on the streets," Miss Williams complained, pointing the steel tip of her umbrella at a paper flying past on a gust of wind.

I refused to look at garbage. "Raise your eyes and look at Notre Dame, Miss Williams," I suggested.

"I know that stone heap by heart," she said resignedly. "We've spent three afternoons staring at it. Let us go back to the hotel, Rosalie. I'd like a cup of tea, and what they call a sandwich in this place."

"Just a few minutes more," I sighed, and gazed on.

Miss Williams was not the optimum companion for a young lady's first trip to Paris. She was a good woman, and the closest thing to a mother I had ever known. She had made Papa and me an excellent housekeeper, me a kind governess and lately friend, but she wasn't Paris material.

I heard her sigh and lean forward to slide the umbrella behind her back, lest someone run past and snatch it. Miss Williams had no good opinion of the human race, of which she considered the French a subspecies. But then life had not treated her kindly. It is a great misfortune in a poor woman to have no looks to recommend her. My companion was thin-faced with hair a mousy brown, shading to gray over the years. The lines in her forehead had increased, and the grooves etched from nose to mouth had deepened to ruts.

One day I would be old too, but today I was young, and in Paris. My heart soared with joy. · What more could anyone ask of life? My mirror told me I was not ugly; my vanity whispered that with the proper clothing and hairdo, I could be beautiful. Blonde curls and deep blue eyes were my major physical attractions. The major detraction was a somewhat lean body, made even more insignificant by a dowdy gown.

My father had been in his grave for a year, but Miss Williams felt that navy blue did his memory more honor than brighter colors. She had given in on this holiday in Paris, so I gave in on the toilette and chose subdued shades. As she so practically pointed out, "They'll be more serviceable when you come home. If you plan to spend so much of your inheritance on a holiday, you'll have to work after you get back, Rosalie."

Yes, I would have to work, but not yet. There were still ten lovely days of breathing in the air of Paris before the return to reality. My father left me all he had, which was enough to eke out a respectable existence in a couple of rooms for the rest of my life. He had worked in India, but had not returned a nabob. As a bank clerk in London after his return, his wages were small. After this reckless trip, I would have to do a little genteel work of some sort—sewing or millinery—unless or until I married.

Willard Henshaw was the major, though not the only, suitor. He came courting two evenings a week to our little apartment on Watling Street, bringing bonbons or a small bouquet of flowers. Some evenings I played the piano and Willard sang, with Miss Williams tapping her toe as she watched us. Willard worked in the bank like my late father. Having started younger, he would rise higher than Papa. But in my deepest heart of hearts, I did not want to rise with him on sparrow's wings. I wanted to soar like an eagle with some romantic stranger. The sort of stranger that could best be met in Paris.

My view of Notre Dame was interrupted at regular intervals by passing pedestrians. I hardly glanced at them, but I happened to look at one young gentleman as he stopped right in my line of sight. My first reaction was annoyance, but as my eyes focused on his back, I felt the rising tingle of interest.

A black top hat, shiny and new, sat at a cocky angle. Below the hat, a pair of blue shoulders stretched wide, before tapering to a neat waist. The man was about six feet tall. My curiosity rose to admiration, and I wished he would turn around. As though attuned to my thoughts, he turned his gaze across the river, revealing a handsome profile. My chest tightened as I stared at a brow high and noble, a Roman nose chiseled to perfection, a strong chin.

This could be the one, my romantic stranger. He turned in an idle way, his eyes just glancing off me. He nonchalantly tapped his walking stick against his gloved hand and walked on, only to stop a few steps further along. He looked English. His fair coloring and blue eyes suggested it. His walk, close to a strut, spoke of a gentleman who kowtows to no one.

"Shall we go now?" Miss Williams asked.

She had been patient with me. "Yes, let us go," I said.

Our hotel, the Vaillancourt, was a modest one on a little side street off Boulevard St. Germain. As we crossed the boulevard, Miss Williams let out a gasp of consternation.

"I've left my umbrella behind!"

"Oh, dear. We'd best go back for it."

"It would be picked up long ago in this place full of foreigners. Why waste good shoe leather?"

I saw what birthday present I must give Miss Williams. "We can share my umbrella if we go out in the rain."

The remainder of the trip back and half our tea were taken up with repining over the lost umbrella. "It was that young fellow loitering in front of us that made me forget it," she said. "I noticed him giving you the eye from yards away, trying to catch your attention. I was happy you didn't look at him."

"He was looking at us? He stopped there on purpose?" I exclaimed, in completely the wrong tone. Wild thoughts were given birth in that instant. He was a stranger in Paris, lonesome like us, wanting to speak but lacking the nerve. I wondered if Miss Williams had given him one of her scowls.

"He was looking in a surreptitious way," Miss Williams added meaningfully.

I soon modified it to a shy way. The man couldn't possibly have any villainous interest in us. We didn't stand out as wealthy tourists, nor loose ladies. If he had looked with interest, it was because I was a young lady, not unattractive. What golden opportunity had I let slip through my fingers?

"The bread is all crust, as usual," Miss Williams said, biting into a sandwich. "And the ham—if it weren't laced with this burning hot mustard, it would be inedible."

I nibbled the delicious sandwich. The ham was nut sweet, shaved to pink slivers and spiced with Dijon mustard. The bread was a heavenly cloud of air encased in crisp crust. I sipped tea, thinking of my romantic stranger. When he actually walked through the door a moment later, I thought I must be dreaming. With his top hat off, his well-shaped head was visible as he turned to speak to the waiter. He glanced around at the tables as though looking for someone.

My heart fluttered nervously and I looked away. It was impossible he was looking for us. Who, then? No one of his station was staying at this modest place. The stranger breathed an aura of monied elegance, utterly out of place amidst the bourgeoisie and poorer class of tourist.

Yet when his eyes met mine, I knew he had found who he was looking for, and my heart hammered like a drum. A soft smile curved his lips; he said a word to the waiter, handed him something, and was shown to a table not far from us. He sat behind Miss Williams, giving him and me a clear view of each other. I didn't taste another bite of my delicious sandwich. The waiter left the stranger and came to our table. My instinctive reaction was joy, tinged with anxiety. Miss Williams wouldn't countenance such a forward request for an introduction.

"The *anglais*, he finds madame's *parapluie*," the waiter said, and handed Miss Williams her beloved umbrella.

Her raddled face broke into creases of delight. "My umbrella! I have got my umbrella back, Rosalie. Who ever would have thought it? What gentleman . . ." She looked over her shoulder and spotted the finder. She lifted the well-worn umbrella to acknowledge its return, nodded, and smiled.

The stranger inclined his head, smiled back at her, and picked up the menu. "I'll thank him on the way out," she said daringly. Excitement lent a livid hue to her lean cheeks.

Over her shoulder, the vision raised its eyes and smiled a smile at me that had nothing to do with umbrellas. There was laughter in it, admiration, flirtation, a tacit statement that we two would meet before long. Excited, I spilt a little tea.

"So kind of him," Miss Williams said a few times. "An Englishman, the waiter said. It is the well-set-up fellow who strolled by when we were at the cathedral." No talk now of loitering or surreptitious looks.

"Is it the same man?" I asked innocently. Without looking at him, I knew every move he made. I saw from the corner of my eye as he spoke to the waiter, saw a bottle of wine being delivered to him, saw him taste it and nod. When the waiter filled his glass, I knew the stranger would raise it to me in a toast. I peeped; he raised the glass, and I hastily looked away. But not before I gave him a smile of encouragement.

Some uncharacteristic streak of friendliness possessed Miss Williams, and she turned around to smile at the stranger too.

It was enough encouragement for him. Within seconds, the waiter was at our table, asking if we would do monsieur the honor of sharing his wine.

"What, bring his bottle to our table?" Miss Williams asked in confusion. "That hardly seems —it would deprive him of a second glass. So gentlemanly. I think we ought to invite him to join us. What do you think, Rosalie?"

I thought monsieur had made the offer to achieve this very end, and lauded his ingenuity. "It seems the civil thing to do," I allowed as if doubtfully.

"He is English—that makes him seem less a stranger. I'll do it," she decided, and spoke to the waiter.

Monsieur wore a face of very well simulated surprise when he presented himself with the easy manners of a gentleman caught in an unusual circumstance.

"Please allow me to introduce myself. I am Mr. Audry," he said, speaking to Miss Williams. One would think from his performance that she was alone at the table. Not so much as a blink acknowledged that he had been flirting with me over her shoulder for ten minutes.

"I am Miss Williams. Pray allow me to present my charge, Miss Cummings," she replied. "Both from London."

"All three from London," he said, smiling, and took a seat. "We foreigners must stick together in foreign lands." It was a sentiment that found agreement with my companion.

"You've spoken the truth there," Miss Williams answered fervently. "I never thought to see my umbrella again, with all those Frenchies milling around the quai. What a stroke of luck that it was found by an honest Englishman."

Mr. Audry's sandwiches arrived and he soon caught up with us. "Are you in France on holiday or on business, Mr. Audry?" Miss Williams asked.

"A holiday," he replied. "I didn't feel like facing the Season at home. And you ladies, of course, are on holiday?"

"We're here for a month," Miss Williams confided. Before the wine bottle was empty, she had confided much more about our circumstances: my father's occupation, his death, Miss Cummings' desperation to see Paris.

"A romantic," he smiled. His eyes were the most beautiful things I had ever seen. They weren't the pale, washed-out blue so commonly seen at home, nor yet the more rare cornflower blue of my own. They had almost a tinge of green, like lapis lazuli, and were heavily fringed. Even Miss Williams was entranced by those frank eyes.

"What line of business are you in, Mr. Audry?" she asked.

"I dabble in various business ventures," he said vaguely. "Most of my capital comes from the East India Company."

"The EIC! Why, Miss Cummings' papa worked

9

for them in India!" she exclaimed. "Rosalie was actually born there." In her excitement, she used my Christian name.

"No!" His exclamation of delight gave voice to my own feelings. "My father worked for John Company too. He was with the governor of Madras province."

"That is where Rosalie's papa worked! This is incredible. Were you born there too?"

"Alas, no. I was born in London before my father left. I've never been to India. I remained at home with my mother."

"I don't remember anything about it," I told him. "I was only six months old when my parents left."

"Imagine, Rosalie, your fathers were very likely bosom bows, and here you and Mr. Audry have to come all the way to Paris to meet," Miss Williams exclaimed.

"But Paris is such a lovely place to meet," Mr. Audry said, with a smile that turned my insides to butter.

It was evident at a glance that Mr. Audry's father had held some exalted position in Madras, whereas my father had been only a clerk. They would not have been bosom bows, but it was possible they had met. My father seldom spoke of India. He was a taciturn man. Miss Williams said it had been so ever since my mother's death when I was three. The only memory I had of my mother was an ivory miniature in a locket, and a few trinkets. In the picture, she was pretty, in a dark-haired, dark-eyed way unlike myself. Her sweet expression reminded me of a dove.

A little later, Mr. Audry said to Miss Williams,

"What are you ladies planning to do this evening?"

His eyes slid toward me as he spoke. Mine slid to Miss Williams, to see her reaction to what I knew would come next.

"We stick pretty close to the hotel at night," she informed him. "Two ladies unaccompanied, you know."

"Paris only comes alive after dark!" he assured her. "You must allow me to show you Paris by night."

Whatever caused staid Miss Williams to accept his offer? Was it just the recovery of her cherished umbrella, or was there enough romance in her to feel Mr. Audry's magnetism? Subsequent events showed she was not totally devoid of feelings. After a judicious examination of her conscience, she agreed that we should accompany him to the opera that night.

Once she got her toe into the rarefied atmosphere of Parisian gaiety, Miss Williams lost all sense of inhibition. She was as eager as I to feast on the treats of Paris. With Fraser Audry—his name was Fraser—acting as our guide, we saw a Paris beyond my wildest imaginings. Every morning his carriage was waiting for us at the door of the Vaillancourt. We were whisked off to see the Tuileries and gardens, Versailles, the Trianon and the Louvre. We had picnics and lunches at outdoor cafés. In the evenings, we went to plays and to music halls and one evening to a private ball.

It was the Paris I had come to see. Nothing was lacking from my best daydreams. When we occasionally managed a moment alone, Fraser called me 'Rosie' and kissed my hand. It took him so long to try for an outing alone with me that Miss Williams and I became impatient with him. We soon had to return to London, but Fraser was to continue his trip on to Italy.

It was by the lake in the Bois de Boulogne that he proposed. I wore a new straw bonnet trimmed with cherries, and a blue sarsenet suit the color of the sky that day. Fraser said the gods had sent down a fragment of sky to clothe and claim me. He said it was my eyes that had led them astray. They had mistaken them for stars, and of course stars needed a sky.

I should have known then that the gods were jealous of me, and would wreak their revenge. No goddess on Olympus could be as happy as I when he said he loved me. A golden rush of joy surged through me. My body pulsed with rapture as I gazed at dear Fraser. So handsome, so gentlemanly, so in love with me that he couldn't wait to go home to London to get married.

"Can it be done in Paris?" I asked. But I knew that Fraser could do anything. He had stolen my heart, and fulfilled every craving.

"It must be done," he said simply. His eyes said more. "Give me your passport and I'll arrange it with the British embassy. You're not a child—you'll be twenty-one in six months. I'll find a British minister to perform the ceremony."

We drove straight to the Vaillancourt and told Miss Williams. Her thin face split wide in a smile.

"I'm so happy for you, Rosalie!" she exclaimed. "And you, Fraser. We'll go straight home and begin preparations."

"We're going to be married in Paris, Miss Williams," I told her, "and have our honeymoon in Europe."

"Oh, my!" she gasped, nearly overcome with my good fortune. "Then I must return home alone."

"No, no," Fraser assured her. "I'll find some English tourists for you to travel with. And after you get home, Miss Williams, you must take care of Rosie's belongings—have them packed up and ready for removal to my place. Your own as well," he added, a smile lighting his lovely eyes. "We insist that you live with us, don't we, Rosie?" His kindness in making this offer set the cap on his consideration and generosity.

"I wouldn't dream of battening myself on newlyweds," she told him, but with hope gleaming on her raddled face.

"We wouldn't dream of anything else," I assured her.

"We just want to be alone for a few months' honeymoon," Fraser said. "You understand, Miss Williams. Newlyweds . . ."

She understood completely, and approved. "How long do you plan to stay abroad?" she asked.

"About six months. I want to show Rosie the continent. Put a little meat on her bones," he added. Fraser insisted I was too slender. He wanted more of me to love, he said.

"Then I shan't renew the lease on the flat," she decided. "Shall I have Rosalie's things removed to your place, Fraser?"

"I've closed my place up and sent the servants off. We'll take care of that when we go home. We don't want to put you to any bother. You're on holiday, Miss Williams."

13

"I don't know if I should—I can always go to my sister after your marriage, Rosalie. We've spoken of it before."

"Nonsense," Fraser exclaimed. "My wife will want a female companion. Someone to go shopping with, and do all those feminine things. You are absolutely essential, Miss Williams."

We were all so happy that day. How the gods must have been laughing at us, from their Olympian heights.

CHAPTER TWO

THERE WAS NO TIME TO HAVE A WEDDING GOWN MADE up, but I was determined to have a new bonnet for my wedding. I chose a finely woven glazed straw with velvet ribbons and sprinkled with tiny velvet dots on the veil. The contoured rim framed my face like a picture. Strange how a trifle like a bonnet can change one's appearance. I looked like a lady of fashion when I stood in front of the mirror to judge the effect.

"It's rather dear," Miss Williams worried.

"Fraser is wealthy. In fact, he wants you to take all the money from our trip that is left, to tide you over in London." My eyes fell to the engagement ring he had given me, an antique solitaire of ten carats, belonging to his mother. For my wedding gift, he was giving me a more modern sapphire

15

necklace. I had already seen it, but he was having the catch repaired.

"How did you come to bring those things with you, Fraser?" Miss Williams enquired when he brought the necklace to show us.

"I didn't. I sent a special courier home for them the day I met Rosie," he admitted, blushing. "Presumptuous of me, but I'm an optimist."

That evening before dinner I modeled the bonnet for Fraser. He loved it. "We'll have some fashionable gowns made up, so that you arrive in London in style," he told me. "We'll have a coiffeur style your hair as well," he added, studying me. "I'd like to see those lovely golden locks waved in front, with a curl hanging over your shoulder, like in that Fragonard painting we saw at the Louvre."

"My hair's not long enough for that."

"Hair grows," he said, smiling. "You will grow it longer, for me." My heart nearly burst when he looked at me. His lapis lazuli eyes glowed with pleasurable anticipation. "I want to shower you with diamonds and furs, with silks and lace and put you in a palace," he said, his voice burred with love.

I felt like the heroine of a novel. Indeed I had always felt like one. A young lady born in exotic India wasn't destined to live out her days in a flat on Watling Street.

Our wedding took place on a beautiful morning in early May. From the window of the British embassy, we looked out on lime trees and a rose garden in bloom. White cotton clouds skimmed across the azure sky. A perfect day to get married—nature herself smiled on our union. Miss Williams and an embassy clerk acted as witnesses. We had no music, no flowers, no relatives, but afterwards Fraser, Miss Williams, and I repaired to the finest restaurant in Paris for a champagne lunch.

Miss Williams was quite tipsy when the Lalondes came to pick her up. Fraser couldn't find an English couple, but the Lalondes, French tourists who spoke English, agreed to see Miss Williams safely to London. Before they all left the Vaillancourt, I wrapped her frail body in my arms and hugged her. "We'll see you in London in October, Miss Williams. Take care of yourself. I am so very happy."

Through misty eyes she said, "You were right to insist on coming to Paris, Rosalie. I've been too cautious all my life, and very nearly destroyed your chance for happiness."

"I'll write often and describe our travels. You write to me too. We'll give you our destination a few weeks in advance."

Fraser joined us to take his leave of Miss Williams. "I'll put a wedding announcement in the London papers," she said. "Your friends will want to know, Rosalie." The name Willard Henshaw floated invisibly between us.

"No," Fraser objected. "I haven't told my family. I'd rather write to them first, if you don't mind, ladies."

We knew Fraser's parents were dead. His family consisted of cousins and aunts and uncles. I wondered if there was a female counterpart of Willard Henshaw in his life, who would grieve to read the announcement. Since the wedding, I felt very possessive about Fraser.

Miss Williams and the Lalondes were off, with a last shower of "bon voyage" and "be sure to write" and "au revoir." Fraser put his hand on my elbow and turned me toward him. "And now, Mrs. Audry, you and I are going to celebrate our wedding."

His eyes pierced me with love. A tender warmth washed through me at the image his words conjured up. In my daydreams, I had always pictured the intimate side of marriage occurring by candlelight. My head whirled from the champagne, and love.

We went to Fraser's hotel, a much grander place than the Vaillancourt, to consummate our marriage. My husband was gentle, and led me by slow degrees to respond to his ardor. It seemed strange at first—more physical and less enjoyable than I had thought, but I was determined to improve. After we made love, we got dressed and went for a sentimental look at the Seine where we had met just two weeks before.

"Imagine, Fraser, if Miss Williams hadn't forgotten her umbrella, you and I would never have met," I said. "I'm surprised you looked twice at me."

"I thought at first you were just a schoolgirl. You're so thin. You must fill out that lovely figure, my dear. A man likes to know he is holding a woman in his arms."

"I looked a perfect dowd in that round bonnet too," I added, more astonished than ever that he had bothered with me.

"We'll soon take care of your toilette. Tomorrow you and I, Mrs. Audry, are going on a marathon shopping spree, before we set off on our honeymoon. I want you to order gowns in every color of the rainbow—bonnets, gloves, slippers, peignoirs. We shall outfit you in the best, as you deserve."

Over the next week, the dream continued. I was

transformed into a fine lady. Our hotel suite was full of boxes and bags.

"I'm sorry for this mess," I apologized when the maid came to tidy us up.

After she left, Fraser said, "You don't have to apologize to servants, darling. They'll think you aren't accustomed to handling them."

"I'm not accustomed to it, Fraser."

"I know, dear. Pray don't take it amiss, but after we're home, you'll have your own staff to handle. It's best to learn while abroad, so that it will come more easily to you later."

"How many servants do you have?" I asked fearfully.

Fraser laughed. "Don't worry your head about it. When you can handle one, you can handle them all. Remember you are the mistress, and they are your servants, to do as you bid."

My life had suddenly changed drastically. Thus far it had been a romantic dream, but after the honeymoon was over, I would have to learn how to run Fraser's household. I practiced my lessons on the hotel servants. When a fashionable lady is staying in the best room, she is treated so regally that authority settles upon her. Yet Fraser thought my tone was not firm enough. "*Tell* them what to do, don't ask them," he said.

In the second week of our marriage my wardrobe was all assembled, and over dinner in the hotel dining room we discussed our wedding trip.

"Tomorrow's Saturday," Fraser said. "Sunday travel is frowned on, so we'll set out next week for Italy. It should be lovely in May. Not too hot, but more than warm."

A couple seated across the dining room had been looking at us while we ate. "Do you know those people?" I asked him. "Just under the window on your left—the lady and her companion."

Fraser glanced unconcernedly. They nodded and smiled at us. He looked displeased at finding them here. "It's the McCormacks, from London," he said. "I ran into them just after we married. They wanted to get together with us, but I put them off. I'm not ready to share you yet."

I was flattered, yet since Miss Williams' departure I hadn't any woman to confide in, and felt the lack. "We're leaving on Monday. We could just have lunch or dinner with them tomorrow," I suggested.

"Very well, if it will please you," he agreed.

The McCormacks got up to leave, and headed toward our table. I couldn't understand why Fraser was so upset, for they seemed a nice young married couple like ourselves.

"We shan't interrupt your dinner," Mr. McCormack said as they stopped at our table, "but we must all get together and lay some plans for exploring. Our room, in half an hour? Would that suit you and Rosie, Fraser?"

Fraser glanced at me. I smiled my agreement. Now that I was a married lady, I found my interest directed more at Mrs. McCormack than her husband. It was a friend and confidante I wanted. She looked a fashionable, good-natured creature.

"Fine, we'll meet in our suite soon then," Mrs. McCormack said. "See you there, Rosie. I hear you and Fraser are off to Italy, like Norm and me." How on earth did she know my name was Rosie? Fraser must have told her—but it was ill-bred for her to use my nickname so casually before we were even introduced. Yet Fraser hadn't blinked an eye when she said it. I began to suspect that the manners Miss Williams taught me would be useless in society. How free and easy people had become!

"We're not sure about Italy, Anne," Fraser objected. "It's just one possibility. You and Rosie can talk it over tonight."

As the McCormacks were blocking the aisle, they stopped for only a minute. Mrs. McCormack, whom I rather felt I should call "Anne," smiled at me before leaving. "We'll convince them to take us to Italy, eh, Rosie?" she said, laughing. "We've never had any trouble getting our own way before. I like your new hairdo," she said as Mr. McCormack drew her away.

Fraser smiled derisively. "Now you see why I wasn't eager to bring them down on your head. Calling you 'Rosie' as though she were a bosom bow, and I hadn't even introduced you yet! Norman's wife is so common. We shan't join them after dinner."

"Oh, let's," I said impulsively. "They seem friendly, and we have no friends here. We needn't see them in London."

We left, and after Fraser had written a note telling the McCormacks that I had a headache, he gave me a little lecture.

"It is always best to start an acquaintance as you wish to continue it. The McCormacks are not our class, my dear. They are vulgar, nouveau-riche merchants. I wouldn't visit them in London, and I will not lead them to invite me in London by calling on them in Paris."

I admitted that Mrs. McCormack's manners left much to be desired, yet it had felt good to hear a friendly voice.

"I'll take the note down myself and shove it under their door. It saves calling a servant to do it," Fraser said.

I was writing my weekly letter to Miss Williams when he returned. "You write the envelope. Your handwriting is so much finer than mine," I said, and Fraser was happy to oblige. He was proud of his flowery script. "My writing looks as though a ladybug fell into the inkpot and straggled across the sheet, leaving tracks behind," I said, frowning at it.

"Miss Williams taught you; she cannot complain. Since you don't do much letter writing, you should just develop a flowing signature, and all the world will think you write beautifully." As he spoke, Fraser's pen whirled across the page in a flourish of arabesques, writing the name Mrs. Fraser Audry.

"I couldn't possibly do all those flowing circles. Design me a more modest but still pretty signature."

It was an excuse to sit with our shoulders touching, with Fraser's hand guiding mine. When I could write Mrs. Fraser Audry in a creditable manner, he wrote Rosalie Audry, in more ornate calligraphy.

"It looks lopsided," he complained. "The first name's too long for the last. Rose Audry is more symmetrical."

"If the signature is to go on something legal, it better say Rosalie Audry, as that is my name."

"Rosalie is just a diminutive form of Rose," Fraser said pensively. "I daresay Rose would be a

22

legal signature for you. In any case, at banks and so on, you leave a specimen signature with them, signed as you will sign in future. Here, how do you like this signature?" he asked, showing me a striking one. The R of Rose and the A of Audry rose high and steeply slanted to the right, giving a dramatic look to the name.

"Oh, I like that! Let me try it."

He smiled fondly on me. "You know what a handwriting analyst would say?" he quizzed. "People who draw the capitals in tall letters want attention. Actors sign like that, I have read."

"You designed the signature for me," I pointed out. "What would an expert say about my own crabbed writing?"

"That you are a little shy, I think. A little backward in claiming proper treatment, but you are coming along."

"You're looking tired," he said a little later. "Travel is fatiguing after a while. What do you say we postpone Italy and go to some healthy spa to rest for a month, darling?" We walked to the sofa and sat down. "There's Karlsbad, Marienbad, Baden-Baden—you choose. We'll go on to Italy later."

The idea surprised me, but as I studied Fraser's dear face, I noticed signs of fatigue on it. He needed a rest. "All right, Fraser. We'll go to Karlsbad," I decided, since it was the only name I could remember.

"Good. We'll get some flesh on your bones yet," he said, patting my wrist. "You remind me of Gretel in the fairy tale. You never put on any weight, despite my stuffing you."

"How morbid! I wager you don't know why the witch was trying to fatten Gretel up? For the slaughter."

"Good God, is that the way the story goes?" he exclaimed. "How gruesome! We shan't tell that story to our children."

A little frisson scuttled up my spine at the words 'our children.' How serious the words sounded, how permanent. Fraser and I had made a lifetime commitment to each other, to raising a family, sharing joys and tribulations, till death did us part.

"Young people are brave, aren't they, Fraser?" I asked, drawing a deep breath and leaning my head on his shoulder.

He knew exactly what I meant. We had reached that stage where mind-reading was a game with us. "Brave and foolish," he agreed. "If they weren't, the human race as we know it would run out in a generation."

We were brave and foolish that night, and very happy. I was comfortable in my conjugal duties now. Fraser was a good teacher, and an enthusiastic one.

In the morning, he was up before me. When I opened my eyes, our trunks were packed. "We're off for Karlsbad," Fraser announced, laughing at my surprise. "Why wait? You're bored, and the McCormacks are haunting the halls, trying to badger us into going to Italy with them. We can be halfway to Germany by nightfall if we catch the late morning train."

No talk now of Sunday travel being frowned on. Fraser's enthusiasm was contagious. I felt eager and excited and brave and foolish, and very much in love. He had ordered what he considered my favorite breakfast, designed to fatten me up. And so it would, if I actually poured that heavy cream on my cereal, or ate both the eggs that sat on my plate. I nibbled one egg, ate one piece of toast, and drank the tea sans cream.

By darting from the hotel without even checking the dresser drawers, we made the late morning train to Germany.

CHAPTER THREE

LIFE WITH IMPULSIVE FRASER WAS A MAD WHIRL OF surprises. We didn't dart straight off to Karlsbad as planned. We liked Switzerland, and stopped there six weeks, touring mountains and lake districts. From there we went to Vienna, to see the Schonbrunn and walk in the parks and drink the coffee with whipped cream and eat pastries. From Vienna we made a leisurely tour of the countryside by carriage and boat.

When we eventually arrived at Karlsbad, we were ready for a rest. It was a charming place, set in magnificently wooded hills, with the Ohre River running through town. Soon we were ensconced in charming rooms at the Pupp Hotel, a fashionable spa where the waters were only a pretext for a holiday. We strolled the Fountain Colonnade, drove in the stunning hills, dined and danced every night, and of course drank the waters in the morning.

What we did not do, however, was meet any agreeable friends who spoke English. French was the *lingua franca* of the international set. Fraser spoke it fluently, and I a little. "It's an excellent chance for you to improve your French," he pointed out.

I was sensitive about the difference in our backgrounds. Fraser should have married a lady who spoke French fluently, and painted and had many accomplishments. My only talent was playing the piano, and Fraser confessed that he wasn't an enthusiast. I did put on weight, however, which pleased him.

"My new Paris gowns are becoming tight. I shan't be able to wear them soon," I mentioned at lunch one day.

Fraser leapt to his feet, smiling from ear to ear. "Darling! You don't mean—you're not—"

Soon I understood that he thought I was enceinte. "Not that!" I exclaimed. The light faded from his eyes. He wanted a child very much. The idea soon took root with me as well.

When you're traveling there's no feeling of permanence, even if you stay two months in one place, as we did at Karlsbad. We had written to Miss Williams the week we arrived, but had no letter from her, which worried me. "I hope nothing horrible has happened to Miss Williams," I said.

"Her letters will all arrive in a batch. It always happens," Fraser consoled me.

I was suddenly filled with lonesomeness for England. I suggested to Fraser that it was time to go home and start raising a family.

"I thought you wanted to see Italy."

"Some other time. Let's go home now, today."

"It takes a little planning, Rosie. Reservations have to be made in advance, and I'm running a little short of cash. I'd have to arrange something with the bank. It might take a week. I had planned to travel alone when I set out."

Two may live as cheaply as one, but they do not travel at the same magical cost. We had certainly traveled in the first style. "I have my bank book with me. Would it help if I withdrew my money to tide us over? It's only two thousand pounds."

"If you're in a hurry to go home, that might be fastest. Of course I'll reimburse you as soon as we get to London."

"I'm not worried about the money, Fraser. You've already given me a fortune in jewelry."

"I've already reserved rooms at Marienbad," Fraser mentioned. "Let's go there. It will give us time to get your funds from the bank, and for me to arrange our trip home."

"All right."

We seemed destined to remain forever in foreign lands. Our first meal at Marienbad made me ill. It was the meat, but Fraser took the idea I was enceinte, and insisted on calling a fierce German doctor, who asked extremely personal questions about my feminine physiology. Fraser, who knew a little German, acted as my interpreter. He paid the doctor and sent him off.

"From what you have told him," Fraser confided when we were alone, "Dr. Stamm believes you have had a miscarriage."

28

"No, I'm sure I haven't, Fraser. I would know."

"You were never ill at this time of the month before. Why take chances? Rest up a few days, and we'll go home as soon as we're certain you're recovered."

I objected, but Fraser insisted. He was like an angel through it all. "Dr. Stamm said a period of despondency is normal after losing a child," he mentioned.

"Oh, Fraser, I didn't lose a child," I told him, smiling sadly. "If you truly want a child that badly, let us go home and I promise you as many children as you want."

"We'll leave as soon as Dr. Stamm says it is safe for you to travel. Meanwhile, you should tell Miss Williams we'll soon be home." I wrote the letter, signing my new signature.

The next morning, we left Marienbad. Fraser went below to tend to the bill and luggage. While I was taking a last look around the room, there was a knock at the door. I called, "Come in," thinking it was a servant.

A strange man entered, smiling at me. He was a tall and slender, pleasant-looking man. "Good morning, Rosie," he said. There was nothing menacing about him, but his boldness in calling me by name surprised me.

"Good morning," I said, trying to think where in our travels I had met him.

"Fraser tells me you're off to London," he continued.

"Yes, we're leaving immediately. In fact, I must go right now." I edged nervously toward the door.

"It was nice to see you again. You're looking a

little peaked, Rosie." He examined me closely as he spoke. "Helen asked me to give you her love. We'll see you in London in a month's time. Shall I give her your best wishes?" he asked.

"Please do." The name Helen rang no bells in my memory.

I was relieved when Fraser came bouncing in. He looked from the man to myself. "Charles, come to wish us good-bye, I see." He smiled. "The carriage is waiting below. Come along, darling." He took my arm. "Give our best to Helen, Charles."

"I shall. And a very bon voyage to you." The man bowed.

We left hurriedly. "Who on earth was that?" I asked. "He seemed to know all about me. I never saw him before."

"Charles Swanson. We met him and his wife in Paris, don't you remember? I introduced you at the Tuileries gardens. She's a mousy thing. You probably don't remember her."

"He thought I looked peaked. If he met me in Paris, I should think he would have remarked on how I've blossomed."

"I had an ale with Charles and his wife here while you were ill. I told them about your miscarriage. Very likely I used your name, and by mentioning your appearance, he was acknowledging your illness without stating the indelicate nature of it. People behave so freely when abroad," he tsked.

"I'll be so glad to get home," I sighed luxuriously.

We went home via Germany and Belgium, stopping in Brussels. Toward the end of October we crossed into France, to set sail from Calais across the Channel home. With porters carrying our trunks and with a loving husband taking care of all the details, I marveled at the change since my arrival at Calais. I had been a frightened greenhorn then, with Miss Williams, more fearful than myself, for a companion.

We spent the first night in England in the inn at Dover. "Tomorrow we'll be home, Fraser!" I exclaimed joyfully. "What is your house like? Is it very grand?"

"I don't live in a house, Rosie," he explained. "I had an apartment, but I decided to give it up. It would have been crowded for three of us. Won't you enjoy choosing your own house, my dear? We'll put up at the Savoy while an estate agent shows us what is for sale. The house is the wife's domain. You choose what suits you, while I tend to business. Don't let money be a constraint. We aren't poor, Rosie."

I was happy with this. A woman likes to choose her own home, and to be told that money is no object is reassuring.

"Where did you get your money, Fraser? You never told me."

"One of my uncles was a nabob—old Alvin Simson. I told you I had family in India. I've invested in various stocks and so on. I must review my investments. You'll have to do a little paperwork as well. We'll go to my lawyers on Monday and sign some things. I want to put my holdings in both our names."

"Monday—that's my birthday!" I exclaimed.

"Did you think I had forgotten?" he asked, with love shining in his brilliant blue eyes. "You'll be twenty-one. I'll get the family heirlooms from my safety box. I want my wife to be the queen of London society." Tears clogged in my throat. All this love, and wealth on top of it. It was surely a dream. "The collection is stunning, but it is entailed," he added.

I began to understand Fraser's eagerness for a child. He wanted a son, to inherit these things. I was eager for one too. "Then we shall have a son first," I promised rashly.

"You must recover after your miscarriage first. A son isn't as important to me as you, my darling."

Fraser raised my hand and kissed my fingers, one by one. We left Dover early the next morning and were whisked off to the Savoy Hotel, where a doorman ushered us into the impressive lobby. Fraser ordered us a suite—"for a week," he told the clerk, who smiled in approval at this lavish request.

"We shall dine in our room this evening," Fraser added. I frowned. "You need your rest. We shall begin our celebration tomorrow—on your birthday. I have to see a few men on business matters this afternoon. I'll stop at the bank and repay the loan you made me. Three thousand pounds, wasn't it?"

"Two! I hope you aren't always so careless with money."

"I'm including interest," he said, with a laughing look.

"While you tend to business, I'll write to Miss Williams, asking her to join us for dinner. You don't mind, Fraser?"

"I should love it. I'll have the note delivered to her."

I wrote the note, and Fraser left. Alone, I began to

plan the evening. I would have the table set up in the living room. Now, what would Miss Williams like to eat? The afternoon slipped by pleasantly with plans and preparations.

When Fraser returned, we decided to make a grande toilette to impress Miss Williams. My hair was long enough to wear in the style Fraser liked best, pulled back in waves with a curl over my shoulder. I wore my blue crepe gown, which showed off the sapphires exquisitely. Miss Williams would be hard-pressed to recognize this elegant lady as her old charge. I looked so sleek, so pampered, so rich. And considerably plumper too, like a fat cat. The extra weight was becoming. It rounded my arms and bosom attractively, and filled in my lean cheeks.

Miss Williams was invited for seven, to allow us a good chat before dinner. She was punctual in her habits, but by seven-fifteen she had still not arrived. By seven-thirty I was worried and spoke to Fraser. His answer was rational, but unsatisfying. "She probably wasn't at home. She didn't know exactly when we were arriving."

"She wouldn't have stayed out this late at night."

"Your Miss Williams has been alone in that apartment for months, no doubt bored to flinders. She has a sister—very likely she went to pay her a visit. If you're really concerned, we'll drive over to the apartment tomorrow and see her. If she's not home, the neighbors will know where she's gone."

The dinner arrived—for three. It was a lovely dinner, the roast beef as tender as butter, the Yorkshire pudding a cloud. I sat across the table from a handsome and loving husband, sipping wine, but some worm of discontent nibbled inside. I wasn't lonesome—how could I be lonesome with Fraser? I was—dissatisfied was the closest I could come to naming my feelings.

Six months spent day and night with my husband and virtually no one else had begun to weary me. I wanted someone different to talk to about my experiences abroad. Fraser knew all the funny stories and odd experiences.

"You seem a little tired this evening," he said as we sipped coffee after dinner. "We'll go to bed early. Tomorrow will be busier—your birthday. We must go out and celebrate with friends. I noticed a sign in the lobby that some ladies' charity is having a ball here at the Savoy tomorrow night. We have that legal business we must tend to in the afternoon. That leaves us the morning to ourselves."

"A ball? Oh, how lovely. I've never been to one!" And to be going with friends. That was enough of a birthday gift for me.

Fraser had brought back the newspapers, and we spent the remainder of the evening examining the houses for sale and let.

CHAPTER FOUR

WHEN I AWOKE THE NEXT MORNING, I WAS ALONE IN bed. The drapes were drawn and the door to the next room closed. Through the drawn draperies slivers of bright sunlight invaded the darkness, picking out the brass trim on dresser and desk, and giving an idea of the elegant, high-ceilinged chamber where I slept. The warm peach of the walls cast a friendly glow. I sat up and stretched luxuriously. From the next room there came a muted murmur of voices and a discreet clinking of china. The door opened, and Fraser came in, fully dressed. He had brought me breakfast in bed.

"Good morning, sleepy head! And happy birthday, my darling." He leaned over to kiss me lightly on the lips.

What a marvelous way to begin your twenty-first birthday. "Thank you, Fraser. You're spoiling me."

"What are husbands for? No, no. Don't get up. I'll pour your coffee." He lifted the gleaming pot, and the black liquid steamed into the delicate china cup.

"I've been up for two hours. You've slept the clock around. And look much better for it," he said, studying me.

I lifted the hot cover and saw a tempting breakfast of fresh fruit, bacon and eggs, kippered herring and hot buns. While I ate, Fraser had coffee and we talked.

"I've been arranging our day. This morning we shall pick out our costumes for the ball. Since it is Halloween, they've made it a costume ball."

I smiled at my husband. "I should go as Cinderella."

"Better not," he laughed. "That would cast me in the role of Prince Charming." As I gazed at him, I felt he was Prince Charming. Hadn't he lifted me from nowhere and made me a princess? "I don't want you disappearing on me at midnight. I shall wear a plain black domino," he said. "My friends will stop by here for a drink to let you get acquainted, then we'll go down together."

"We were going to call on Miss Williams today."

"I knew it was worrying you last night, so I drove over to Watling Street myself," he said. "As I suspected, Miss Williams is visiting her sister for a week. I left word with the neighbor where we're staying."

"That was thoughtful of you, Fraser." But I was sorry I had not been with him.

He cocked his head at a mischievous angle and

said, "You haven't even asked what I plan to give you for your birthday."

I disliked to mention it when Fraser had bought me so many beautiful things, but what I really needed was a winter coat.

"What is it?" I asked, eager as a child.

"I shan't tell you," he teased, "but you'll have it by noon. Now finish up your breakfast. Come out when you're finished. I have something to show you."

I knew by the twinkle in his eyes the "something" was an extravagance. Fraser was inordinately generous. In my excitement, I couldn't eat any more. I slipped my blue velvet dressing gown over my nightie and went into the next room, just as Fraser was putting a leather case on the sofa table.

"I knew you wouldn't be able to wait!" he said, laughing. "I'm eager to see what you think. Come, they're for you, my darling. I got them from the bank this morning. The family heirlooms."

I was trembling as I went to sit beside him on the sofa. "Family heirlooms" had an almost magical sound to it. It was a large case, fifteen inches long and six inches in width and depth. If it were half full, it would hold a king's ransom.

"Open it," he urged.

With unsteady fingers I lifted the lid and gasped in astonishment. An emerald necklace was in the center of the box, spread out on pale yellow satin. It was a lavish piece, the emeralds interspersed with oval diamonds, with a large pear-shaped emerald suspended at the front. There were earrings to match, also with pendants. Ranged in little niches along the satin were other expensive pieces—a diamond necklace and bracelet, a peacock brooch featuring many sapphires. And that was only the top layer. Below there were three drawers, each full of jewels—pearls and a ruby ring, diamonds in various pieces.

"Oh, Fraser!" I gasped. "These look like the crown jewels!"

"My nabob uncle assembled the collection in India. He paid a pittance for some of these rare pieces. The diamonds are the most valuable," he said, lifting the diamond necklace. "But not the most beautiful." He looked at the emeralds.

I had to try the pieces on. The stones felt cold, alien against my skin, but in the mirror I looked like an empress.

"Of course they weren't meant to be worn with a nightgown," he said, smiling. "Which shall you wear tonight?" I gazed at the collection, speechless. "That will depend on what costume you choose, I daresay. Let us go and choose your outfit now. There's a place that rents them on Hill Street. We'll take a cab till I set up our carriage. I ought to do that today, if I can find time."

My thoughts scurried in a hundred directions as I went to dress. I had known that Fraser was a well-to-do gentleman, but this jewelry collection—it was priceless. And he told me to buy any house I wanted, money no object. I had married a millionaire, and I began to fear that I wouldn't be up to the job of managing his social life.

This party tonight, for instance—how many people would be coming? Would they be lords and ladies? My fingers shook as I arranged my hair. I chose my blue suit for our shopping. I would wear a crinoline to the costume ball. I was eager to get into a swaying crinoline, that looked so lovely and impractical.

I selected a French bonnet with a rolled brim and a big tie under the chin. Beyond the windows, the autumn winds blew in gusts that set men running for their hats. I ought to take my coat, but its simplicity would look ludicrous with this bonnet. I really must get a proper coat.

When I went to join Fraser, he stood smiling enigmatically as he studied me from head to toe. His eyes lingered on my bonnet and the curl hanging artfully over my shoulder. It is difficult to explain that smile. There was more than satisfaction in it; he looked almost gloating. No doubt I wore the same expression as I looked at my uxorious husband.

"Fraser, do you think I'll be cold? I can't seem to find my coat—"

"Here's your coat—and your birthday present," he said, and led me by the hand to the closet. He opened the door, and there hung a long sable cape, shimmering in the shadows.

As he lifted it from the hanger, an iridescent play of light danced over the luxuriously thick pelts. He hung the coat over my shoulders, then led me to the mirror. I didn't recognize the lady there. She was no longer me. She had stepped straight out of a fashion magazine.

"Oh, Fraser! I—" Words caught in my throat. What good were mere words to convey a thousandth of my feelings? Hot tears stung my eyes. I blinked them away and ran my fingers over the silky-smooth sable.

"You like it?" he asked softly.

"I love you," I hiccoughed. "You must have read my mind. I knew my old cloth coat was not fashionable enough for—"

"I hope you don't mind, Rosie. I left your old clothes behind at Marienbad. We had such a lot of luggage, and I knew you wouldn't be wearing them here. I gave them to the maids."

I was surprised that he had done it without asking me, but this wasn't the moment to cavil at such a detail. My life had turned into a fable. I imagined I could even smell the light, pervasive scent of violets coming from my coat. It must have come from my suit. Fraser had bought me violet perfume, his favorite scent, at Karlsbad.

"Why don't you wear a brooch on your suit?" he suggested.

"The peacock! Would it be too grand for day wear?"

"Perfect." He got the peacock and pinned it to my jacket, where it looked stunning. It was done in blue, and to me it was the bluebird of happiness.

"I'll have the case put away in the hotel vault," Fraser said. "Oh and by the way, Rosie, I have your three thousand pounds here."

"*Two* thousand, Fraser. I can't take so much."

"You'll get used to it, Mrs. Audry," he said, laughing. "If you don't plan to spend it, why don't you let me invest it for you? But meanwhile, here is the money."

He gave me the envelope—of three thousand

pounds. "Invest it for me," I said, but for the meanwhile we put it in the vault with the jewelry.

The doorman hailed us a carriage and we were taken to the costume shop on Hill Street.

"I am dying to wear the new crinoline," I said.

"That will hardly be a costume, Rosie. It's contemporary."

"I don't care," I decreed grandly. "A lady in sable and sapphires may wear what she wants."

"That's the spirit! Show your claws."

I was not the only lady who wanted to wear an alluring crinoline, no matter if it was historically inaccurate. French panniered gowns of the eighteenth century had been converted to swaying crinolines. The costume shop suggested high headdress and feathers to go with it, but I meant to wear my hair as Fraser liked. I chose an ice-blue silk gown, low-cut in front and edged with panels of white embroidered with gold flowers. The shop would deliver it to the hotel.

Afterwards, we stopped for lunch at an intimate café, and Fraser explained the afternoon's business with the lawyer.

"I've arranged the details. You'll just have to sign a few papers. My cousin Mycroft Harlow will be there as the executor of my uncle's estate. That's the nabob who assembled the jewelry collection and left me his money." I nodded.

"About Mycroft—he's a bit of a strange bird. Jealous, to tell the truth. He thought Uncle Alvin would leave his fortune to him, and when he didn't, he took me in dislike. I believe the disappointment actually disordered his mind. One never knows what he may say or do. Don't pay him any heed."

I could see that Fraser was upset about the ill feelings in the family. "Can he do anything to keep your money from you?"

"No, of course not. It's mine, whether he likes it or not. The fact is, Mycroft isn't at all happy with my marriage."

"How does he know about it?"

"I wrote and told the lawyers. When I married, I changed my will to make you my heir if anything should happen to me. Today we just have a few incidental papers to sign."

"Why is he unhappy with your marriage, Fraser? He doesn't know me. Is it because I—I don't have any money?"

Fraser gripped my hand in a painfully tight grasp. "Don't let him upset you, darling. It's true the family would have preferred I marry a cousin, to keep the money in the family. But they'll love you once they meet you. I call Mycroft 'Cousin.' It might please him if you do the same. We shan't have to see much of him. Once this legal business is over, he'll go back to Thornbridge, his estate in West Sussex."

"If he has an estate, he shouldn't begrudge you your uncle's money. Is it a small estate?"

"Thornbridge?" he asked, staring. "Good God, no. It's a showplace."

"Were Mycroft's mother and your mother sisters? I'm just trying to sort out all these new names."

Fraser frowned. "I'm not much good at this first cousin once removed business. Mycroft is a distant cousin. I never met him till five years ago, when my uncle died. I can't say I cared for him—unpleasant chap. Now, how about some dessert?" he asked, and the bothersome subject of Mycroft was dropped.

"I want to buy violets for your fur," Fraser decided when we left the restaurant. "There must be a flower vendor somewhere about. Let us walk a little and show off your new fur. We'll have the carriage follow us."

This novel extravagance was employed till we found a flower woman selling violets, in October! From some commercial conservatory, no doubt. Miracles are possible in our age of science. Fraser pinned the flowers on my cape, and we returned to the carriage to go to the lawyer's office. I could sense that Fraser was nervous. He mentioned Mycroft Harlow a few times in such disparaging terms that I began to fear I would meet a lunatic. I was trembling when the carriage pulled up in front of a stone office building and we entered the offices of Hibbard and Sons, Barristers and Solicitors.

Fraser stopped a moment at the door. When I looked at him, I saw he was a little pale, and his lips were clenched in a grim line. Knowing how he doted on me, I understood his feelings. He was afraid this odious Mycroft Harlow would say or do something to offend me.

"Come along, Fraser," I urged, and we went in.

CHAPTER FIVE

WE WERE GREETED BY MR. HIBBARD, A THIN WHIP OF A man with spectacles and mutton-chop whiskers, who rushed forward officiously to greet us.

"My dear Mrs. Audry! And Mr. Audry! Welcome back to England. Did you have a nice trip?" He pumped our hands and led us toward a meeting room where a long table with chairs on both sides awaited us.

"Very nice, thank you," I said, as it seemed to be myself who received most of his attention.

From the corner of my eye I saw another man standing at a window that looked out on the street. He would have seen us arrive. The strange way he studied me gave rise to the impression that he had been examining us even before we entered. He was intensely interested in us—or rather, in me. He hardly glanced at Fraser. Was this Mycroft Harlow?

44

He didn't look insane, but he certainly looked bad-natured. He also looked passionately curious.

"Cousin Mycroft, nice to see you again," Fraser said, and went forward to shake his hand. Over his shoulder, Fraser added quietly, "Best come and make your curtsey to Mycroft too, Rosie, or he'll be offended."

This gentle hint reminded me of Mycroft's uncertain temper. I took the man's measure before going to him. He was taller than Fraser, and a little heavier in build. A good, solid build, broad of shoulder, well formed and elegantly tailored. Hair as black as jet and as straight as a ruler was brushed severely back from his high forehead. His weathered complexion hinted at a life out of doors. And his eyes—they made ink look pale, they were so dark a blue. A slash of black brows gave him a somewhat menacing look. His lips formed a grim line, and his nose was aquiline. The haughty set of his head announced he had a generous share of pride.

When Fraser forgot to introduce us formally, I said, "I'm happy to—"

Before I could say I was happy to make his acquaintance, Fraser broke in nervously. "You're looking well, Cousin. How is everything at Thornbridge? The cousins are well, I trust?"

"Quite well, thank you," Mycroft replied, with a dismissive glance at Fraser before he turned his gaze back to me.

He looked at me—oddly—passionately, so closely I would have felt I was under a microscope, had it not been for something else in that look. There was an intensity to it that made me feel weak.

I had the oddest sensation that this man either hated me or loved me. Reason told me it had to be hatred—because of my marrying Fraser, and because of Fraser's having inherited the nabob uncle's money.

"Good afternoon, Mrs. Audry. Welcome back to England," he said with a stiff bow. "I hope you had a pleasant trip?" And still he stared—at my eyes, my hair, my new sable coat, the violets pinned to it.

I curtsied, also stiffly, and said, "Very pleasant, thank you, Cousin."

Mycroft's thin lips eased from grimness to tentative amusement at my cool voice. I called the man 'Cousin' once to please my husband, but as he called me 'Mrs. Audry,' my next address to him would be more formal.

He was still examining me with that scalding intensity that seemed out of all proportion to the occasion. Finally he said, "You're looking well."

If it was intended as a compliment, it seemed rather gauchely worded. How did he know my usual appearance? But I was out of patience with the man and replied, "Marriage agrees with me," to annoy him.

Mycroft's reaction was surprising. I thought he would have kept his temper under better control. A flame of anger leapt in his dark eyes, and his nostrils dilated, but he said nothing. I noticed my husband smiled in approval. Encouraged by Fraser's smile, I continued acting haughty to please him. It occurred to me that Fraser encouraged this haughty attitude to inform his cousins that I was indeed a worthy lady. He wouldn't want his wife to go cowering before them.

I turned my back to Mycroft Harlow and spoke to Mr. Hibbard. "Shall we get on with signing the papers?" I asked. "My husband and I are very busy." As I spoke, Fraser came and took my fur wrap. Mycroft continued examining my suit and the sapphire peacock as closely as he had scrutinized my outer wrapping. I walked in a businesslike way to the long table.

Mycroft wasn't a step behind me. "I had hoped you and Fraser could spare us a week at Thornbridge," he said. How he expected anyone to accept such a bristling invitation was beyond me. I knew that Fraser didn't want to go, and if the cousins were all as stiff as Mycroft, I didn't want to go either.

I looked to Fraser; he shook his head firmly behind Mycroft's back. "We have a dozen things to do, settling in after our trip," I told Mycroft.

"What pressing matters are these, that can't wait a week?" he demanded angrily.

I rather wished Fraser would answer, but the question had been put to me, and I said curtly, "We must arrange living accommodations."

Mycroft turned to my husband. "Buying up property so soon, Fraser? You don't waste any time." Then he turned back to me. "Shall we all have dinner together this evening? You can't look for a house at night."

"I'm afraid our plans are already made. We are busy with friends this evening," I informed him coolly.

"I have come all the way from Thornbridge to see you! Is this the answer you want me to take back to Aunt Sophie and Gertrude? That you're too busy to spare me an evening?" Mycroft's glaring eyes made me consider seriously whether he wasn't deranged with jealousy, as my husband had jokingly said.

What were a parcel of unknown in-laws to me? Fraser didn't want to go, and that guided my reply, but civility urged me to coach the refusal politely. "West Sussex is not that far. We shall all meet another time."

After I was seated, Mr. Hibbard opened a black folder and began sorting through a batch of official-looking papers. "These will require your signature, Mrs. Audry, and of course your husband's. Mr. Harlow has already perused them and finds everything in order. If you'd care to read them before signing . . ."

A set of pens and ink pots was on the table. "I'm sure I couldn't make head or tails of the legal mumbo-jumbo. Fraser, do you want to look these papers over?"

"If Mycroft has already done so, there's no need. As you said, we're in a hurry, Rosie." He took up one of the pens and turned to the last page of the first document to sign, then passed it along to me.

"Should I sign Mrs. Audry, or—"

"Just sign the signature you always do—Rose Audry," Fraser said. His pen blotted, and he muttered a curse under his breath.

"Would that be legal?" I asked. Rose might be more symmetrical, but for a legal document I rather thought my full name would be necessary.

"Of course it's legal. It's your name," Fraser said.

Mr. Hibbard considered it a moment and suggested I sign Mrs. Fraser Audry, with Rose in brackets after. Fraser was busily flipping pages of the other papers and scratching his signature, then passing the pages along to me for my name. Mr. Hibbard took them, added his signature as witness, and set his seal on them.

"You seem in a great hurry to hand over a fortune," Mycroft said stiffly. "I think you ought to read the papers and be aware of exactly what you are doing."

I felt a hot sting of anger at the man's infernal interfering. What was it to him if Fraser was signing half his property over to me, and making me his legal heir? Enough of the property was entailed that he need not worry at its going out of the family.

I took time from my signing to give him a blistering stare, and found him still examining me. "It is the custom for a married couple to share things, is it not, Mr. Harlow?" I asked.

He didn't say anything, but only gave me a reproachful, accusing look. I could see the anger in his eyes. Mr. Harlow was a very poor loser, but as he had lost, he might at least have tried to control his feelings in front of us.

The signing was finished inside of two minutes. Mr. Hibbard gathered up the papers and returned them to the black leather case. "I think that takes care of things for the present," he said, smiling in satisfaction. He rose and turned to Fraser. "If you need any help in handling estate matters, Mr. Audry, Hibbard and Son are always at your disposal. I daresay there will be investments you'll want to take a look at, and so on. You'll want cash for that house you mentioned."

"Yes, yes, you'll be hearing from me," Fraser said, and stood up. He pulled my chair and gave a sigh of relief that the business was finished. It remained only to escape before Mycroft suggested some other social activity for us.

"As Rosie mentioned, we're busy today, so we'll be running along. Nice seeing you again, Mycroft." Fraser shook hands with him and stood a moment chatting with Mr. Hibbard. Mycroft went into the outer office.

When we joined him, he was holding my sable wrap, gazing at the violets. He looked preoccupied when he saw me watching him. More than preoccupied, he looked almost guilty, but covered it by coming to put the wrap over my shoulders. I was intensely aware of his closeness. Something akin to an electrical charge emanated from the man.

"I notice you're wearing the sapphire peacock," he said as he set the wrap gently over my shoulders. The angry sting was gone from him. He sounded a little sad.

"Yes, it's my favorite piece of the collection. Not the most valuable, but the prettiest, I think."

"You didn't waste any time getting the collection out of the vault."

I turned and stared at him. "This happens to be my birthday, Mr. Harlow. I plan to wear one of the pieces at a ball this evening."

"I haven't forgotten it's your birthday, Rose. Your twenty-first birthday is a very special day. Aunt Sophie and Gertrude have sent you a little gift." He took a small box from his pocket and handed it to me. "There's something from me as well," he added.

If I hadn't known better, I would have believed he

was embarrassed. The anger in his eyes had softened to regret, and his voice was gentle. The way he called me Rose—it was the first time he had done so, yet it sounded natural. 'I haven't forgotten your birthday' was a strange thing to say. 'I know it's your birthday' would have been more appropriate. Caught off guard, I just looked. Mycroft shoved the box into my hands. Our fingers touched. Our eyes flew together in a moment of piercing confusion. We both pulled back as though burned.

"Thank you. And thank Sophie and Gertrude," I said, rigid with embarrassment.

"You ought really to write and thank them yourself. But I'm sure you will do everything that is proper in that regard." There was an ironic sting in the way he said it, an implication that I had no familiarity with propriety. I felt an urge to flare up at him, but controlled it.

Hibbard had cornered Fraser and was bending his ear about some business detail. I could see that Fraser was frantic to save me from Mycroft, and smiled to show him I had the situation under control. When I looked back at Mycroft, I was astonished at the expression in his eyes. They were black with regret. The man really was unstable in his emotions. I felt uncomfortable, and suddenly wanted to get away.

"Rose, are you all right?" he asked gently. "Are you happy with Fraser?"

"What on earth are you talking about? Of course I'm all right. I've never been so happy in my life."

"You don't seem quite yourself. The miscarriage, I daresay."

It was extremely disconcerting to be such an object of curiosity to people I had never met. He knew all about me—my birthday, the so-called miscarriage. What did he do, live at Hibbard's office, asking questions about me?

"I am perfectly happy. Fraser is a model husband. He treats me like a queen."

"Well he might!" Mycroft inserted angrily. "And as to his being a model husband—we both know his reputation—"

Before I could launch into a counterattack at this charge, Fraser managed to detach himself from Mr. Hibbard and came to rescue me. He smiled heartily. "Once again, thank you for your interest in all this business, Mycroft. I hope it wasn't too inconvenient for you, having to come up from Thornbridge."

"I was happy to do it, for Rose," Mycroft answered blandly. "As to inconvenience, I happened to be in London in any case. I'll be staying a month, on business. I'll look you both up. The Savoy you're staying at, isn't it?" He even knew that!

"We look forward to it," Fraser said with a smile and gripped me by the arm. He hurried me out the door, with Mycroft staring after us.

The carriage was waiting for us below. As I got in, I looked up to the window where Mycroft had been standing when we entered the office. I saw a dark head at the window, looking down.

"That man is eerie," I said to Fraser.

"What did he say?"

"Nothing special—it's just that he's been looking into my background. He knew it was my birthday.

He knew we were staying at the Savoy."

"Hibbard probably told him. Hibbard knew."

"He even knew about the miscarriage—which wasn't actually a miscarriage at all."

"Did you tell him that?" Fraser asked sharply.

I could see that Fraser was vexed with his cousin, and quit the subject. "I didn't bother."

Later I would tell my husband about that slighting remark on his 'reputation.' I didn't bother telling Fraser about the birthday gift either, as he was upset. I just slid it in my handbag to open later.

"I have some business to attend to, dear," Fraser said a moment later. "Why don't you go home and look through the newspapers for houses for sale? Tomorrow we'll see an agent and start looking in good earnest. And if Mycroft should call while I'm out—"

"Surely he won't!"

"I shouldn't think so, but if he does, don't let him in. Tell him you're not feeling well. You don't even have a woman to stay with you yet. It would be improper to let a jackanapes like Harlow into your room."

A little shiver scuttled down my spine. Why was it so easy to believe that Mycroft was a womanizer? I thought of those darkly brooding eyes. Yes, there had been rampant interest in me as a woman. That was what had set my teeth on edge when I was with him. Mycroft despised me for having attached Fraser, but he was interested in me as a woman. A flutter of excitement quivered through me, flushing my cheeks. Some primitive part of me responded to his interest.

I remembered the way he had examined my face, my eyes, my hair. He had looked with keen interest at every part of me, from my stylish bonnet to my patent slippers. I shook the thought away and spoke of other things.

"How many people are coming to our party tonight, Fraser?"

"Party? Why, I just invited one other couple. The Ramplings, Margot and Oliver. We'll save our large party till we have a proper house for entertaining. You couldn't get fifty or a hundred people into a couple of hotel rooms."

"Oh." I was a little disappointed, but even one couple was of interest. "What are they like?"

"They're lively—fun. I think you'll find them amusing. You might speak to the people at the hotel and ask them to serve wine and some snacks before the ball. The Ramplings are coming at eight-thirty. You'll want to choose some jewelry to wear to the ball as well. Why don't you call in a coiffeur and have your hair done, darling?"

"Perhaps I shall. How long will you be out?"

Fraser took my hand and squeezed it. He gazed deeply into my eyes and said, "Not a moment longer than necessary. I want to be alone with you before the Ramplings come." He seemed excited, almost feverish.

A warm rush of love surged through me. All thoughts of Mycroft Harlow and his peculiar, insinuating manner fell away. It was still my birthday, and a birthday like none I had ever had before. The best part of it still awaited me. Fraser and I, alone before the Ramplings came. And afterwards, the costume ball. How Miss Williams would smile to hear all this. I was lonesome to see her again.

When I was in my room, I took the little box from Mycroft to the sofa and opened it. Inside were three separate items, each wrapped in silver paper. The first two were tiny carvings, one in jade of an elephant from Aunt Sophie, one in ivory of Buddha from Gertrude. They were dainty little pieces, very well done, but the card left me pondering.

"A small addition for your collection, Rose. And very best wishes on your twenty-first birthday. All our love."

Where had they gotten the idea I collected these little miniatures? Even while I puzzled over this, my fingers went to the other silver wrapping. It was smaller than the first two. When I opened it, I saw one perfect pearl, about a third of an inch in diameter. It glowed a pinkish-opal in the fading light of afternoon. It had been drilled through, as though to hang on a necklace. What an odd present!

I knew that some young girls were given a pearl for each birthday, which eventually made up an entire necklace. But to start such a procedure on one's twenty-first birthday seemed unlikely. I would be ancient before there were enough pearls to complete a set. I couldn't make heads or tails of it, but I appreciated the thought.

I would ask Fraser the address of these ladies, Sophie and Gertrude, and thank them. Of course I must add a note thanking Mycroft as well. But really it would be a very strange note: "Thank you for the pearl." I returned all three items to their silver paper to show Fraser when he returned. I looked in the wrappings, thinking there might be a note from Mycroft explaining if the gift had some significance, but there was nothing. Just that one, perfect pearl. It was as inexplicable as everything else about Mycroft Harlow.

CHAPTER SIX

FRASER JUST LAUGHED AT MY PRESENTS FROM SUSSEX. "Since none of them gave us a wedding gift, they're using your birthday as a pretext to ingratiate themselves with me. They wanted to give something without putting themselves to any expense, and sent along things that were lying about the house. These trifles are as much an insult as anything else. Mycroft didn't come while I was out?"

"No, thank goodness. I didn't care for him in the least." Since Fraser was in a prime mood, I decided to tell him Mycroft's opinion of his reputation. That too Fraser brushed aside with contempt.

"Much I care for Harlow's opinion of me. He's jealous as bedamned, that's the top and bottom of it. Moreso than ever now that he's seen what a beautiful bride I found for myself," he said, pulling

57

me against him. "He was just trying to put a wedge between us."

The rag manners of Fraser's cousins were really laughable, and we laughed together over it. They couldn't touch us. We were insulated from such petty jealousies by our love, and Fraser's money. Yet I was sorry his relatives were so disagreeable, as I had none of my own.

"We'll say we're busy if Mycroft comes calling, trying to set up an evening together," Fraser decided.

"For a whole month? He'll certainly become suspicious."

"Let him." Fraser shrugged. Nothing could dim my husband's good mood that evening. He seemed flushed with victory.

We were still in good humor as we prepared for the ball, I in my beautiful crinoline gown and Fraser in his unimaginative domino.

"Why don't you wear the diamonds tonight?" he suggested.

He had the case brought up, and I tried various pieces before settling on the diamonds. The necklace contained beautiful stones, but the cumbersome setting didn't do them justice. They looked like something Queen Victoria might wear on a state occasion.

"I'll wear these matching earrings," I said, picking up a dainty drop diamond. "Oh, where's the other? There only seems to be one."

"What—is it missing?" Fraser asked, and searched all through the box.

"Perhaps there was only the one," I suggested.

"No, there were a pair. I'm sure they were both

there when I put them in the vault."

"You're not suggesting an employee at the hotel took it?"

"No, I meant the bank vault." Fraser rubbed his neck and paced the room, frowning. "I may be mistaken. I might have left one—"

"Left it where? I don't suppose you wear earrings."

"I had the collection at my apartment before I went abroad," he explained. "I told you I had the sapphires and emeralds reset. The other earring must be put away with my own jewelry. It's still stored. I'll have a look before notifying the insurance company."

"I'll wear the emeralds instead. They have these lovely earrings. What do you think?"

He held them up to my neck and examined me. "The green interferes with the color of your eyes, but with that mask, no one will notice."

As we had dressed early and didn't want to go downstairs in our costumes, we had dinner served in our room again. At eight-thirty the waiter was just wheeling out the table when our guests arrived, and I looked with interest to see what kind of friends Fraser had.

My first feeling was dismay that Mrs. Rampling should be so beautiful. She was a statuesque red-head with green eyes and a full figure. Her costume of Venus rising from the waves left very little to the imagination. Hair streamed over her shoulders like a veil of flame, and when she came in, she kissed Fraser on the cheek.

Fast! was my immediate assessment of her character. I stole a glance at her husband, and saw he was undismayed at his wife's manner. So this was how London society behaved—much more freely than I had imagined. Mr. Rampling made do with shaking my hand and saying, "By Jove, you're even lovelier than Fraser said. And he said you were a vision beyond words."

Mr. Rampling lacked the striking looks of his wife. He was slightly less than average in height, with waved brown hair and pale gray eyes, but he was not ugly or unpleasant.

Then Fraser presented Margot Rampling to me. From the first look, we disliked each other. Her smile was broad and insincere, like my own. She examined my toilette longer than my face, which showed where her real interest lay. She wanted to see if I was fashionable.

"Lovely gown, Mrs. Audry," she admitted, but it was on the emeralds that her eyes lingered covetously. She wore no real jewelry, just a blue ribbon around her neck with a crystal pendant, which she explained was a drop of water to symbolize Venus's emergence from the waves.

"Thank you, Mrs. Rampling. Yours is very original."

"Ladies, ladies!" Fraser said, smiling. "Let us dispense with Mr. and Mrs. We are all going to be fast friends. Rosie, shall we have some drinks for our friends?"

I found myself rising like a servant to pour wine. It was ridiculous to resent it. I was the hostess, and we hadn't yet arranged for servants. But when I saw Margot take up a seat beside Fraser and engage him in some bantering conversation, my temper flared.

"Why don't you pass the hors d'oeuvres, Fraser?" I suggested, to get him away from her.

I sat next to Margot myself while he was up. "And how did you like Europe, Rosalie?" she asked.

Though Rosalie was the name I had been called all my life before meeting Fraser, it sounded odd. How did she even know my name was Rosalie? Fraser always called me Rosie.

"I loved it, but then of course my memories are colored. We were on our honeymoon, you know."

She smiled, with a gleam of jealousy in her green eyes. "Karlsbad is magnificent," she told me. "I knew Fraser would take you there. I hope he didn't make you drink that horrid water."

"We drank champagne mostly," I replied. "Have you been to Karlsbad, Margot?"

"Oliver and I usually go every year. His aunt enjoys poor health, and takes us along with her for company. Aunt Mildred is wealthy," she added, to explain their compliance. "Of course I'd much prefer Paris, but what can one do?"

As she finished this speech, she leaned in front of me to speak to Fraser at my other side. "Did you see the Broughams there, Fraser? Edna and Harold were going to Karlsbad."

"No, we didn't run into them."

"We met Helen and Charles Swanson at Marienbad," I mentioned. I hadn't even seen Helen, and Charles was only a rather frightening memory of an intruder, but I wanted to establish my place in Fraser's life and dropped the names as though the Swansons were my bosom bows.

Margot's green eyes grew wide with surprise. "Really!" she exclaimed, and looked a question at Fraser. Now what had I stumbled into? There was definitely some meaning in the look Margot leveled at my husband. The awful idea popped into my head that there was something between Helen and Fraser. That was the sort of look it was that passed between them—questioning, slightly amused, brightly curious.

"Rosie didn't actually meet Helen. I met them downstairs once, and Charles popped in to say goodbye as we were leaving," Fraser explained.

"Oh, I see." Margot's lips curved in a knowing smile, and her eyes as she looked at Fraser were full of meaning.

I suddenly felt like an outsider. This evening that was supposed to be wonderful was fast degenerating into misery. I knew full well that the burning inside me was jealousy, pure and simple. I thought of Mycroft's offhand remark: 'We both know his reputation.' I didn't know it, and I didn't want to learn it, not on my birthday.

I turned to include Oliver in the conversation. "Have you both known Fraser long?" I asked.

"Five years, is it?" Oliver asked, looking at his wife.

"Yes, exactly five years," she agreed.

That 'exactly' made me wonder. She must be keeping very close track of the friendship to pinpoint it 'exactly.' I was ridiculous, imagining meaning into every word. Jealous of Margot, jealous of Helen Swanson, whom I had never even met. I was behaving as though Fraser were some kind of monster. Fraser, the kindest, most generous and loving husband in the world.

I looked at him and caught him examining me. He smiled intimately and his lapis lazuli eyes glowed, but in that first glimpse he had looked more—assessing. That was the word. He looked as though he were wondering whether I suspected anything. And he wouldn't look like that if there was nothing to suspect. I should have known that a handsome, eligible bachelor would have women in his past. What did I think, that he had never looked at another woman before me?

While these troublesome thoughts whirled in my mind, Fraser held my eyes, still smiling, reassuring. I felt he knew what I was thinking, and wanted to calm me. I couldn't doubt his love. The past was done, and we would go on from here together, faithful and true to each other.

"Is anyone ready for another glass of wine?" Fraser asked, and busied himself filling our glasses.

The next half hour passed pleasantly enough in talking about our trip. When the bottle was empty, we all rose to go down to the ball. The haunting melody of a Strauss waltz came through the lobby and up the stairs to greet us. I held my feathered mask up as we descended. The crinolines lent a touch of glamour to the occasion. They seemed to have a life of their own, bobbing and gliding like waves on the sea as I walked, with Fraser holding my elbow.

The Ramplings went in front of us. I was happy to see that Margot looked rather common from behind. Her flaming hair had separated into strands at the back, and her shoulders had spots that had been powdered over.

"How do you like my friends?" Fraser asked.

"Charming," I said through thin lips. "I expect you have many other friends as well?"

"Oh, certainly, but the Ramplings are my closest friends. That's why I invited them tonight. I hope you and Margot hit it off. We'll probably be seeing a good deal of them. Charles wants me to go into a business venture with him. A shipping company," he added vaguely.

"I see."

Nothing was definite. If I found I truly disliked the Ramplings after tonight, Fraser wouldn't insist upon inflicting them on me. This wasn't the time to worry about the future. We were at a ball, celebrating my birthday, and I would enjoy every minute of it.

I did enjoy the colorful throng of guests, waltzing gracefully under the chandeliers. We were shown to a table, and Fraser ordered champagne in honor of my birthday. After toasting me, everyone wanted to waltz. It was like a dream, wafting in Fraser's arms to the romantic music of Strauss, with emeralds at my throat and my crinoline standing out around me, bouncing with every movement. After the first dance, we changed partners and I waltzed with Oliver, who danced superbly. I could forgive his dull conversation, he danced so exquisitely.

I truly didn't mind when Fraser asked Margot to dance with him again. I disliked her less after the second glass of champagne. Oliver and I watched them leave.

"You're stuck with me, Oliver," I said playfully, and offered him my hand.

"A pleasure, madame," he smiled, but he didn't take my hand, or stand up.

We had all been drinking freely, and Oliver's bleary eyes told me he had had more than he could handle. When he finally did rise, he excused himself and said he thought he could use a breath of air. I sat alone, holding my glass, watching the others dance. Later, I looked around at the unescorted gentlemen, of which there were several standing on the side lines, in black dominoes and masks. Two or three of them were looking at me. An unescorted lady was of interest to them, but I looked away quickly, to discourage any advance.

My real interest was Fraser and Margot. I looked back to where they had been waltzing. Though I looked all around that general area, I couldn't see them. They were gone. It was Margot's flaming hair that finally caught my eye. They weren't waltzing now. She had Fraser by the hand, hastily leading him off the floor toward the exit. She stopped and looked up at him, smiling softly, and I saw him reach down and just touch her lips with his finger. The gesture was more familiar than a kiss. It was possessive. It spoke of long, close intimacy. I knew as sure as death they had been lovers. I sat, frozen, staring at the now empty doorway.

I didn't see Mycroft Harlow as he came toward me. I didn't even recognize him when he stood, silently staring at me. "I don't want to dance," I said gruffly, to get rid of whatever forward gentleman had come to pester me.

"Neither do I, Rose," he said.

I recognized his deep, authoritative voice at once, and when I looked at him, I recognized his head and general build, though he still wore his mask. He pulled out a chair and sat down. "Having a happy birthday?" he asked ironically.

"Very happy," I said through grim lips. I lifted the bottle and poured myself another glass of champagne.

"This is a strange marriage," he said mockingly, "when a wife's idea of a perfect husband is one who leaves her alone at a public ball, prey to any hedgebird who cares to molest her."

Fraser wasn't there to receive my wrath, so I took it out on Mycroft. "But then we didn't know you planned to attend, Cousin," I said in icy accents.

Mycroft smiled satirically. "Mrs. Rampling didn't waste any time reclaiming her prize," he said. There was infinite satisfaction in his voice.

My instinct was to attack, but my thirst for knowledge was even stronger. Mycroft knew! He knew all about Margot and Fraser, and I had to discover the truth.

"Reclaiming?" I asked archly. "You sound very well informed on my husband's peccadilloes." It was an invitation to reveal what he knew, and I didn't think Mycroft would fail to respond.

He didn't answer immediately. He reached for the champagne bottle and said, "May I?" before pouring himself a glass. He drank half the glass, then set it on the table and looked at me. It was impossible to see anything behind his mask, but his lips were grim.

"Fraser's affairs are no secret. I should have

thought he could wait till after your birthday, however."

"You know about him and Margot?"

"The whole town knows about it."

"Tell me, Mycroft. Tell me everything. I must know." I didn't realize I was holding on to his sleeve till he pulled away.

"It's a little late for that, Rose," he sneered. "You should have asked me before you signed those papers."

"Damn the papers! What has that got to do with anything? Tell me. How long have they been lovers?"

He just sighed and patted my hand. "I don't know how long, and it doesn't matter. Before Margot there were others, and after Margot there will be still others. You must know by now what Fraser is."

It's strange I believed him so quickly. Had I not seen what I had just seen, I wouldn't have believed. But I had seen Fraser gently touch Margot's lips. Longingly, lovingly—as he had often touched me.

"Men, there's no trusting them, Rosalie," Miss Williams used to say, before the advent of Fraser into our lives. She never said it about him, but she had been right all along. I, in my youthful arrogance, thought her only an embittered old maid, but Miss Williams had been right.

A hiccoughing sound caught in my throat, and I suddenly realized that my eyes were wet behind the mask. I stood up and fled the room, heading for the same door that Fraser had left by. Halfway there, I realized I might meet him, and turned back. I stood in the middle of the busy dance floor, feeling more abandoned than I had ever felt in my life. My own father's death hadn't affected me so cruelly as this betrayal. A waltzing couple bumped my shoulder and sent me reeling. I thought I would hit the floor, and didn't care a groat.

Before this happened, a strong hand gripped my elbow. Someone put an arm protectively around my waist and piloted me out a different door into a dark, quiet room, filled with empty tables, each wearing a ghostly damask cloth. I knew before I looked that it was Mycroft, but at that instant he was my rescuer, and I was no longer angry with him.

"Come now, don't cry. This is your birthday, Rose," he said gently. Light filtered in through the partially open door. Mycroft had removed his mask. Shadows distorted his appearance, casting a blur over his lower face. While I stood trying to control my sobs, he reached out and removed my feathered mask. He held it in his hand, looking at me.

It must be the shadows that make him look so fierce, I thought wanly. To judge by his eyes, one would think he felt the urge to kill, but his voice was soft.

"Shall I kill him, as I've always wanted to?" he suggested. It was a mocking question, obviously not serious, but with an edge to it. "That's the only way to keep the estate, you know. Divorce won't do it."

The estate—that's all Mycroft was interested in. No doubt much of it would revert to him if Fraser died without leaving an heir. I wasn't angry enough to listen to him, not angry enough to think of murder, but I was angry enough to want revenge. I also wanted to hide from Mycroft how deeply I was hurt. Pride demanded that much of me.

"Don't be ridiculous," I scoffed, tossing my head. "One doesn't commit murder for a little indiscretion."

"There's more than a little indiscretion going on here, my dear. But I see you're determined to put on a brave face, as I knew you would. I'll bring some champagne and we'll stay here till you're ready to face the music."

Mycroft left. I went to the door and peered through the milling throng to our table. There was no one there, not even Oliver. I didn't want to stay here with Mycroft, yet I didn't want to sit alone at a public table either. I shouldn't have had any more champagne, but my nerves needed a strong tonic to get me through the rest of that hellish night. When Mycroft returned with a bottle and two glasses, I didn't object.

I would get tipsy, and flirt with this cousin, whom my husband despised. One more glass was enough to do it. "Why are we hiding in shadows, Cousin?" I said coquettishly. "Let us join the party and waltz."

Mycroft examined me curiously. His first look of surprise changed to amusement. "Planning to use me to make Fraser jealous, eh, Rose? Take care what you're about—I might demand payment. You're no longer protected by maidenly youth and innocence," he cautioned.

I was in no mood for caution. The night had gone beyond such tame stuff. "And what payment would you demand, sir?" I asked archly.

His eyes stared into mine unflinchingly. "Just what you think, Mrs. Audry."

A wave of warmth rose up over my shoulders, up my neck to stain my cheeks. I tried to look confused, but there was knowledge in the long look we exchanged.

Mycroft placed my hand on his arm—possessively. My fingers trembled, but his were calm and steady.

"No, don't wear your mask. I want to see you," he said when I began to attach my mask.

I flushed at the way his eyes caressed me. This man could indeed be dangerous—not in the way Fraser had intimated, but as a lover. It was the same sort of look Fraser had bestowed on Margot, and I was seared by it. It went straight through my flesh and touched my spirit. I couldn't draw my gaze away from him. I don't know how long we stood staring at each other as though hypnotized. I trembled when he put his arms around me.

Then the music swelled and we began a swirling dance, crinoline swaying as my feet moved on wings over the floor. Of course it was the champagne that lent that touch of madness to our dance. That feeling that nothing mattered but the music and the waltz and being in Mycroft's arms. Especially being in Mycroft's arms, where I felt safe. It was about the most treacherous place I could possibly be, but the solidity of his warm chest against mine, the strength of his arms holding me, his very presence was a bulwark against despair.

As the music slowed I leaned back and said, "No more circles, Cousin. I'm giddy!"

His black eyes were devouring me. We were back at the door where we had begun. He spun through the opening and pulled me hard against him. Before I knew what was happening, his head came down and his lips plundered mine in a ruthless kiss. I tried to push him off, but he was too strong, and too determined.

"I'll have one kiss, dammit. You owe me that much, Rose," he growled in a husky voice.

It was too much to resist. Between the champagne, my anger with Fraser, and Mycroft's strength, I was overborne. At first I only submitted. As his lips burned on mine, as one hand began an exploration of my back and the other pressed me against him till I could even feel the buttons of his jacket pressing my breasts, submission escalated to encouragement. My arms were around his neck. My fingers reveled in his crisp black hair, and the quivering excitement at my vital core warned what would come next. Passion crouched, ready to spring and undo me. How fatally easy to be unfaithful! Perhaps I had been too hard on Fraser.

I pulled free and stood panting. Mycroft looked drunk with desire. I felt the same way. "We shouldn't have done that," I said in a quavering voice.

Mycroft grabbed my two hands. "Rose, if you ever want to be free of him, if you ever need me, you know I'll be waiting for you. You have only to write me at Thornbridge, or come to me. Promise me you'll do it."

In total confusion, and wanting only to get away I said, "Yes, I'll remember, Mycroft."

"Why do you call me Mycroft? You make me sound like a stranger. Call me Mike, as you used to."

"What?" I frowned at this strange speech. I couldn't remember calling him Mike. Through the partially open door, I spotted Margot's Titian hair and blue gown. She was still with Fraser. They were at our table, looking all around for me. The music had stopped, but people still milled around the floor.

"I must go back," I said.

Mycroft looked out and saw Fraser too. "Are you sure you want to?" he asked.

"Of course I'm sure. Don't come with me, Mycroft. He'll wonder—"

"No, he won't wonder. He'll know, and I for one don't give a damn." He pushed open the door, but I didn't wait for him. I fled alone to the table and smiled gaily, as though I hadn't just been in another man's arms. And my husband in another woman's. Fraser and Margot were experienced enough that they looked innocent.

"What have you done with my husband?" Margot asked lightly.

"Oliver stepped out for a breath of air." No one asked me where I had been, and I didn't tell them. They seemed to assume that Oliver and I had just parted.

"More champagne, darling?" Fraser asked.

"I've had my quota. Fraser, would you mind if we go upstairs now? I'm frightfully tired."

"Very well, dear. I'll find Oliver for Margot first. We can't leave her alone."

Fraser went off in search of Oliver and soon

72

returned with him. While he was gone, Margot said, "We must get together tomorrow and go shopping, Rosalie. I'll write a note and set the time."

"Fine, you do that, Margot," I smiled. And I shall throw your note into the closest grate.

Fraser and I went upstairs, arm in arm. It wasn't till the door was closed that I turned on him like a Fury.

CHAPTER SEVEN

AFTER THE SHOUTS AND TEARS, THE ACCUSATIONS AND rebuttals, Fraser admitted he had been intimate with Margot Rampling. "It happened a long time ago, Rosie, long before I knew you," he told me. By that time we had settled down. We sat close together on the sofa, holding hands. Fraser was like himself again, smiling and loving, but something had gone out of our perfect marriage. It was no longer the bright and beautiful thing it had seemed that morning. It was touched by reality—and I felt old and disillusioned.

"Tonight I told her it was all over between us," Fraser confided. "I couldn't do it in front of you and Oliver, obviously. That's the only reason we left the ballroom. We only went into the lobby. You sound as though—"

74

"It was the way you touched her, Fraser, and smiled."

"What you saw was regret, my dear, for something that should never have been. I promise you, it will never happen again."

But it had happened once, and that shattered the charm. "How could you bring her here and expect her to be my friend? I don't want to go on seeing them. It would be too uncomfortable."

"If that's the way you feel, then you'll never meet the Ramplings again. Oliver is involved in a very interesting shipping deal—we could make a fortune on it, but I'll find something else instead. Your happiness is all that matters to me."

I forgave him—in words, but my heart was still sore. We cuddled and made up, and later Fraser said, "Who were you waltzing with, Rosie? It just occurred to me, Oliver was out sobering up. The man looked taller than Oliver."

Guilt set like a ton of lead on my breast. I wanted to confess about Mycroft, yet dreaded to do it. "It was Mycroft Harlow," I said reluctantly.

The name was like a goad to Fraser. He jumped up, fire flashing from his eyes. Language I never heard before came gushing from his mouth, making me blush. I decided at that moment that my confession must remain forever unspoken. If he ever suspected what had passed between Mycroft and me, I honestly feared he would kill Mycroft. This was how men saw marriage—a wife was their sole and unique property.

"What did he want? What did he say?" he shouted.

"Just mocking things about you and Margot—

that you were her lover." It gave me a sense of power to make the charge against him.

"You see what kind of a trouble-maker he is? What sort of a man would tell a young bride her husband was unfaithful? Mycroft Harlow is poison, Rosie. I want you to promise me you'll never speak to the man again."

Looking at Mycroft's behavior from a little distance, I found there was some truth in Fraser's assessment. Why had Mycroft told me about Margot? Oh I had asked him, of course, but a friend would have told a polite lie. A real gentleman wouldn't have made love to his cousin's wife. He wouldn't have taken advantage of a young woman's emotional turmoil to try to turn her against her husband. Yet he had seemed genuinely concerned for me. . . . My inexperience with men left me confused.

"I promise, Fraser. If I hadn't been alone at the table, I wouldn't have danced with him. Other men were looking at me. You must be patient with me. I find London manners so—so different from what I'm used to. We never had any trouble like this when we were traveling." I frowned over this. "Of course when we were traveling, we didn't have much to do with other people, really. I'm a greenhorn. I've lived in London all my life, but I have the naiveté of a country-bred girl. It will take me a while to find my social sea legs."

Fraser looked rather sad. "I love you just as you are, darling. It was your sweet innocence that attracted me. I hate to think of you becoming all sophisticated and spoiled. I'd like to carry you off to the country and lock you in a rose-covered cottage, where the world will never get at you."

We laughed at the idea that night, but by morning it had taken root in Fraser's mind.

"Rosie, what do you say we buy a country house instead of a London one?"

"But your business—don't you have to be in the city?"

"We'll need some sort of pied-à-terre in town, but I'd like to make the country our permanent home. A fine estate, where we could ride horses and raise our children in the healthy country air. We could come to London for the Season and shopping and so on."

"I never thought of living in the country," I said.

The idea, once I did begin to think of it, had some charm. The country would be lovely during the summer, and if we had an apartment in town, it wouldn't become tedious. I felt instinctively it would be a more healthy moral atmosphere, especially for Fraser. He had so many city friends, and no doubt they were all similar to the Ramplings. There was that Helen Swanson mentioned last night. I suspected she was another of Fraser's flirts. Yes, the country began to look better by the moment.

Fraser clapped his hands in excitement. "I have an idea! Let's hire a house in the country for the next few months and see how we like it. Some friends of mine are letting their place for the winter while they go to Italy. It's only a cottage, really, but it will give us the feel of the country. Are you willing to try it?"

"I'll give it a try. And if we find it doesn't suit, we'll have someplace to stay while we look for a house in town, and fix it up as we like."

"It will be perfect." Fraser smiled excitedly. "Longbeach isn't far from London."

I knew that Fraser's family lived in West Sussex, and as he used the word 'beach,' it occurred to me that this house for hire might be close to Thornbridge, and Mycroft Harlow. "Where is this house, exactly?"

"It's in Norfolk, near Heacham. It sits on the mouth of the Wash, that bay in the North Sea. We could buy or borrow a yacht. Have you ever done any boating?"

"No, never. Isn't Norfolk rather far from London, Fraser?"

"It's only a hundred miles. With a good team we could make it in under two days. Or there might be rail service. I'll look into it."

"Why don't we try to find someplace a little closer—say in Kent or Essex, if you want to be by the sea?"

"Longbeach is standing idle right now. And it would do my friends a favor. They could use the money."

"They don't sound purse-pinched if they're gone to Italy for the winter."

Fraser's regard was rebukeful. "It isn't a pleasure jaunt, Rosie. Mrs. Halton had to be taken to a warm climate for her health. I'd like to do something to help them, and renting Longbeach would help us as well. A sort of practical philanthropy."

"Have you seen the house? Is it a nice place?"

"I haven't seen it, but from what I've heard, it sounds ideal. It's small, just a cottage. It comes with servants—a married couple. We haven't hired any servants yet, and this will save us the bother for the time being."

I hadn't considered the hiring of servants a "bother," but a treat. "What about Miss Williams?" I asked. "Will there be a place for her as well?"

"Of course there will," he said, laughing. "It's a spacious house. When I used the word cottage, I didn't mean to imply it only had a couple of rooms."

The difference in our backgrounds sometimes led me astray. I should have known that Fraser's idea of a 'cottage' would resemble my notion of a country estate. As though he'd be willing to live in some shambles of a place, or take me there!

As we talked, I began to see that Longbeach had its advantages. I especially liked the fact that it would keep Fraser from his fast friends. Autumn wasn't the best time to spend by the sea, but it would be a novelty for me, and if we liked it we could eventually settle on some part of the coast. Right after breakfast, Fraser went to make the arrangement with the estate agent, whose name he knew from his friend.

"You might as well begin packing," he told me. "Ask the hotel to send up some women to help you, Rosie."

His cheery smile put me in a good mood too. I felt rather self-righteous, agreeing to go off into the country with my husband. In the superior moral climate provided by nature, the little crack in our marriage would heal. We hadn't unpacked much yet, and I decided to do the packing myself, as I had nothing else to do that morning. I received a note from Margot Rampling suggesting we meet for lunch, and sent back an answer telling her that we had decided to remove to the country. I wondered what she'd make of that.

"Mycroft hasn't come to call?" were Fraser's first words when he came back. Even before he told me he had hired the cottage.

"No. I doubt he'll come." In the sane light of day, I had decided that last night was a moment's madness. Mycroft probably regretted it as much as I. "Did you hire Longbeach?"

He took an envelope from his pocket. "Here's the lease. If we leave this afternoon, we can be there by tomorrow evening. Is everything ready?"

"All set," I said. "There's just one detail, Fraser. What shall we do about Miss Williams? We'll leave word, of course, but how will she get to us?"

"I'll send her money to hire a private carriage. We won't want her buffeted about on the public coach."

These thoughtful, generous gestures were the real Fraser. Even hiring Longbeach was an act of kindness to help a friend. I sensed he would be happier closer to London.

"In fact, I'll leave off a letter and the money this afternoon before we go."

With several details to be attended to, we had lunch in our suite. I wrote the letter while we ate, and Fraser gave me money to enclose. I hoped Miss Williams wouldn't be disappointed at the idea of moving to the country.

"Oh, incidentally," Fraser said, "you are now the proud owner of three thousand pounds' worth of Consolidated Annuities. I invested your money this morning."

"Really! I own Consols!" I smiled fatuously at being such a financier. "Do I get some certificates or something?"

"They'll be sending them along in the mail. Hibbard will handle it for us. I got three percent interest for you. Not much, but Consols are as safe as the Bank of England."

After a hasty lunch, Fraser went downstairs to dispatch Miss Williams' note, arrange for the carriage, and settle up our account at the Savoy. He planned to tell the hotel to forward any mail to us at Longbeach. I smiled softly to consider how I had outwitted Margot Rampling.

When Fraser came back he had servants with him to take the luggage down. "We're off!" he exclaimed. "You'll want to wear your new sable, Rosie."

He held the luxurious cape for me. The bouquet of violets was still attached, all wilted now. I took them off and threw them in the wastebasket. Their scent permeated the cape. Footmen bustled about as we swept through the lobby. The hotel manager came personally to say good-bye and tell us how he looked forward to our next visit. A frisky team of four were chomping at the bit to be on the road. I rested at ease against the velvet squabs of the elegant carriage and looked at London passing by, taking my leave with no regrets.

"What did you do with the jewelry, Fraser?" I asked.

"I didn't think you'd want it at Longbeach. I took it back to the bank vault this morning. I had to go there on business. You have your sapphires and diamond ring if you want to lord it over the provincials in Norfolk," he said, smiling.

"I would have liked to have the sapphire peacock too."

With an intimate smile, he reached in his pocket and handed it to me. "I thought you might," he said.

As I didn't want to pin it on my fur cape, I put it in the deep pocket. My fingers encountered something hard and cold as I reached in. Curious, I pulled it out.

"Look, Fraser! It's the other diamond earring!" I exclaimed. "How on earth did it get there?"

Fraser, to fool me, appeared stunned. I realized at once what had happened. He had found it and put it there to surprise me. "You found it!" I said, and kissed him. "Where was it? We looked all through the case yesterday and it wasn't there."

"It was still in the safety box at the bank. I opened the case before bringing it home yesterday. Careless of me to drop it. I hope you take better care of the family heirlooms than I do."

"Did you bring the other with you? I can't very well wear one earring."

"I forgot!" he said, and clapped his forehead with the heel of his hand. "Damn! I meant to bring it. You don't have any good earrings with you. I thought the diamonds would go well with your sapphires when we entertain or go out."

"It's not important," I assured him.

The trip to Longbeach was like a continuation of our wedding trip. Just the two of us, but being alone suited me now. I had come to realize the danger of exposing my highly desirable husband to society.

I was content to gaze out the window at the gently undulating series of green hills and valleys, interspersed with villages and towns. The air was clean and fresh in this unindustrialized part of the island. As we continued northward the second day, the land began to flatten out to marshlands. The closer we got to Longbeach, the flatter and more isolated the landscape became. Of hills and valleys there were none, but only hedgeless acres of fen recovered from the sea. As we approached the sea, even the sparse gorse petered out to sand, stippled here and there with stringy grass and reeds. It was desolate in the extreme.

"It's rather dreary countryside," I mentioned.

"I find it peaceful," Fraser said.

He looked peaceful. I had to wonder how long it would take for peace to become boredom. Longbeach would require some extraordinary degree of charm to seduce me into liking it. After the ever-changing novelty of travel, the stark landscape was stultifying. I kept looking for some interesting buildings, some people, or even a tree. There was an occasional meager tree.

We smelled the sea before we could see it. As we drew near, a small white-washed, thatched cottage came into view. It consisted of three pitch-roofed rectangles pulled together, the short ends of two backed against the long side of the third. The two backed against the long side were uneven, one shorter than the other and a story less high, giving a chopped, unsymmetrical, and unlovely look to the whole. There was no formal landscaping. Patchy, sparse grass wandered around the house, and at the water's edge there were reeds nodding lazily in the breeze.

"Whoever lives here might be able to direct us to Longbeach," I suggested.

"This is Longbeach," Fraser told me.

I stared, my heart sinking to my shoes. Then I looked at Fraser, hoping to see a smile break, hoping that he was teasing me. I saw only mild interest as he stared out at the house.

"It's not quite as spacious as I had hoped, but the view is lovely," he said, gazing out to sea.

"Fraser, there isn't even a stable! And no garden."

"We'll put in a garden. It will be a hobby for us. There is that little spinney behind the house, you see, so things will grow here."

We wouldn't be starting a garden in autumn, however, and my hope was that we would be out of here long before spring.

We got out of the carriage just as the front door opened and the housekeeper came to greet us. She was a stern-looking woman of middle years, with black hair skimmed into a knob. She wore a clean white apron and decent black dress.

"I'm Mrs. Warner. I've been expecting you. You'd be the Audrys," she said. "Come on in."

Fraser went to speak to the groom, and I went along with him. "How did she know we were coming? There hasn't been time to send a message," I mentioned.

"I had a message sent down the morning I signed the lease. I wanted the place to be cleaned and ready for us." He turned to speak to the groom. "You'd best take the carriage into Heacham and find a stable after you unload our trunks. Come back tomorrow morning."

The groom began to untie the trunks, and Fraser turned to me. "We'll have to hire some mounts, and possibly set up a jig. I can't leave the carriage out, exposed to the weather."

"Yes," I agreed doubtfully.

A day or two here would surely show him the error of thinking that we should live here. At the moment I was tired, bone weary and hungry, and I expected Fraser felt the same way. Twilight was falling, but there was no beautiful sunset on the sea. We were on the east coast. A purple haze with golden reflections hung over the lapping water. Sunrise might be interesting, though.

We went inside, and Mrs. Warner showed us to our bedroom. She proved to be a taciturn woman. I noticed that her upper lip sprouted an incipient moustache, giving her a masculine look.

The house was built with so little thought to convenience that the master bedroom didn't even overlook the water. Our view was flat marshland, with only a few straggling blades of wild grass. It would be impossible to grow a garden on this salty soil.

"This looks cozy," Fraser said heartily.

It was a country bedroom, with a few incongruous city touches. The plain bed had a blue brocade canopy and blue drapes at the window. There was a well-worn carpet on the floor. The nap was all gone, but imbedded in the threads were the remnants of a pattern of intertwined flowers. The furnishings were heavy, dark mahogany from the past century. They had never been fine; now they were just old and distressed. I felt tired just looking at the room.

We spoke little as we freshened up for dinner. It seemed a joke to dress up, so we went below in our traveling clothes. Mrs. Warner had set the table with decent china and silver and candles.

"I don't do fancy cooking," she warned us. "Just mutton and potatoes and vegetables, but there's plenty of it."

Fraser looked askance at the table. "Is there no wine?" he asked.

"Aye, I'll have my husband get up a bottle."

She left and returned soon with a dusty bottle of port. The dinner was fair, with little variety. The only vegetable other than potatoes was carrots.

"What's the matter, Rosie?" Fraser asked. He was trying to put a good face on this mistake, and I tried to abet him.

"I'm just tired."

"I admit Longbeach isn't exactly what I expected," he confessed, "but it will do for a while. I'll hire a yacht, and we'll get mounts. The bracing air will do you a world of good, after your miscarriage." That again! Good gracious, I thought I was through with hearing about that illusion.

"I've never ridden, Fraser."

"Then it's high time you learn!" he said. "This is the spot for it, with no one to see your spills. You don't want to take your first falls in Rotten Row, with everyone seeing you. We'll send off to London for some good books too, and when the weather turns cold, we'll huddle around the fire and catch up on our reading. You'll have Miss Williams to keep you company."

More importantly, I would have Fraser. If he

wanted a spell of peace and quiet after our bout of travel, I wouldn't spoil it for him. Perhaps it wouldn't be so bad. And if it became unbearable, we could always leave.

"It will be fun," I answered.

"I'm sure you'll come to like it."

Chapter Eight

The next morning we awoke to no marvelous sun-rise but a drizzle of rain from leaden skies. The little cottage was unutterably dreary. Unpacking the trunks seemed pointless. Surely we wouldn't be staying.

"Fraser, let's have the trunks put on the carriage when it comes and go back to London," I suggested. We sat in the little living room, shivering and unable to get close to the grate because smoke hung like a fog around the fireplace.

He laughed as though I were joking. "You're letting one bad day put you off. You're not a quitter, Rosie. Tomorrow the sun will shine, and you'll love it here. I'll drive into Heacham when the carriage comes and hire our mounts. I'll see if I can find a yacht for hire as well. I won't ask you to go out in this downpour. You unpack, and we'll talk about it some more this afternoon. If you truly dislike it here after giving it a good try—a week say—then I'll take you back."

When Fraser returned, he was mounted on a fine chestnut gelding, leading a mare for me behind him. He had the name of a gentleman who had a yacht for hire. When the weather let up, he'd go and speak to him. Unfortunately, the weather didn't let up. The gelding and the bay were sheltered under an overhanging roof at the back of the house, with stout blankets to keep them from freezing.

As bad as the days were, the evenings were worse. They were interminable. We had no books, no magazines. There weren't even any cards in the house. After a mediocre dinner, Mrs. Warner told me she had a sewing box, if I would care to mend anything. My clothing and Fraser's was all too new to require mending, so I mended a rent tablecloth till my eyes became sore and my head ached.

"What are you doing, Fraser?" I asked. He was at a desk, poring over some papers.

"I'm just reading some literature from Mr. Hibbard. Since you don't want me to go into the shipping venture with Rampling, I must find something else to invest our money in. If you're bored, why don't you write to Miss Williams?"

It was a change of occupation at least. I tried my hand at making rain and a small cottage in the wilderness not sound dreadful, which was best done by ignoring them. I wrote of the sea, and the yacht, and our mounts, but these would be little consolation to Miss Williams. I foresaw infinite boredom for her. It would be kinder to warn her of the truth.

The next day it rained again. My headache was

no better and I felt sluggish. As there was nothing to do out of bed, I stayed in it. Fraser got me some novels at the circulating library at Heacham, and I fell in love again with Miss Bronte's Rochester. I also asked Fraser to pick up *Wuthering Heights,* that I might wile away the next day with Heathcliff.

The next morning we awoke to sunshine and I got up, ready to tackle riding. I had no riding habit, but was willing to sacrifice my blue suit to the cause. When I got outdoors, the wind cut through me like a knife. I was still a little feverish and not feeling at all well. Fraser was so disappointed.

"Belle should be exercised, Rosie," he urged. "See what a beauty she is. Look at those eyes, and the deep chest on her."

"You go ahead and ride, Fraser. I really don't feel up to it. Later in the day I'll take a stroll and begin investigating the neighborhood. The little spinney . . ." So meager were the delights of the area that a spinney no bigger than a city block loomed as a rare treat.

"You'd best stick to the shore, Rosie. Warner saw a fox in the spinney last night."

My shoulders sagged in disappointment and I sighed deeply.

"Darling, are you ill?" Fraser asked, staring at me wild-eyed. "What a brute I am. I can see you're pale as a ghost. I'll send for a doctor at once."

"No, no. I'm just tired after that little bout of flu." I called my illness flu, though there was no cold associated with it. "I'll go back to bed for a few hours. You go ahead and ride. Please do. There's no reason for you to sit beside me all day."

"I see what it is," he joked. "I have competition

—it's that Rochester fellow you were reading about yesterday."

I finished *Jane Eyre*, then slept. I got up for dinner but couldn't eat much. I felt tired and listless, as though the life were washing out of me. I spent half the time asleep, dreaming wild and horrible dreams. The next day I was no better. Fraser sent for a doctor to examine me. The man's name was Dr. Agnew. He was a provincial who held no truck with modern medications. He prescribed an old-fashioned tonic that was three-quarters whiskey. It was flavored with cherry syrup, and quite tasty, but left a bitterness behind.

"A good rest is what the young lady needs. Plenty of fresh air and sunshine. Wrap her up warm and put her out in the sun, where she'll trap the salubrious sea breezes in her lungs. She'll be right as rain in no time," the doctor asserted.

My constant companion during the ensuing days was a friendly collie called Scout. He sat at my feet while I read, and thought, and looked out at the dreary water. Most of the time I was half asleep. The sun on the water gave the illusion that the ocean was on fire. Strange, imaginary monsters loomed up out of it to menace me. Then I would jerk myself back to reality and realize the monsters were only the shadows of clouds.

There were some fishing boats to amuse me, and a few sailboats. Fraser sat with me sometimes, and he also did those things gentlemen do in the country. He wrote letters, rode, bought a gun and looked for something to shoot, and when he had his fill of that, he rode into Heacham.

We had been at Longbeach for one week when he

announced, "I have to take a run into London on business, Rosie. I wish you could come with me, but—" I sat huddled in a blanket before the fire, sipping wine.

I looked up, excited at the news. "I can! I'll go, Fraser. I'd love to."

"Don't be foolish. You're not up to the trip," he said, rather harshly.

I gave a gasp of surprise at his angry tone. Fraser immediately became contrite. "Forgive me, dear. I am worried about leaving you—you look worn to the socket. But I'll do something you will like. I'll see if I can renege on this lease while I'm there. The property was misrepresented to me. We'll go somewhere livelier. Brighton perhaps, in a week or two."

Really I didn't feel up to going with him. "Stop at Watling Street too, will you please, and see if Miss Williams is there. I thought she would be here by now."

"She probably extended her visit with her sister. I'll go after her and drag her back with me if she's there."

"How long will you be gone?"

"I only need a few days in London."

But with two days to get there and two days to return, it would be nearly a week. And I would worry every moment about Margot Rampling.

"You won't see *her*?" I asked.

"Who?" he said, but when he lifted his eyes and met mine, the image of Margot was between us. "Rosie, don't you trust me?" he chided. There was hurt in his blue eyes as he examined me reproachfully. "Didn't we come here to get away from the sordid city life? I shan't see anyone but businessmen. I'll be back before you can say Jack Robinson. What would you like me to bring you, other than Miss Williams? Books, embroidery, bonbons?"

It was strange that Fraser didn't worry about my loss of weight. He always used to be urging me to fill out. I had lost a few pounds since coming to Longbeach, but he didn't seem to notice, or care. Did all marriages dwindle to this in the end?

"I can afford to eat bonbons now," I decided. "Bring any new novels you can lay your hands on. I'm half finished with *Wuthering Heights*. And perhaps some embroidery equipment. I've never done it, but I have plenty of time to learn now."

We didn't make love before he left, as I thought we would. And to tell the truth, I was relieved. It was my tonic that made me so disinterested and sleepy and I nodded off almost before Fraser had gotten undressed and joined me. He left early in the morning. I was awake, but he asked me not to get up.

"The day will seem long enough without even me here for company," he said. "Don't forget to take your tonic, dear. I want to see the roses back in your cheeks when I return. And, Rosie—if Mycroft should come sniffing around—"

"Mycroft! Fraser, he won't come here!" I had almost forgotten Mycroft Harlow. A sharp image of his navy blue eyes popped into my head at hearing his name. My pulse raced at the memory.

"But if he should, have Warner run him. Remember, you promised me you wouldn't speak to the man. I don't want him pestering you."

"He won't come. How could he know where we are?"

"I wouldn't put it past him to hire someone to follow you. In any case, don't see him if he comes."

"I shan't."

Fraser kissed me goodbye and left. I went to the window to watch him ride away. He looked so handsome astride that Bay gelding, yet the little smile on my lips was due to a memory of a different handsome gentleman. Did all wives harbor these foolish dreams of some other man than their husbands? What if I had not married Fraser, what if I had met Mycroft first . . .

I pushed the thought away. Fraser was riding into Heacham to get the carriage. I felt a little better, as I often did in the morning. I even felt strong enough to tackle Belle, but I would wait till Fraser returned to help me. Before I got dressed, Mrs. Warner was at the door with a tray.

"Mr. Audry said you should stay in bed," she announced. She set the tray on the dresser with a commanding eye.

As she had gone to the trouble of carrying the tray upstairs, I decided to oblige her and eat in bed. "I shall take luncheon downstairs, Mrs. Warner," I told her.

"We'll see how you feel. Don't forget your medicine." She put the bottle on the tray for me. "It's a nice day," she mentioned, looking out the window. "I'll have Warner take your chair outside later."

I felt stout enough to do more than sit today. I thought I might go for a walk along the coast, and perhaps meet some neighbors. It was lonesome eating breakfast alone, gammon and eggs and strong tea. I took my medicine and got dressed. When I got downstairs, my energy was sapped. All I felt up to was sitting in the sun, rubbing Scout's furry neck, nodding and having my vivid dreams. I ate lunch downstairs, but by evening I was so tired I had dinner in bed, and only nibbled at it.

For the next few days, things continued in the same vein. I didn't get worse, but I didn't get better. The only soul I saw other than the Warners was an old fisherman who stopped to show me a long, silver fish one afternoon as I sat in the pale sunlight.

"There's a tasty dinner then, Mrs.," he said, smiling. Half his teeth were missing. I smiled back. "It's nice to see you up and about again, Mrs. Sorry to hear about your wee one. But you're young. You'll fill your nursery yet." He winked and nodded and went on his way.

I pondered his disjointed speech. He must have heard in the village that I was ill, but surely Fraser had not been prating of my 'miscarriage' there? The man's rough speech and vacant smile suggested he might be the village idiot. I yawned and forgot him.

His mention of filling a nursery gave rise to an interesting possibility, though. It occurred to me that I might really be pregnant. Miss Williams said some women were very tired and sleepy and grouchy and felt ill in the early months of child carrying. That was the way I felt—but what could account for my weird, rather frightening dreams?

When I complained of the cool breezes, Warner found me a sheltered nook behind a sand hill, from which I was invisible from the house. I enjoyed my rest more then, for I disliked the feeling of always being watched by the Warners. A new twist was added to my reading. Heathcliff had magically turned into Mycroft Harlow.

When it was too wet or too cold—and the weather was getting quite cold—I stayed inside by the grate, reading and dreaming. Increasingly there was more dreaming than reading. I blamed my lethargy on Fraser's absence. When he came home, I would have more incentive to become active.

The week passed swiftly, considering how little I had to amuse myself. On the seventh day the wind from the sea was milder and I went out after lunch. Scout curled up at my feet, offering his warm fur as a rug. I felt quite happy. Fraser would be home this evening, if all went well. Miss Williams would be with him. I told Mrs. Warner to cook a special dinner for three. With the sun warming my shoulders, I dozed off after an hour, dreaming of Brighton, hoping we could go there.

I was wakened by a hand on my shoulder. I looked up in surprise, sure it would be Fraser, to see Mycroft Harlow's dark and probing eyes examining me. He leaned close over me, so close I felt his breath fan my cheek. He looked as surprised as I felt. In my first shock, I thought he was a dream.

"My God, Rose, what's happened to you?" he asked harshly. "You look like death."

The breath caught in my lungs, and I was unable to speak. I had thought my reaction to this man was due to champagne, and anger with Fraser, and a dozen other things. I wasn't tipsy now, and I wasn't angry with my husband, but my heart pounded with excitement. It was his presence that did it, and the awful concern in his eyes.

"I've been ill," I said, and noticed how light my voice was.

"I can see that! What's the matter with you? Have

you seen a doctor?" He grasped my hand, and began feeling my pulse. His fingers were like fire on my cool wrist.

"Yes, of course. I'm taking a tonic."

The wind had grown colder while I dozed off. The sun was gone under a blanket of clouds and a stiff breeze lifted whitecaps on the sea, which looked bleak and cold and gray.

"What are you doing out in this gale? You should be in bed."

"The doctor prescribed sea air. Mycroft," I said nervously, "please go. Fraser doesn't want you here."

His face turned to stone. "Fraser's in London."

"No, he'll be home today."

"I doubt that. He has tickets for Drury Lane tonight."

"No!" I shouted angrily. "He hasn't! He'll be home today. How do you know—"

"I make it my business to know what Audry's up to. He's painting the town red with his friends."

The clenching of my heart was painful. It wasn't true! It was only Mycroft trying to poison my mind against Fraser. Why was he so horrid? But he had told the truth the last time he spoke to me. Surely he hadn't come pelting all the way to Norfolk only to make mischief.

"Why are you here?" I demanded angrily.

He gazed at me, long, intently. "Why do you think, Rose?" he asked. His voice was a caress. I noticed he was holding my hand, and I didn't pull away, but lowered my eyes.

"How long have you been ill?" he asked gently. His gentleness touched a chord deep within me. It was reassuring to have someone care about me.

"It started the day after we arrived here. Why?"
As though they had a will of their own, my eyes
lifted and met his probing gaze.

"Tell me about it," he urged, and I found myself
pouring out my tale of woe to this near-stranger,
whom my husband had forbidden me to speak to.

"Let me see this tonic. Do you have it with you?"
he demanded.

"I have it here in my handbag with my novel," I
said, and showed it to him.

He opened the bottle, smelled it, and poured a
drop in his palm to taste it. "I never heard of
whiskey and cherry juice curing anything. And
what is that bitter aftertaste?" He put the top back
on and stood, frowning out over the cold sea.

When he turned back to me he said, "I don't like
the looks of this, Rose. I'm taking you away from
here before he succeeds in killing you."

I just shook my head in wonder. Mycroft really
was deranged. Killing me—it was absurd. Fraser
loved me. "Please go," I said.

There was thunder on his brow and lightning in
his eyes when Mycroft turned on me in a rage.
"Don't you see what he's doing? He's got the money
now. That's all he ever wanted from you. I knew the
son-of-a-bitch didn't love you, for all his simpering
act, but I never thought he meant to go this far. I
thought he'd only neglect you. I'm taking you
home, Rose."

Fear began rising in my throat. The man was a
dangerous lunatic, even worse than Fraser knew.
His ranting made no sense. I had no money for

Fraser to steal. What 'home' did he plan to take me to? This was my home now.

"Please go," I repeated, and stood up. In my fear and confusion, I tripped over my bag and was only stopped from falling by Mycroft's arms, which flew out to save me.

They folded around me, pulling me against his strong, warm chest. The sensation of fear dissipated swiftly as his gentle fingers stroked my shoulders and back. His arms were a haven from the raw coastal winds, and from my recent worries. As the tension eased from my body, I relaxed against him and looked over his shoulder at the indifferent sea and the expanse of white-capped waves.

His arms moved, and warm fingers caressed my neck, tilting my face up to his. His ink-dark eyes probed mine with a scalding intensity. It was strange to see such tenderness in those eyes when his jaws were locked in a grim grip and his lips were thinned in anger. As we gazed, his lips softened and slowly descended to mine in a fleeting brush, like the passing of a bird's wing against a flower.

My lips tingled with the foretaste of his embrace. All resistance washed from me, and a warm glow of anticipation welled inside. I closed my eyes and waited, but felt only the flutter of his breath. When I looked up, he was staring at me, frowning.

"Poor Rose," he said, soft as a sigh. "We never thought it would come to this."

Disappointment lent a sharp edge to my words. "You'd best get in your carriage and leave, Mycroft," I said, and pulled away.

As I looked all around, I saw there was no

carriage or even horse nearby. How had he got here? He must have left the carriage down the road and come on foot. The Warners didn't know he was here, which was good. They wouldn't tell Fraser.

"The hell I will," he growled. "It's time you open your eyes and see what he's doing to you. He's poisoning you, Rose. He only married you for your money. We all told you so. Sophie, Gertrude, myself."

"I don't have any money. I never had any money. I don't know what you're talking about. I don't even know Sophie."

Mycroft looked stunned. Blank incomprehension settled on his features. He spoke slowly, as if to an idiot. "I'm talking about your inheritance from Uncle Alvin Simson, of course, and the jewelry collection."

"But they're not mine! They're Fraser's. I had nothing but two thousand pounds from my father."

His bewilderment grew deeper. Mycroft gulped as he gazed at me. He looked actually frightened of me. "How did he do this to you?" he asked. His voice was light, rough-edged, disbelieving.

"He didn't do anything. You're mistaken, Mycroft. Please go now, before he comes."

"I'm taking you with me."

He advanced a step, I retreated nervously. "I don't want to go. You can't make me. I love Fraser."

He stood, helpless, but not looking at all violent. He just looked infinitely sad. "You're right, I can't make you, but the law can. I'll consult a lawyer. There are laws against this sort of thing. I'll be back with a court order, and you can tell your precious Fraser that if he dares to be here, he'll pay for this.

You're coming back to Thornbridge."

"I've never been to Thornbridge."

"I mean the Manor, of course," he answered impatiently. A new name to conjure with.

I watched as he took the bottle of medicine and slipped it in his pocket. "If they give you any more of this stuff, don't take it," he said grimly. "I'm going to have it analyzed."

With a last, long, black look, Mycroft bowed and left. I watched to see how he had come. He walked westward along the shore, his head bent in thought, till a bend in the coast took him out of sight. I sat down again, panting, feeling as if I had just escaped death.

Strangely, what I thought of was how I could explain my missing medicine. Mrs. Warner was always at me to take it. I'd tell her it fell and the bottle broke. It didn't seem to do any good in any case. When the trembling stopped, I gathered up my blanket and went inside.

"Feeling better, Mrs. Audry?" Mrs. Warner asked politely. She was always polite, but never friendly.

"A little, thank you. I'm going upstairs."

"I'll take up your dinner at six. A nice broth and some cold mutton."

"Mrs. Warner! You didn't forget my husband will be home for dinner, along with Miss Williams! Don't tell me you aren't prepared?"

Her guilty face told me she had forgotten all about it. She wouldn't be talking about broth and cold mutton if she had remembered.

"Of course I'm prepared," she said firmly.

I knew she was lying, but it would be up to her to get something ready in time. She didn't ask anything about Mycroft, which made it clear she hadn't seen him. In my room, I felt so weary I just lay on the bed in my gown, and soon fell asleep. When I awoke, it was pitch black outside. A small, cold-looking moon peered in the window. It seemed to be a million miles away.

I lit the lamp and saw it was nine o'clock. So Fraser hadn't come, or he would have wakened me. Mrs. Warner must have heard me moving about. She came up within minutes with a tray, holding the broth and cold mutton.

"Your husband didn't make it home, Mrs. Audry," she announced. "I decided to hold the chops till tomorrow, when he comes. I can cook you one if you like."

"No, thanks. The cold mutton will be fine."

"Will you be coming downstairs after dinner?"

Down to sit alone before the smokey grate? "No, not tonight."

"Don't forget your tonic, Mrs. Audry. Your husband told me to remind you."

I nodded, and she left, wearing a very satisfied expression. I was coming to dislike Mrs. Warner. There was something crafty in the woman. She knew Fraser wouldn't be home. That was why she hadn't prepared dinner.

I looked at the tray and felt ill. My mind was confused. Had I dreamed that Mycroft had come to the beach that afternoon? Surely it was a dream. I looked in my handbag and saw that the tonic was missing.

What strange things Mycroft had said. He thought I was rich, that Fraser had only married me for my money. He actually thought Fraser was trying to poison me. He mentioned going 'back to Thornbridge.' Then he had mentioned the Manor. But worst of all, he had said Fraser was going to the theater tonight, that he was seeing his friends. I knew what friend he meant. Margot Rampling. Tears scalded my eyes, and I went to the window to look up at the cold moon. It had turned all fuzzy around the edges from my tears. I looked up the empty road, hoping to see carriage lights, but there were none.

Fraser didn't come. After I had drunk the tea and eaten half a slice of bread, I lay down again and slept.

CHAPTER NINE

WHEN I AWOKE, THE ROOM WAS PERFECTLY DARK. I knew it was the middle of the night, but strangely, I wasn't tired. I felt more awake than I had felt in days. The lethargy that usually enshrouded me had gone, leaving me clearheaded. And hungry. The kitchen would be cold—I could wait till morning. I just lay in the darkness, thinking. Mainly, I thought I was getting better. I felt a little weak, but much better. Tomorrow I would really go for that walk. I'd walk down the road and perhaps meet Fraser on his way home.

Fraser. A welter of emotions swarmed over me at the name. Jealousy mingled with love and uncertainty. Why hadn't he come home? Was he with Margot? I saw that haunting image of her smiling at him, him touching her lips with his fingers, familiarly, lovingly. Was it my fault? Was I too cold to Fraser? I had thought that, away from London, we would grow closer together, but we had only drifted further apart. He didn't seem to love me as before —that was the awful truth.

Why had he really decided to come here to Longbeach? Was it not to get away from the sordid city, but only to get *me* away from it, so that he might return and be with her? And Mycroft . . . I wasn't blameless either. If he had kissed me this afternoon, I would have let him. Who knew what else might follow? I had never thought marriage was such an uncertain thing. I believed that people got married and lived happily ever after.

A person shouldn't lie in bed at night wide awake. She is prey to such wretched imaginings. Miss Williams had trouble sleeping. She always kept a book by her bed, to fight off the "night devils" as she called them. Miss Williams—why wasn't she here? What had happened to her? She never spent more than a day or two with her busy sister, whose house was already full of half a dozen children and a husband. "I'm always glad I'm single when I come back from that madhouse," she used to say. She would have leapt at the chance to visit the sea; she would have come running to join me and Fraser. Had Fraser forgotten to send my letter—or purposely not sent it? Oh, I really was running mad. Kind, dear Fraser—I was behaving as though he were a monster.

I turned over to escape my thoughts, and heard a sound in the hallway. Fraser! was the first thing that came to mind. In his eagerness to see me, he had driven all night. I leapt out of bed and went to the door. With my hand on the handle, I heard a strange, dragging sound outside, and stopped. A gruff whisper came through the door—Mrs. Warner's voice. It was the impatient, commanding tone she used only to her husband.

"Be quiet, you great clod. She'll hear you."

"It's heavy," he grunted. "She's had her medicine, hasn't she?"

"That she has. She was out like a light last time I looked," Mrs. Warner replied with satisfaction.

Then the dragging sound continued, as though they were moving some great weight. My heart hammered as I stood, listening. Though I was mistress of the house, I was afraid to open the door and speak to them. There was menace in their rough voices, talking about me as though I were an enemy. What on earth were they doing that they didn't want me to hear? And why did they count on my tonic to keep me asleep? That wasn't its purpose —was it?

"Fraser said to put it in the attic with the other things so she wouldn't see it. We'll never get it up those stairs," Mr. Warner complained. I was the only other 'she' in the house. What was Fraser hiding from me? And why were the Warners calling my husband 'Fraser' so familiarly?

"Not with my back, we won't," she agreed. "We'll shove it in the spare bedroom till he comes back to give us a hand. He should be here in a few days. It's only his own things, so it doesn't matter."

No, he should have been here yesterday! Mrs. Warner had known he wasn't coming. I stood without breathing, listening at the keyhole like an intruder in my own house, afraid of my servants. I heard the spare door being opened, and the heavy weight being pushed in. The door closed, the key turned with a click, and the Warners stood gasping for a minute.

"I'll be glad when this is over," Mr. Warner said. "How long do you figure it'll take?"

"Fraser doesn't want to rush it," his wife said vaguely. "I'm for bed, Jack. Let's go."

The Warners' bedroom was downstairs, off the kitchen. I listened as they crept quietly past my door and down the stairs. When they were gone, I tiptoed to my bed and sat trembling on the edge. Fear clutched my heart. A terrible panic came over me, a fear for my very life. I wanted to run out the door and keep running till Longbeach was miles behind me. I wanted to go home, back to Watling Street and Miss Williams.

I wanted to go to the spare room too, and see what secret Fraser had hidden so carefully from 'her,' his wife. What could it be? Would the Warners be asleep yet? I'd wait half an hour to be sure. The dark was dreadful, but if they peeked up the stairs, I didn't want them to see an edge of light around my door, so I sat in the darkness, waiting and thinking.

Nightmare thoughts swooped like bats through my mind. Black wings of doubt and fear disturbed the edges of sanity. I was going insane, that was it. Or I was dreaming the whole thing. I used to be afraid I'd wake up and discover that Fraser was a dream. I pinched my arm, but the nightmare didn't stop.

So many little things I had overlooked in the first flush of love seemed suspicious now. Fraser's falling in love with me seemed most suspicious of all. If he loved Margot Rampling—if that vulgar, gaudy woman was what he liked—then he couldn't possibly love me. Yet he had married me, and whatever Mycroft Harlow might say, I had no money. I had never had any money but my little dowry of two thousand pounds. Fraser had spent five times that on our honeymoon. He had borrowed it and returned three thousand. Well, he said he had returned it, though the receipt for the Consols had never come.

But it certainly wasn't for a measly two thousand pounds he had married me. Of that at least I was positive. The jewelry alone was worth a fortune. He had given me a sable coat for my birthday. I remembered the diamond earring in the pocket. Fraser had looked shocked when I pulled it out. I had assumed he hid it there for a surprise, but what if he hadn't? What if he hadn't known it was there? No, he must have known. Who else could have put it there, in a brand new coat? Yet the new coat had smelled of violets . . .

Fraser liked the scent of violets. He had given me violet perfume in Paris. It wasn't my own favorite, but I wore it to please him. I had changed in many ways to please Fraser. He had disliked my weight, he wanted my hair longer and worn in a special way, he chose my gowns—he even modified my behavior. 'I love it when you show your claws.' 'Be haughty, Rosie.' He had changed everything, even my name and my signature. It was almost as though he were trying to turn me into someone else.

When enough time had passed that I thought the Warners would be asleep, I lit my lamp and tiptoed down the hall to the spare room. It was locked, but the key from my room opened the door. I went in and saw one of Fraser's trunks shoved against the far wall. It was locked too, and I was afraid to pry it open, even if I could. I didn't want them to know I had been searching. It wasn't the trunk he had used abroad. It must be one of those he had stored when he gave up his apartment.

Frustration battered in my breast. I had to discover what was going on. There were more things in the attic, the Warners had said. I closed the door, locked it, and went to the attic. Every stair squawked, but with the door closed I didn't think the sleeping Warners would hear. The attic was long, dark, airless, and strewn with the debris of generations. Racks of old clothes covered with dust cloths lined one wall. Below, there were trunks and all sorts of lumber pushed against the walls—chairs and odd tables and garden pots, frames and pictures and some discarded china. Most of these things must belong to the Haltons, who owned the house and lived here.

Yet Fraser had stored some things here to hide them from 'her.' We hadn't brought them from London with us. When had he put them in the Haltons' attic? Maybe this wasn't the Haltons' house at all . . .

I must seek till I found what belonged to him. One portion of the clothing rack was covered with a newer dust cloth than the rest. I lifted the covering and found myself staring at a whole row of the most stylish and expensive ladies' clothing imaginable. There were suits and morning dresses, ballgowns and afternoon gowns, a fur jacket. When I disturbed the gowns, an aroma of stale violets wafted toward me. My flesh crawled at the scent. It smelled like my new sable coat.

Who did all these beautiful things belong to? Not Mrs. Halton; they were purse-pinched, and in any case she would have taken them with her. The gowns weren't out of fashion by any means. I lifted one particularly lovely gown in ice blue satin from the rack and held it up to me. It was the proper length. The width was a little greater than my own. If I put on a little weight, it would just fit. And Fraser was always after me to put on a little weight.

The color suggested that the owner had blue eyes. I had chosen the same shade myself for the masquerade ball. Was the owner a blonde, like me? Did she wear her blonde hair in a curl over her shoulder? I swallowed hard and with trembling fingers hung the gown back on the rack. I felt as though I were handling a ghost, or a shroud.

What else looked as though it had been recently added to this vast collection of debris? Fraser's additions would probably be farthest from the wall, and easiest of access. I tried the lid of the closest trunk; it had no lock, it was the sort of household trunk used for storing blankets. I lifted the lid and crouched down to examine the contents, which were all individually wrapped in newspapers. Every object I unwrapped was beautiful and valuable. There was a chased silver dresser set, engraved with the initials R.C.—my own maiden initials, for Rosalie Cummings.

There were delicate crystal perfume bottles and ink pots, fans and hand mirrors, fine linen handkerchiefs and kid gloves. It looked like the contents of a rich lady's vanity. In the bottom, not wrapped in paper, was a cardboard box. I lifted the lid, now knowing what to expect, and saw a jumble of tiny carvings, some in ivory, some in jade, like those given to me by Fraser's Aunt Sophie and Gertrude for my birthday. 'For your collection,' the note had said. For this collection, not mine. I recognized them as Indian carvings.

My God, who did they belong to? Whose personal effects was I rummaging through? At the bottom of the box was a fine gold chain, the front portion of it holding pearls of the sort Mycroft had given me. I counted them. There were twenty. Mine, given on my twenty-first birthday, would make twenty-one. It's impossible to describe the sensations that surged through me. Utter confusion, amounting almost to madness. Were these things mine? The dresser set had my initials, the gowns nearly fit me, but I had never seen any of them before in my life. I had never owned anything so exquisite.

I carefully wrapped everything up, returned it to the trunk, and closed the lid. I hardly wanted to see more, but it would be difficult to come up here with the Warners always watching me, so I'd best finish the job. I found a trunk full of lovely lingerie, and at the bottom of it a small brown cardboard box, about two inches by four. My fingers shook uncontrollably as I lifted the lid. There were calling cards, and embossed daintily in gothic script the name Mrs. Fraser Audry. The box was half empty—they weren't new cards, made up for me. I dropped the lid as though it were a live coal.

It didn't seem possible that that attic could hold any more shocks for me, but before I left, I happened to glance at the pictures and frames against the wall. Those on top were faded landscapes, poorly done and not worth saving. Toward the back of the pile, one frame gleamed more brightly than the others. I set the others aside till I had uncovered it. I was too numb to scream, or even tremble. I think I half suspected it would be a portrait of myself.

I saw myself standing against a misty scene of sky traced with lacy leaves. My golden hair was waved at the front, pulled back, with one curl hanging flirtatiously over my shoulder. At my neck the sapphire necklace glowed. I looked well, a little extra weight rounding out the bones of my shoulders and arms. I was a little surprised I wasn't holding a bouquet of violets. In every other respect I must have pleased my husband very well. My head was held at a haughty angle, defying the world. The painting wasn't signed, but I recognized the work of Monsieur Corot, from France. I had been to France with Fraser before, then, in my earlier incarnation as Mrs. Fraser Audry.

After memorizing every line of the portrait, I piled the other frames in front of it, took up my candle, and tiptoed downstairs to my room. Whatever was concealed in Fraser's trunk in the spare room, it couldn't be more conclusive, or more damning than what I had already seen.

Fraser had been married before. By accident he had come across me in Paris, and decided to recover his dead wife. By accident? No, our meeting was not so fortuitous as that. He *knew*. Somehow he knew that a living replica of his wife walked the earth, and had sought me out. He knew I was in Paris. The casual stroll before me, the loitering to obstruct my view of the Seine, the snatching up of

Miss Williams' umbrella to find an excuse to follow us—all carefully planned.

The courting and wedding were all done up with a haste that seemed less romantic than suspicious now. Miss Williams had been turned off and sent packing home—why? I must get to Miss Williams. A shiver of apprehension rippled up my arms, lifting the hair. The beautiful honeymoon was no romantic interlude but his Pygmalion's trick of transforming Galatea. Karlsbad and Marienbad were chosen to avoid the usual crush of English tourists, who might discover his stunt. He didn't want me seen till the transformation was complete. That's why we had had no friends except foreigners.

Those people in Paris who had called me Rose— the McCormacks. They knew this other Rose, obviously. That was what accounted for our impetuous departure. The Swanns too. And still I had to wonder why. Had he so loved his other R.C. that he wanted only to replace her? Was he a poor, demented man, heartbroken by the loss of his lovely wife? If that were true, there wouldn't be such women as Margot Rampling in his life. What had happened to her, that other Mrs. Fraser Audry? How had she died—if she was dead.

'It's nice to see you up and about again, Mrs. Sorry to hear about your wee one.' The old sailor wasn't talking about my imaginary miscarriage. He was talking about the other Mrs. Audry. Rose—her name must have been Rose. That's the name Fraser re-christened me. Had Rose lost not only a child but her own life as well? Was that it? If people knew she was enceinte, it would be well if I had been too, in case anyone mentioned it.

113

Mycroft had mentioned the miscarriage. Mycroft, who had warned me about Fraser, and I thought it only the ranting of an insanely jealous man. Mycroft knew everything. He knew all about that other Rose. I rather thought he loved her. Even loving her, he had believed I was she. The resemblance must be truly remarkable. Could it possibly be that convincing? If I appeared with Fraser wearing Rose's sable coat and Rose's diamond ring— but no. It was my face he had examined. Perhaps he hadn't seen Rose for years, or never knew her terribly well.

'Call Mycroft Cousin. It will please him,' Fraser had said. Was that to prevent me from calling him Mr. Harlow? Had Rose called him 'Cousin'? Fraser had interrupted me when I was about to say I was pleased to make Mycroft's acquaintance. He had been extremely nervous about that whole meeting at Hibbard's office, and flushed with victory afterwards. Why had he bothered arranging it? It was only to sign his will making me the beneficiary. Something about giving me a share in his fortune.

Or so he said. I hadn't actually read the papers. 'Don't you know what he's doing? He's got the money now, that's all he ever wanted.' It was *her* money, Rose's. Was it her birthday too, her twenty-first birthday? Obviously it was. Mycroft had brought gifts from the family. That was the traditional age at which a young lady's fortune was turned over to her. And if she was married, then it would be turned over to her husband. Fraser had certainly been eager to get the money. He couldn't wait one day, but went prancing off to Hibbard's on my birthday.

114

Once the money was in his hands, he had been just as eager to hustle me out of London so that he might have his way with Margot. Or was it fear of Mycroft that caused the haste? 'Promise me you won't speak to Mycroft.'

Mycroft, another enigma in this puzzle. A vital piece. His interest in Rose was strong enough that he had hounded after her to Norfolk. Or after Fraser, whom he clearly despised. Was it the money that motivated Mycroft too? There seemed to be a great deal of money involved. Those dainties in the attic were the accoutrements of a very wealthy woman. I should have listened to Mycroft yesterday afternoon. I should have asked him more questions. I should have known he wasn't a lunatic. How could I know anything, drugged as I was with medicine? I could hardly hold my eyes open.

Why did Fraser want me to be bedridden? I hadn't really been ill till I started taking the tonic. Was he afraid I'd get up to the attic and discover his secret? Or was it something else—the spinney, perhaps, where he said there was a fox, to keep me away? Then why bring me to Longbeach at all? To escape Mycroft, of course, but he could have chosen somewhere else. He had brought the other Rose here too. She had been with child—that might account for it. She would want peace and quiet. Somehow I didn't think the haughty lady in the portrait would want this much peace and quiet. Had he brought her here to— No, I wouldn't think that. Not murder. Fraser wasn't the loving husband I had thought, but he couldn't be capable of murder. Yet the spinney would make a good secret burial ground, and he had warned me away from it.

A week ago I couldn't have believed him capable of anything but love. That love almost smothered me at times. It was too much. Why hadn't I seen he was overdoing it? All the shower of gifts—just to convince Hibbard and Mycroft I was the other Rose. The blithe suggestion that I pick out a house for us, money no object—he never had any intention of buying a house. It was all play-acting to keep me in thrall till the papers were signed. This was what he intended all along, shuffling me off to the country while he enjoyed himself and his women in town. But still he couldn't be capable of murder. Not his other wife, and not me.

'I'll be glad when this is over. How long do you think it will take?' 'Fraser doesn't want to rush it.' How easy to believe the worst, once the spell was broken. I had to escape before the 'few days' that would bring Fraser back. How did he plan to do it? Was it to be a sudden and regrettable overdose of medicine, or a long, lingering decline? Either way, I couldn't stay and face him with the knowledge I now held. I wasn't as clever as Fraser. I wouldn't be able to hide my true feelings. And once he knew I knew, I thought my loving husband would be quite capable of 'rushing it.'

Escape, then, but how? We were in the middle of nowhere, with no carriage, and the Warners forever watching me like hawks. Dare I wait for Mycroft's return, and risk Fraser coming before him? Mycroft might go to visit his lawyer before he had the medicine analyzed. He wouldn't want to have the analysis done locally, he'd probably take it to London, in which case he wouldn't be back for days. Oh God, what could I do? There was Belle. I had never ridden in my life. I might fall and crack my skull. Was that why Fraser had got the mare for me? A riding accident would look perfectly innocent.

When I looked toward the window, I noticed a gleam of red on the horizon. The sun was rising already. I must get away, before the Warners were up. I slipped off my nightie and began to dress quickly. Money—I'd need money. How much did I have? My handbag held only a few French coins. I had given everything to Miss Williams, and since coming home I hadn't needed money. Fraser paid for everything.

I was already hungry, and without a sou to my name it would be hard to make it to London. I'd have to pawn something. My diamond ring? No, that would be too conspicuous. Questions would be asked. Should I wear the sable coat? How odd I would look, rattling along alone on a mare in a sable coat. But I had nothing else. Fraser had given away all my clothes at Marienbad. All traces of Rosalie Cummings were gotten rid of. I wondered what he had done with my passport.

I grabbed the sable coat and put it on. I remembered the diamond earring and the sapphire peacock in the pocket. Maybe I could pawn the brooch? I fished in the pocket and found it gone. Fraser had taken it and the earring. They must be in the room somewhere. I looked in his jewelry box and grabbed up its contents, a pair of cufflinks and a tie pin. They were modest enough to be sold without any questions. But where could the brooch be? I ran to the clothespress and searched Fraser's pockets. I didn't find the brooch, but there were letters in the inside pocket of one jacket.

I snatched at them eagerly to see what I might learn of his plans. They were both addressed in my hand to Miss Williams. He hadn't posted them! The invitation to dine with us at the Savoy and the letter telling her of our remove to Longbeach were both in his pocket. The second letter had been slit open. I looked inside and saw he had removed the money that was supposed to pay for a carriage to bring her to Longbeach. No wonder she hadn't come! His artless story that she was visiting her sister—all lies. He hadn't even told her we were back in England. Poor Miss Williams, what must she be thinking?

This new evidence of Fraser's long-planned treachery sent me into a tizzy of nervousness. I was more anxious than ever to get away, but took time to search every pocket for money, or something to pawn. I found two shillings. Better than nothing. They would buy me breakfast. I stuffed them into my pocket, took up my handbag, and tiptoed to the door.

When I opened it, I felt a gust of cold wind sweeping up the stairs. Before I had taken a step, I heard the front door close and peered through the bannister railing. The worst that occurred to me was that Warner had gone out, and I must evade him. Imagine my horror to see Fraser standing there. All I saw was his bottom half, but there was no mistaking his coat. It was the same one he had worn to London. His feet began to move, and I darted back to my room, threw off my coat, and scrambled into bed, still wearing my day gown.

If he pulled back the covers, if he wanted to make love! A tremor of revulsion shook me. I must close my eyes and pretend I had taken my medicine. Oh dear, and he'd look for the medicine. As I lay cringing, I heard his footfalls mounting the stairs.

CHAPTER TEN

THE BEDROOM DOOR OPENED, AND I LAY, SCARCELY daring to breathe. Please, God, let him just look and go away. Beneath the blankets, my hands clenched into fists. The air caught in my lungs, suffocating me with its painful pressure. I tried to stop the flickering of my eyelashes, but it only made them quiver more. The soft, menacing footsteps came closer, right up to the bed. He must see my anxiety, he must feel the tension surrounding me. Why didn't he say something?

Behind my closed eyes, I was aware of a shadow as he leaned over me, his head blocking out the light from the window. Tension mounted to an unbearable height. If he didn't say something or do something, I would scream. Then his fingers touched my brow, and he emitted a light grunt. I felt the stirring of the air as he stood up. From the ensuing silence, I knew he was either staring at me or looking around the room.

When his steps receded, I knew he was examining the room. What guilty traces had I left to betray my interrupted flight? The sable coat, thrown in a heap. I heard the telltale susurrus as he lifted it, the soft plop as he threw it aside. He walked to the dresser —he'd see his jewelry was gone. There were more rapid, light footsteps, then the click of my handbag being torn open. An ugly curse rent the air. He had found the cufflinks and tie pin, and he knew.

In three swift, angry steps he was back at the bed. The covers were whipped away and I lay exposed in my day gown.

"I know you're awake, Rosalie," he said in a tight, angry voice. He hadn't called me Rosalie since before our wedding.

God only knows what was happening to my face. I was so frightened I just lay like a board. His fingers jabbed at my eyes, forcing the lids open. If I were unconscious, what would I do? I felt my eyes roll up, showing the whites. It seemed to confuse him. He slapped lightly at my cheeks, calling "Rosalie" a few times. I forced myself to remain absolutely lifeless.

As I lay, breath suspended, I felt his warm finger curl around my neck. A tremor started at my vital core, but by a supreme act of will I suppressed it. I felt as if my very life depended on quelling that tremor. When I could no longer hold my breath, I exhaled lightly and inhaled. His fingers weren't gripping tightly enough to prevent breathing. I thought then, and I still believe, that Fraser hovered, at that instant, on the brink of strangling me. I think my lifeless act was all that deterred him. Better to make it a more natural-looking death. Strangulation would be difficult to explain, if anyone started asking questions.

As suddenly as he had come in, he left the room. As his steps receded I took a deep breath and looked from lowered eyelids at his retreating back. He left the door open. I heard him go pelting downstairs to the kitchen after the Warners. Every instinct told me to run for my life. But common sense, and paralysis, held me on the bed. I wouldn't get ten yards before they were after me. Whatever they suspected, they would know the truth if I tried to run. I would hardly have had time to reach the front door before Fraser was back, with Mrs. Warner trailing behind him.

I closed my eyes and listened as he came stomping in, with no effort at silence or secrecy. "Look at this!" he said. "She had my jewelry in her purse." It was hard to believe that this rough voice was coming from Fraser. Anger and anxiety combined to wipe away his polite veneer and reveal the villain beneath. "And her coat, ready to run. She's fully dressed." The blankets were still pulled down around me.

"I expect she fell into bed before she got undressed," Mrs. Warner said. "She was out like a light last night, Fraser. She hardly touched her dinner."

"Has she been taking the medicine regularly?"

"She never misses. I keep after her."

"Where is it? Let me see how much is gone."

They began searching the room, while I lay palpitating in terror. I heard them searching about,

moving things on the dresser, looking in my handbag, finally opening drawers.

"It's gone!" Fraser exclaimed.

"It can't be."

"I tell you it's gone."

"But look at her—dead to the world. Maybe she
left it down by the beach yesterday."

"She should have taken some last night. She
didn't talk to anyone while I was away?"

"Not a soul, Fraser. No one's been here. Is it
Harlow you're worried about?"

"Of course it's Harlow. The bastard's been following me around London, asking questions. He
suddenly disappeared—I was afraid he'd come
here. He knew I brought Rose here before. I should
have gone somewhere else."

"I wish you had, son," Mrs. Warner's tired voice
answered. Son! Good God, was she Fraser's mother? "I don't care for all this business."

"Did the trunk come from London?"

"Yes, we put it in the spare room last night while
she was asleep."

"You're sure she didn't see it?"

"I'm positive."

"Then, by God, she's been to the attic. She
knows. She was planning to make a run for it.
Harlow let something slip when he was with her."

"You're imagining things. Maybe the medicine is
under the blankets."

"And maybe she put my jewelry in her pockets in
a delirium? I don't think so. I'm going to have a
look upstairs. Stay with her."

Terror subsided to plain fear when he left, only to
return as I considered how carelessly I had covered

my traces upstairs. Had I put the covering back on the gowns? Had I left the trunks as I had found them? In a moment I knew I hadn't been careful enough.

Fraser came pelting down. "She's been up there all right," he said grimly. "She's been into Rosie's trunks. What are we going to do? We can't let her talk."

"This has gone far enough, son," Mrs. Warner said. "I won't stand still for murder. Stop while you can. Rose's death wasn't your fault. A miscarriage is often fatal."

"I can't stop!" he shouted angrily. "Don't you see that? She knows about Rose. She'll go running to Harlow, and I'll end up on the gallows. Is that what you want?"

Mrs. Warner—or whatever her name was—gave a strangled sob. "What will you do?" she asked in a tired, defeated way.

"I'll have to get some more opium into her, to keep her out till I have time to think. Where is it?"

"I'll get it, but don't give her a fatal dose. Just keep her tranquil till we have time to plan something. Maybe you could send her away," his mother suggested doubtfully.

She left, and I lay on, pretending to be unaware of what had passed. He wouldn't give me a fatal dose while his mother was there, but once I was drugged, I wouldn't be able to help myself. How could I keep from taking the opium? If I rebelled, he'd know I was conscious, and I dreaded to think what his temper might lead him to do.

Too soon she was back. "Here it is," she said.

"Help me hold her," Fraser ordered. He spoke to

his mother as though she were a servant.

Mrs. Warner was a strong woman. She held my head and one arm while Fraser held the other arm and tilted the bottle to my lips. It was a strong alcoholic tincture of opium, sugared to hide the bitter taste. I pretended to be asleep, to give an excuse to let it run down my chin.

"Hold her nose," Fraser ordered.

Mrs. Warner's fingers pinched my nose till I had to gasp for breath. Then Fraser rammed the bottle into my mouth and tilted it. I tried to hold the solution in my mouth, but inevitably some of it trickled down my throat.

"That ought to keep her quiet for a while," he said with satisfaction, and dropped my head to the pillow.

I let my head turn to one side and pushed the opium out with my tongue, down my chin on the pillow side where they wouldn't see it. It was so strong my tongue was numb.

"Lock her door," Fraser said.

"She won't be going anywhere, poor thing," Mrs. Warner replied.

They left, and I lay quietly, wondering if I had swallowed enough to paralyze me. At least I hadn't swallowed as much as they thought, but it was terribly strong. If I felt drowsy, I'd soon recover and plan my escape while they thought I was asleep. Meanwhile I'd let my eyelids flutter shut and rest a bit. It was so peaceful now, so still and quiet all alone. If only the world would stop spinning in these reeling circles that made me ill. Just rest a minute—then you must go. Hurry away. Had a minute passed yet, an hour? What was time? My eyes felt glued shut. I saw a vast tunnel opening before me. I'd escape by the tunnel. Down this vast corridor of timeless time and out the other end in a second. It was as quiet as the grave, and as dark. How long did death last? Was it over yet? I was still in the dark tunnel. Time flew, and stood still. Time was irrelevant. Was it day or night—there, morning was coming through the purple mist at the end of the tunnel. Was it a window there?

I'd have to leave by the window. That would be amusing. Perhaps I'd fly to London—fly on gilded wings, out the window and into the bright red, phosphorescent sky. How red the sun was, like the dawn of creation.

A whole new world spread before my unseeing eyes. Golden steeples soared through crimson clouds beyond the heavens. Now celestial music thronged the universe, where mortal never trod. It wafted on a zephyr, with tinkling bells and rippling harps. It was brighter than possible, yet grew steadily brighter and brighter till my whole head hurt with the glow. The heat from that brightness scalded my face and burned my shoulders. Was this heaven, or hell? What unknown force devised this hellish paradise?

Prehistoric creatures slithered in at the periphery of my vision. Black, prehensile claws reached for me, tore me up from the bed and carried me aloft on beating wings. They let me go—I was falling, legs flailing the air, arms beating, but nothing kept me aloft. I heard a scream catch in my throat. Fraser came to rescue me. He was there, all worried and concerned.

"We've given her too much!" he shouted.

'Too much! Too much! Too much!' It echoed down a long chamber, reverberating in my ears.

"You've killed her, Fraser!" 'Killed her, killed her, killed her.'

"Fraser, help me!"

I clutched at his hands. Thank God for dear Fraser. He wouldn't let me die. He loved me so, but he was smothering me in love.

"Get some coffee—black. Cold water for her face. She can't die yet." Oh, but I was dying, going into the void of the unknown, where those awful echoes pounded my ears.

The water was like ice against my scalded face. I was pulled along a heaving, shifting carpet, with the flowers all faded to threads. "Drink this!" Hot burning coffee.

"Try to make her wretch."

"They never wretch with opium. It depresses the reaction."

"Walk, Rosalie. Just to the end of the room."

That far? It was miles away, the other wall a waving darkness in the infinite distance. No one could walk that far. It would take a lifetime. And each foot weighed a ton. My toes seemed to be growing into the floor. They uprooted me and dragged me along, my arms slack, legs turned to rubber.

"Fraser, help me."

"Open the window. The fresh air . . ."

Now was my chance. I'd fly out the window. I had to escape Fraser. He wanted to make me live. "She's trying to jump out the window."

"Look at the color of her. She won't last another hour."

127

"If it weren't for Mycroft I'd let her jump."

Mycroft—hang on till he comes. He'll take you home to Thornbridge.

"I'm calling the doctor."

"No, Mother! Get her back to bed. She's less white now. She'll pull through."

Back to bed. Hands unfastening my gown. Gentle hands, a woman's hands. Was that a tear in her eye? Had I died, then? Poor Fraser, he'd miss me so. Sleep. Deep, dark, oblivious sleep. Waking still in the darkness, with a candle burning.

"Eat this, Mrs. Audry."

The broth tasted scorched. How did anyone burn broth? "Water, please."

"Just one more spoonful of this nice broth. I made it specially for you. There's a good girl. Now you can sleep."

Daylight filtering through the curtains. Fraser nodding on the chair, looking all unkempt. I'd never seen him unshaven before. Darkness descended again, and when I opened my eyes, Fraser had become old Mr. Warner. He was smoking a pipe. Much later, Fraser was himself again, watching me. He looked as though he hadn't shaved for three or four days. There was rain slashing against the windowpane. I had thought it was going to be a nice day. What had happened to that red sunrise?

My mind was a big gray cloud, with shafts of sunlight nibbling round the edges. I felt that if the sun could eat up the cloud, I would—know something. A something so vital it contained the secret of the universe. I didn't even know what day it was.

Mrs. Warner's head appeared at the door. "Is she awake?"

Yes, yes! I cried, but no sound left my lips. Fraser must have discerned my efforts to speak. He jerked to attention and came to me. "Rosie, how do you feel?" he asked.

My eyes closed and my head drooped like a dead flower. I couldn't lift it to reassure him.

"She's going to be all right, I think," he told his mother. "We won't give her any more for another day. Then just a small dose, getting gradually stronger. We'll make sure to dilute it. I didn't realize the drops were so strong."

"I don't like it," his mother said, with the weary air of long repetition. What didn't she like?

"I have to get back to London," Fraser told her. Ah, that's what she disliked. I disliked it too. Stay, Fraser, I begged silently. "I was supposed to be there yesterday. Hibbard has everything ready for me to sign. The cash will be easier to handle than stocks and bonds. I'll arrange for Italy while I'm there."

"She's not well enough to travel," Mrs. Warner objected.

Oh, but I wanted to travel! Sunny Italy! We had planned to go sometime.

"She only has to make it one way," he replied.

Were we moving permanently to Italy then? How nice! Margot would never find us. Mrs. Warner clicked her tongue in disapproval and said, "Go ahead. We'll handle things here."

"Keep her door locked, and put Scout outside her window. If she tries to leave, or if Mycroft comes, we want some warning."

"Don't worry, Fraser, your dad will take care of everything. He's as bad as you are."

"Mother," he said cajolingly.

Under partially lowered lids I saw Fraser kiss her on the cheek. She pulled her head away. Such a cold, unnatural mother. Fraser left, and she stood looking at me and shaking her head a moment before leaving. I heard the key click in the lock when she left.

Then I felt safe. No one could get in to harm me. Peaceful sleep stole over me once more.

CHAPTER ELEVEN

LONG INTERVALS OF TROUBLED SLEEP AND HORREN-
dous nightmares were broken briefly by flashes of
lucidity. Occasionally I would open my eyes and see
where I was. I recognized the shabby bedchamber
as being at Longbeach. I knew that the woman who
came to feed me broth and give me my tonic was
Mrs. Warner, but why did I loathe and fear her?
Why did I cringe and cower at her approach? She
was really quite kind. The periods of lucidity
became less lucid. Even when I was awake, the
room was no longer quite right. The ceiling had
grown very high, and the walls tilted in so sharply I
felt they would fall on my head and suffocate me.

When he came, I thought it was one of my
nightmares. He looked twelve feet tall, dark as
Satan, with a snarling, demonic mask for a face. In
the white mask, his navy blue eyes burned like live

coals. Worst of all, he had a pistol, which he waved at the Warners and me as he shouted, "I'll see you all hang for this, and you can tell Mr. Audry so." He had come to kill us, then. Why hadn't Scout saved me from Mycroft?

I was torn from my safe bed, bundled in a blanket, and swept up into Mycroft's arms. The Warners didn't try to stop him when he carried me downstairs and put me in a black carriage. Mrs. Warner was crying. The cold wind from the sea set me to shivering. It caught my hair and blew it around my shoulders, till Mycroft pulled the blanket up. It was warm in the carriage, with the blanket and Mycroft's arms around me. I felt his fingers stroking my hair, and was soon lulled by his soothing words.

"You're safe now, Rose. I'll take you home. It's all right, darling. Don't cry."

I felt warm tears clotting my lashes and oozing down my cheeks. I didn't know why I was crying, but I couldn't stop.

"I'll take you to a doctor at King's Lynn. He'll make you better. It's all over, Rose."

The gentle swaying of the carriage, the warmth of the blanket, and Mycroft's crooning voice eased me off to sleep. When I awoke, I was in a different room and a strange man wearing spectacles was leaning over me. He held a light to my eyes and peered closely at me.

"Massive doses of opium—for a fairly long period of time," he announced.

Beyond his shoulder, staring at me with a frown of concentration, stood Mycroft Harlow. "Will she be all right?" he demanded. He sounded like a haunted man.

"Eventually. There are bound to be repercussions—bouts of hallucination, perhaps loss of memory—but no permanent brain damage. I think you caught her in time. Is she an addict?"

"An involuntary one," Mycroft answered, in a voice as tight and metallic as a coiled spring.

"She's undernourished. That's quite common in addicts. She'll need plenty of good food, fresh air, sunshine, some mild exercise. My advice is to build up her strength for a few days, then take her home and let her family look after her. No excitement is advised. Just keep her quiet but contented."

"Can you recommend a woman to tend her here, till she can be moved?" Mycroft asked.

"I can recommend a nurse. I'll send Miss Piggott along, if you like. She's a cheerful soul. I often use her for this sort of work."

The doctor put down his light and the gentlemen moved toward the door. I couldn't hear their conversation, but it was lengthy, terminating in the passing of money to the doctor. Then Mycroft returned to the bed. His demonic frown had vanished, leaving a residue of regret, tinged with contentment. He stared at me so closely I felt nervous.

"Where am I?" I asked. My voice sounded weak.

"You're safe in a hotel at King's Lynn. We'll set out for Sussex in a few days' time."

"Why did you take me away?"

"We'll talk about that later, Rose. The doctor says it is better for you to relax and not worry."

"We must notify Fraser."

Something in his eyes closed like a shutter. His expression was perfectly impassive when he answered, "Fraser will learn soon enough."

"We were going to Italy," I murmured.

I closed my eyes, but not to sleep. My thoughts were so jumbled I couldn't think with Mycroft staring at me like a sphinx. Tattered shreds of memory hung in my mind like cobwebs, diaphanous, insubstantial, menacing. Mrs. Warner holding my nose, that bittersweet liquid being forced into me. The burning sun. Being propelled along the threadbare carpet, the floor heaving. The window, escape. 'If it weren't for Mycroft I'd let her jump.' Fraser dozing in the chair, his face covered in whiskers. Fraser's fingers curling around my neck. 'Then, by God, she's been to the attic. She knows.' The attic, rows of gowns, trunks, R.C. on the chased silver dresser set. The portrait.

I drifted into sleep, and when I awoke I lay quietly with my eyes still closed, arranging the shreds of cobweb till I had sorted out the past. The dreadful truth was like a tomb resting on my spirits. But the nightmare was over. I was alive—somehow, magically, I had been rescued by Mycroft.

I heard scuttling sounds around me, and when I opened my eyes, a strange woman in a white apron and mob cap was bustling around the room. Her brown hair was bunched up behind. Snuff-brown eyes peered at me from a rosy face, with a little turned-up nose and a broad mouth. She looked so delightfully normal I wanted to touch her, to reassure myself this wasn't a new dream.

"Here we are then," she smiled. "Awake at last

and hungry as a bear, I warrant. Tonight you shall have a good thick soup, and tomorrow Dr. Dahl says you may have meat and potatoes if you like."

"Where's Mycroft?" I asked.

"He's downstairs having his dinner, Mrs. Audry. He'll be back up soon enough. My, your cousin is attentive!" she said with a suggestive lift of her brows.

She went across the room where a burner had been set up on a table. I looked around to appraise my new room. It was large, high-ceilinged, and elegant in its appointments. Two tall windows were curtained in gold brocade. The mahogany furnishings had been polished till they glowed in the firelight.

The woman came back with a steaming bowl of soup and some bread. "My name's Piggott," she said, smiling. "Shall I feed you, dear, or can you manage the soup yourself?"

"I can manage, thank you."

Piggott sat beside me, monitoring every bite. The thick soup was like a stew, with vegetables and meat floating in it. It tasted delicious. I ate every drop, and felt so full I could burst.

"There's a good girl!" Piggott smiled and took away the dishes.

"Now you'll want to freshen up before Mr. Harlow comes back. We don't want him to see us looking like this!"

I gazed down at what I had on. It was a remarkably soiled lawn nightgown. Stains of various hues decorated the front of it—'tonic,' broth, tea. "Good gracious!" I exclaimed in dismay.

"You've been sadly neglected, dear," Piggott

chided. "How your family could let a poor invalid lie in such filth is beyond me. I've ordered hot water for a bath. You'll have to make do with one of my nighties for tonight."

There was a tap at the door, and two servants brought in a cauldron of hot water and towels. Piggott was an extremely efficient woman. She scrubbed till my skin glowed pink from rubbing. It felt wonderful, as though all the soil of my marriage were being scoured away by her capable hands. She slid a plain flannelette nightie over my head. It fit like a tent. Next she took her brush to my hair and brushed till my scalp stung.

When she was finished she stood back and regarded her handiwork. "That's more like it. You're beginning to look halfways human," she complimented. I was beginning to feel half human too.

"Would you like me to bring my mirror?" she asked. "I darted straight off home and brought some things when I learned you were here without a sign of bag or baggage."

Curiosity glowed in her brown eyes. Before long, Piggott would want a complete accounting of my unusual condition, but not yet. "Yes, please."

She brought a hand mirror set in bone and held it before me. I stared, horrified, at the poor wretch who gazed back at me. I didn't recognize her. That pale, slack-cheeked hag with dark circles under her eyes wasn't me. It couldn't be! I looked fifty years old. "No!" I exclaimed, and pushed it away.

"You look better than when I got here, dear," she assured me with a vigorous nod of her head. "I never saw such a nightmare. It's the opium. You want to stay away from that nasty stuff. It's slow poison. I don't know why they allow the chemists to sell it."

With this admonition, Piggott pulled the bell cord and had the dishes and bath water taken away. Soon there was a tap at the door and Piggott said archly, "That will be your cousin, Mrs. Audry. You're a widow, are you, dear?"

In confusion, I just smiled wanly. How much of my past I should reveal I didn't know, but my feeling was, the less, the better. Piggott went to the door, and Mycroft stepped in. He was an elegant, commanding figure. His twelve feet had shrunk to half that, and his demonic scowl had been transformed to a tentative, worried smile. I liked the way his dark hair swept up from his brow. There was no noticeable resemblance to his cousin Fraser, for which I was grateful.

"Now she's looking more like herself, I daresay," Piggott told him, looking brightly for a compliment.

"Much better. You're a wonder, Miss Piggott," he replied without looking at her. His gaze flew straight across the room to me.

Piggott retired demurely to the grate, where she took up a journal, which she peered over with the liveliest curiosity toward the bed.

I felt embarrassed to appear before Mycroft in such an unbecoming guise. The fashionable, pretty lady he had waltzed with had dwindled to a shrunken invalid in a flannelette nightgown with dirty hair streaming over her shoulders. Yet when he examined me with an intense look, I saw no disapproval. His dark eyes glowed.

He didn't take the chair but leaned over the bed

and grasped my hands. "Rose, how are you feeling?" he asked gently.

"Much better, thank you." My gaze flickered to Piggott. "We have to talk, Mycroft."

"I know, dear. I know, but there's no great rush about that. You're safe now."

"And Fraser?"

His brows drew together and he looked at me doubtfully. "You can't expect him to walk away from this with impunity. He was trying to kill you." He spoke low to hide his words from Piggott, but his tone was fierce.

"Where is he?"

"He was back in London when I left. The analysis of your tonic revealed a massive dose of opium. When I learned that, I went back to Longbeach as quickly as I could. I didn't think you'd want it reported to the police. Since he has reduced you to a shell, however, I hope to convince you I did the right thing in reporting him here, in King's Lynn. Officers have gone to Longbeach to arrest the Warners, and to London after Fraser."

"The Warners are his parents," I said.

"I suspected as much. He said he was taking you to his parents when you became enceinte last January. I supposed at the time it would be a decent house with servants. I was astonished to see that hovel—and no parents there."

The newspaper in the corner rattled. I looked over and caught Piggott staring at us with the greatest interest. "We can't discuss it here, but you don't know the half of what is going on, Mycroft," I said in a low tone. My mind boggled to consider the monumental chore of convincing him I was not the

Rose he had known. The truth was too bizarre. I couldn't begin to understand it myself.

A blaze of interest leapt in his eyes. "What do you mean? What has he done?"

I wanted to pour out the whole story, but fatigue was already creeping over me. I hadn't been awake this long in days, perhaps weeks. "It's about Rose," I said.

Mycroft frowned. He looked deeply disturbed. "What about you?" he asked.

I had to give him a hint of the shock that was in store for him. "I'm not Rose," I whispered. "I know I look like her, but I'm not Rose. I think—" Oh God, how could I tell him Rose was dead? He loved her. Every move he had made since I'd met him told me so.

"Rose!" he exclaimed. A frown of terrible anxiety seized him. My fingers were crushed in his grip.

I couldn't convince him tonight. I was too tired. "We'll talk tomorrow," I said, and yawned.

His frown receded and he patted my hand. "Yes, you try to get a good night's sleep, and we'll talk tomorrow. Good night, Rose."

Before he left, I overheard him say to Piggott, "I'm going to have a word with Dr. Dahl. I'll speak to you before you turn in, Miss Piggott. It's rather important." A worried glance was cast over his shoulder toward my bed before he left.

Chapter Twelve

After breakfast the next morning, Mycroft came with a new dressing gown for me. It was pale blue velvet—Rose's favorite color, and mine. A high collar kept out the autumnal chill, and the flowing robe was lined with pale gold satin, rather like my hair. It was a luxurious thing that would have been at home on that rack in the attic at Longbeach. Mycroft was intimate with Rose's taste. He had made an effort to choose what would please her. I wondered if Rose had appreciated how much this man loved her.

Why hadn't she married him? What had led her to choose the treacherous Fraser? I not only had an interesting story to tell; I had one to hear as well. Rose C. intrigued me. Now I could discover her maiden name!

Piggott claimed first audience with Mycroft, to

relate how I had 'slept like a top' and eaten gruel for breakfast, 'licking the bowl clean.'

"Gruel?" he asked, staring in astonishment. "But Rose hates gruel. You're a magician, Miss Piggott, to convince her to eat that."

"Why, she said she liked it. She always had it for breakfast at home."

That disturbed frown appeared on Mycroft's forehead again as he looked across the room at me. "I wonder if you would be kind enough to do some shopping for Mrs. Audry," he said. "We left the house in a rush, and she has nothing with her. You will know what a lady requires."

I did need clothing, but Mycroft chose this moment to buy it in order to give us some privacy. Piggott deemed it more modest to get me out of bed and into the dressing gown, sitting by the grate, before leaving us alone. As soon as the door closed behind her, Mycroft and I exchanged a conscious, tense look.

"Well, Rose, I'm happy to hear you had a good night's sleep," he said with that forced heartiness people use toward invalids.

I pinned him with a firm eye and said, "I have a very strange story to tell you, Mycroft. I told you last night I'm not Rose. It's true. I'm not."

He sighed wearily as he stared into the leaping flames. I wanted to reach out and smooth away the lines of anxiety that pleated his brow. How could I tell him the awful truth? He slowly turned his head and smiled, a sad, wan parody of a smile.

"Dr. Dahl mentioned there might be bouts of hallucination—loss of memory. I daresay the past is a terrible confusion inside your head, Rose. Let us speak of pleasant things. Sophie finally managed to breed Fiona," he said.

"What?"

"Fiona, you remember that Scottish sheep dog she idolizes."

"Mycroft, you've got to listen to me! You have to understand. Rose is dead. I'm not Rose. I don't know Sophie."

"It will all come back to you in time. What *do* you remember, Rose?"

I took a deep breath and tried again. "I'm Rosalie. My name was Rosalie Cummings before I married Fraser. I lived on Watling Street in London with my father and Miss Williams. Oh dear! I must be in touch with Miss Williams. She'll be worrying about me. Fraser never sent her the letters, you know. I found them in his jacket pocket."

Mycroft looked at me bewildered, then jumped to his feet. "I'm going to call Dr. Dahl," he decided, and turned away.

I jumped up too and grabbed his arm to pull him back. "No! Wait! Dr. Dahl doesn't know anything about me. How could he? He never saw me before yesterday. I'm telling you the truth, Mycroft, you have to believe me. Rose is dead. I think she died in childbirth at Longbeach. Fraser has all her things stored in the attic. He was furious when I discovered them. That's why he was trying to kill me. 'She knows!' he said. And that's when he gave me the undiluted medicine that nearly killed me."

I could sense Mycroft's frustration, and knew he was only humoring me when he asked, "What things did you find in the attic?"

"Her portrait—and she does look remarkably

like me. We could practically be twins. People do say, you know, that everyone has a double walking the earth. When Rose died, Fraser found me and tried to turn me into Rose. He made me put on weight and dress my hair like her. He even called me Rosie, and devised a signature for me. It must have had something to do with her money. He told me it was *his* money—that the papers I was signing at Hibbards would give me some share in his fortune. And there was his will too, making me his beneficiary for the things that weren't entailed."

A glazed, incredulous gloss came over Mycroft's eyes. He didn't believe me, and the more I talked, the less he believed. He thought I was hallucinating, but he asked a few questions, perhaps to discover the extent of my mental derangement.

"When did you think—or learn you aren't Rose?" he asked diffidently.

"I never thought I was her! I didn't know she existed till I saw her things in the attic. Who is she, Mycroft? What was her name?"

"Comstock," he said dully. "Rose Comstock. Y—she lived neighboring my home, Thornbridge, in Sussex. The family is wealthy. A nabob uncle—Alvin Simson—left his entire estate to Rose, and of course there is her own family inheritance as well. The Manor and its farms were left to her when her father died. Her Aunt Sophie reared her. Gertrude—my aunt—was like a second mother."

"Fraser said Alvin Simson was *his* uncle!" Mycroft just looked at me. "He said you were jealous because Alvin didn't leave the estate to you."

"To me?" he asked, staring in surprise. "Why the

devil should he leave anything to me? I never knew the man, and he's no relation to me. Alvin's fortune and jewelry collection are entailed. If Rose died without issue, they wouldn't go to Audry, but to a male cousin. Rose's own fortune, however, came to her on her twenty-first birthday. Till then she had only the interest. I was her guardian till that date. Her father left her in my care. The papers you signed turned the money over to her husband, and the will made him her sole beneficiary. It was what Rose insisted on, against my better judgment." He leveled an accusing glare at me.

"The fool!" I exclaimed. "How did she come to marry him, Mycroft?"

Black accusation and deep pain were in his eyes. I noticed his hands were clenched into white-knuckled fists. "Only you can answer that, Rose," he said harshly. "You can't evade the responsibility by pretending to forget. It was you who ran off with Audry—when you were betrothed to me! Once he had accomplished his aim, there was nothing for it but to let you marry him. Why did you do it?" he demanded. His misery was still as acute as it had been when Rose first deserted him, if not greater. Time hadn't eased the burden, perhaps it had compounded it.

"Why did you do it?" he repeated, more loudly. It was my hands his white knuckles crushed now, till I winced with the pain. The flames of torment in his eyes betrayed how deeply he had loved—how deeply he still loved Rose Comstock.

"It seems we'll never know," I told him sadly.

"The hell we won't! *Tell me*! Why did you do it?"

"You're hurting me!" I wrenched my hands away

and rubbed them to ease the cramps. "If you won't believe me, there's nothing more to say. Look at me, Mycroft. Can't you see I'm not Rose?"

He studied me minutely. His hand rose and touched my hair. His fingers gently traced the structure of my bones, from eyes to jaw, as he gazed at me. "Not Rose?" he asked softly. "Do you think I don't know every line of your face? Haven't I lived with the hellish memory of you for two years? Those eyes—no other woman has eyes that exact shade and shape. They aren't exactly the same, your two eyes. One has that golden fleck at the edge of the iris. And your hands," he said, taking my hands and holding them.

Love echoed in every word; it beamed from his dark eyes and engulfed me in a golden glow.

"Only Rose had those peculiarly shaped finger-nails," he continued, fondling my hands. "The nails are more highly arched than most. They always reminded me of a Chinese mandarin's fingers. Where is your ring?" he asked, glancing at my third finger.

I looked, and noticed for the first time that it was gone. "Fraser must have taken it. He only gave it to me to convince you and Hibbard that I was her."

"Stop it, Rose!" he barked angrily. "Of course you're her—you. You wore her sable coat—my God, you even wore the violets you always wore."

"I didn't always wear violets! I hate violets!"

Mycroft stood up impatiently. "This is pointless. You refuse to acknowledge that you've made a great, thundering mess of your life. You always were headstrong, but I never knew you to be a coward before, Rose. Just admit that you made the wrong choice in marrying Fraser, and go on with your life from there. Divorce isn't impossible nowadays—" He stopped suddenly.

I looked and saw him examining me doubtfully. Divorce him and marry me, was what he was thinking. It was there in the air between us in the still room. My interest must have been evident, or he wouldn't have put his arms around me. He wouldn't have cradled my head against his chest and let out that regretful, inchoate sigh from deep in his throat.

It was strange, being in Mycroft's arms. I felt safe and cherished. I didn't want him to let me go. I wanted to be Rose Comstock, the woman he loved.

"I'm sorry if I was brusque, Rose," he said, speaking softly in my ear while his hand stroked my back. "The doctor warned me you might have trouble remembering. Opium is pernicious, especially in such large doses as you had. When the effects have all worn off, you'll remember everything. And I'll be here to help you pick up the pieces."

I breathed a sigh of relief to hear it, and raised my head to see him. "You *will* be here? You *will* help me, Mycroft?" I asked.

"Always, Rose," he said, and kissed me.

It was a gentle kiss, poignant, piercingly sweet. After he left, I lay down and began to wonder if Mycroft was right after all. I had heard Dr. Dahl talk about hallucinations and loss of memory. It wasn't possible there were two women so much alike that the dearest friend of one mistook her for the other. That was as incredible as what I believed to be the truth. I was still very weak. A part of my recent past consisted of gaping holes. I couldn't remember very much about the opium—just lying endlessly in that bed, and the horrible nightmares.

It could be a nightmare, this notion that I was Rose Cummings. Some of my nightmares were frighteningly real to me. Mycroft would help me forget the past and get better. He would take me home to Thornbridge and Aunt Sophie, and everything would be all right.

That afternoon I tried on the clothes Piggott had bought for me. The gown was one of the new 'off the rack' outfits, not of the finest material or cut, but the ill-fitting blue sarsenet was made elegant by the mink-trimmed cape and dashing bonnet that accompanied it. I was newly outfitted from undergarments to slippers and stockings. I was not allowed to go out, however. Dr. Dahl came and decided my pulse was too weak to permit me out in that cold wind.

Mycroft brought cards and we played quietly by the grate, with Piggott peeping in at us from the next room. Conversation was very much inhibited by her busy ears.

"Piquet?" he suggested, shuffling the cards and discarding the low numbers.

"I don't know how to play piquet. Miss Williams and I usually played All Fours, or Pope Joan."

"It will come back to you. You usually beat me at piquet," he said blandly, and dealt me three cards. I looked at them, not knowing what to do.

"What have you got?" he asked.

I showed him my hand. "Carte blanche! You have no court cards! Ten points for you," he said, and wrote it down.

"It's no good. I don't know what you're talking about," I exclaimed in frustration, and threw the cards aside.

"Tell me about Miss Williams," Mycroft suggested nonchalantly. I suspected that Dr. Dahl had suggested he question me about my 'hallucinations.'

I described her. "She's tall and thin, with mousy hair turning gray. She's rather—rather tart, though not really bad-natured. She came to look after me when my father brought me home from India when I was six months old. Mama died a few year later. Miss Williams is the only mother I've ever known."

"Do you have any brothers or sisters?"

"No, I'm an only child."

Mycroft nodded, appearing quite satisfied. "You have just described your Aunt Sophie as this Miss Williams. Sophie took over your care when your mother died. She's the only mother you've known, and her appearance is like your Miss Williams. You've remembered everything but the name. Rose was born in India too, and left while still a child. You remember all that. Rose's father was stationed at Madras. Where was your father stationed?"

"At Madras," I admitted.

Confusion was mounting. It really did begin to seem I was wrong about myself. I searched my mind for some proof, one way or the other.

"You're beginning to remember things now, Rose," he encouraged. "Soon you'll get the names and places right too. It is only a matter of time, and we've plenty of that. All the rest of our lives. Dr. Dahl will be happy to hear of your progress."

I looked hopefully across the table. "But I don't

think I could have so completely forgotten *you*, Mycroft," I said. The thought was uttered before I considered how forward it sounded. I hadn't meant it to encourage his love; it just didn't seem possible I could forget being engaged to Mycroft.

He smiled, happy with what he obviously took for a great compliment. "I'm here to make you remember, Rose," was all he said, but his eyes were more speaking than his voice, and they spoke of love. Love not only past, but present. I bathed in the warmth of that look, and a smile trembled on my lips.

"What did we do together?" I asked.

"Everything. We rode, walked out, went on picnics by the seaside, danced, argued. I tried to interest you in philosophy and you tried to interest me in novels. Do you still harbor your great love for Heathcliff?" he smiled.

I could almost remember being with Mycroft in the ways he suggested. I wanted so very much to recapture the past. "Yes, I still love Heathcliff," I admitted.

"Stiff competition," he replied, gazing deeply into my eyes while I blushed with pleasure. "Thank goodness he's confined to the pages of a novel."

One of the pastimes he suggested sounded quite alien to me. "I don't ride," I told him.

"You gave it up when you became enceinte—wisely so, but when we go home we'll get Belle saddled up for you. I took her to Thornbridge. I've been exercising her when I have time."

"Belle? A chestnut mare?"

"Of course! You *do* remember!" he smiled.

"I—I seem to remember her from Longbeach.

149

Fraser hired her, but I was never once on her back."

"You're still a little confused. It's wishful thinking that she was at Longbeach. If she'd been there, you'd have been astride her."

I remembered very clearly seeing the large mare chomping the grass under the overhanging roof at the side of Longbeach cottage. But then I remembered with equal clarity a golden castle piercing crimson clouds, and celestial music—things that obviously never were. If Belle had been there when I arrived, I felt I would indeed have been astride her; riding held a fascination for me—perhaps because I used to do it well before I became enceinte?

My own memories of the past whirled in my head with those lovely times Mycroft spoke of. And alongside both there were cavernous holes. Had reality sunk into those gaping holes, and some treacherous demons crawled out to bedevil me?

"Mycroft—you mentioned a dog, Fiona. Describe her to me."

"Why don't you describe her to me?" he countered.

"I remember sitting with a sheep dog at my feet, a big collie. Scout I called him."

"That was the dog from Longbeach. It was with you when I saw you there," he said, a little disappointed.

"You know, there's a very easy way to discover whether I'm imagining things or whether I'm right," I suggested tentatively. "Why don't we go to London and see if Miss Williams is on Watling Street? If she's there, then we'll know."

"We could do that," he agreed. His easy acceptance told me he thought Miss Williams was a fabrication, and if so, I was as eager to learn it as he.

"I really should be in touch with her. Fraser didn't post the letters I wrote—she'll be wondering what happened to me."

"What's the number on Watling Street?"

"Twenty-eight. It's the gray frame house on the corner of Watling and Elm. We lived on the second story."

"We'll be passing through London on the way to Thornbridge in a day or two. We'll be there as quickly as a footman could go and return."

"Did the doctor say I could travel that soon?"

"I twisted his arm a little," he confessed. "Aunt Sophie is so eager to see you, Rose. It will do you a world of good to be home. You'll remember everything once you're there."

One subject more unpleasant than the rest had to be brought up before he left. "Have you heard anything from the police yet?" I asked.

"Fraser's parents have been taken into custody at Heacham. The Warners, it seems, are his parents, though he gave us to understand they were well off. I haven't heard anything about Fraser from London," he answered briefly. "The trial will be very messy. I'm going to go after Fraser to recover your fortune. Faced with the evidence of Dr. Dahl and myself, he'll knuckle under, I'm sure. In any case, the law doesn't permit a man to profit from his crimes, and his attempt on your life was certainly to gain control of your fortune. A good lawyer shouldn't have any trouble."

Mycroft soon left, as the doctor prescribed early nights for me. He came back the next day and we talked again, leading to more confusion. I felt a little stronger in my body, but the uncertainty of my past left my brain weak. I truly didn't know who I was.

"How could there be two Roses, both from India, both born on the same day, both identical in every physical detail, both married to Fraser Audry?" Mycroft pointed out reasonably. "It's not as though you were adopted or something, Rose," he added.

It was true I wasn't adopted. It began to seem I truly was Rose Comstock. When we went to Watling Street, we would both know.

CHAPTER THIRTEEN

MISS PIGGOTT WAS CAJOLED AND, I SUSPECT, HEAVILY
bribed to accompany us to London.

"Oh my!" she exclaimed when the notion was put
to her. "Leave King's Lynn! Go to London! I've
never been farther than Cambridge, and that only
to visit my sister once a dozen years ago. What
would folks say?"

The brightening of her eyes hinted at approval of
the idea, however, and when Dr. Dahl added his
encouragement, she accepted. It was as well I had so
little luggage, for Miss Piggott took every stitch she
owned. She watched from the bedroom window as
her trunk was strapped aboard Mycroft's carriage.

"I daresay you've been to London a dozen times,
Mrs. Audry?" she asked.

"I've lived there most of my life," I answered
automatically.

Mycroft gave me one of those doubting, sideways looks he gave on such occasions when I refused to be Rose Comstock.

"Mrs. Audry spent the better part of the past two years in London," he said firmly.

With the increasing vigor that each day brought, some hardy sprout of sanity told me I was not Rose Comstock, no matter how much I wanted to be, and how much Mycroft wanted me to be. Truth was not so obliging as that. It was a hard virtue to grasp, and harder to hold. It had once seemed true that Fraser Audry loved me to distraction. I would have staked my life on it. And now it seemed I was Rose Comstock—so many details substantiated it. But deep within me, that hardy doubt continued to flourish.

Much rested on what would be discovered at 28 Watling Street. If Miss Williams was indeed there, the affair was over. Truth, stranger than fiction, had produced two identical girls in India on the same day, both featuring 'Rose' in her name.

The trip south seemed endless. Heavy gray skies, which too often opened to drench the earth, did nothing to lighten the trip. But Mycroft's carriage was excellent, free of drafts and well sprung, so that tedium and restlessness were the major discomforts. Actually the presence of Miss Piggott was more annoying than anything else. All the important matters Mycroft and I wished to discuss had to be postponed till we had some privacy. Miss Piggott knew only that I had been ill. I imagine she suspected that I had left my husband under harrowing circumstances, but I didn't reply to any of her hints on this matter.

We arrived in London after dark on the second day of the trip. "I'll take you to a hotel immediately," Mycroft decided.

"No! Let us drive to Watling Street first," I said.

He gave a meaningful little look to Miss Piggott. "I'll hire our rooms at the hotel and Miss Piggott can settle you in while we drive to Watling Street," he countered.

That was what we did. Miss Piggot stood with big eyes staring at the elegant facade of the Savoy. Mycroft went inside and arranged our accommodations. When we left, Miss Piggott had recovered and was browbeating the footmen into handling her tattered old trunk with the greatest respect.

"Where is this Watling Street?" Mycroft asked.

I knew it was in Holborn, far east of this fashionable part of the city, but had no idea how to get there.

"It would be better to wait for daylight," Mycroft said.

I was in a fever to learn the truth and insisted we go that night. For well over an hour the carriage prowled the cobblestoned side streets of London, while we peered through the gaslit fog to read street signs.

"We don't even have a map," Mycroft said. "Surely to God if you had lived here for twenty years, you'd recognize something in this area."

"There! Gray's Inn Road! We're getting close. And Staple Inn—we have only a few blocks to go! I recognize the Elizabethan Hall. Miss Williams told me Dr. Johnson wrote *Rasselas* there."

Mycroft's shoulders relaxed. "Fraser Audry also lived there before he married you and moved up town," he announced. "That's why you remember it. No doubt he drove you here to see where he used to live."

I didn't think Fraser would do any such a thing. This wasn't a place to brag of. He had always made much of his wealthy background. Besides, every building was familiar to me. Barnard's Inn I remembered very well. The Mercers' School was there. I wouldn't know all that from one visit.

"Turn left here on to Watling," I directed.

Mycroft pulled the checkstring and gave the order. The carriage turned into the dear, familiar street. I couldn't have dreamed the host of memories that washed over me. Walking here with Papa and Miss Williams, the hollyhocks growing by the little brick house where the woman kept a gray cat. I didn't know her name, but she always smiled when I walked by, and once when I was still in pinafores, she had offered me one of her cat's litter. Papa had a dog at the time, so the offer was regretfully declined.

"You'll see the house where I lived at the end of the next block, on the left," I told Mycroft. "A gray frame building, two stories high. As I said, we lived upstairs."

We both craned our necks out the window, looking for the house. And when we finally got there, there was no gray frame house, but a brick commercial establishment. 'Moorehead Custom Printing' the sign said. 'Business Stationery, Invoices, Cards.' I felt as though the bottom had fallen out of my stomach.

"I don't understand! This is the place. I was

raised here. Mrs. Fletcher lives just across the road!" I said earnestly.

Mycroft shook his head. There were no lights burning in Mrs. Fletcher's house. It was after ten o'clock, and too late to call.

"Accept it, Rose," he said, and took my hand to comfort me. "You've obviously been here with Fraser—perhaps you visited someone in that house. In your delirium, you imagined you lived here. Dr. Dahl said—"

"I lived in a gray frame house on this corner," I insisted. "Mrs. Beecham owned the house and lived downstairs with her married daughter. She made fish every Friday, and had just installed a new blue carpet on the stairs. I'm not imagining that, Mycroft! I'm not! *I'm not!*"

My hands were pulling at his jacket, shaking him into believing me. Tears stung my eyes and oozed in frustration down my cheeks. I must have looked the very pattern of a Bedlamite. Of course he didn't believe a raving, bawling woman. I was coming to disbelieve myself. My house wasn't there—a printing company was there. If I had imagined the very house where I lived most of my life, then I must have imagined the rest too. Miss Williams was Aunt Sophie, and Belle was at Thornbridge. I was Rose Comstock, and I could ride and I could play piquet.

A wave of helplessness washed over me. Why was I fighting it? I wanted to be Rose Comstock, the rich, pampered beauty that Mycroft loved.

"Come, we'll go to the hotel," Mycroft said gently.

He held me in his arms during the drive home. I

closed my eyes, and the gentle swaying of the carriage made me sleepy. In the darkness, his fingers held mine firmly. This was reality. Mycroft was here, flesh and warm blood. He believed I was his Rose. He said he knew. Who was I to argue? I was the victim of hallucination and loss of memory, as Dr. Dahl had said all along.

After such a shock, I didn't expect to sleep. Miss Piggott had settled us in by the time I returned. She consulted with Mycroft and they ordered me a posset. The hot milk was laced with sugar and spices, and was tasty, but I think there was more wine than anything else in it. After a second glass, I couldn't keep my eyes open.

My sleep was disturbed by strange dreams. I, who had never been astride a horse in my life, cantered through flower-strewn meadows with Mycroft. In the distance, a lovely old stone mansion loomed, but to reach it one had to leap over a bridge of thorns. Happiness lay on the other side of the bridge. I urged my steed faster, faster, but the closer we drew to the bridge, the wider it grew, till at last it was no longer a bridge, but a road, all littered with flowering thorns and writhing snakes. I woke in a cold sweat, panting.

In the morning, Mycroft came to take breakfast with me. My suite this time wasn't so grand as before, but there was a sitting room where the waiter set up a table. Miss Piggott was two rooms away, with my bedchamber intervening so that we could speak quite openly.

"I'm going to have a doctor look at you this morning, Rose, if you have no objection," Mycroft said. "I'd like to take you home as soon as possible.

After last night's shock, I thought you might want to stay in London another day. It will give me time to enquire about Fraser."

"I want to go back to Watling Street," I told him. His eyes darkened in displeasure, and I hurried on to persuade him. "We couldn't see very well last night. We should go back in daylight. It might have been on the wrong block, or—" But it had been the right block. It was just the wrong building.

"We've pandered to these phantoms of yours long enough," he said sternly. "Forget the illusions that haunt you, Rose. They are only illusions. Your pride is preventing you from acknowledging the truth—that you misjudged Fraser. He didn't love you. He married you for your money. The past year has been hard on you, not only losing a child, but discovering the truth about your husband as well. It's enough to push anyone over the edge."

He regretted that last speech as soon as it was out. "Not that I mean to imply you're deranged," he added hastily. "You are confused. The peace and quiet of home will be the best thing for you. The doctor recommended by Dahl is excellent at this sort of case. His name is Lattimer. He studied with Breuer in Vienna. Feel free to speak to him quite freely about your hallucinations. He might help. Till you accept the past, you can't go on with the future."

Dr. Lattimer came at ten thirty in the morning. He was an elderly gentleman with young eyes that danced merrily behind his spectacles. He made only a cursory physical examination. He seemed more interested in talking than examining. We ordered coffee and sat on the sofa as though we were friends, chatting. I did as Mycroft suggested and spoke freely of my 'hallucinations,' which I still feared were the truth. But doubts were taking root now.

"Mr. Harlow has given me the facts of your case," he said bluntly. "It was hard, losing the baby, eh Mrs. Audry? You wanted the child very much?"

"Not particularly. I don't even think I was enceinte, in fact. It was an idea my husband got into his head."

"Women usually want a child. Why did you not?"

"I said I didn't particularly want one. I had no special aversion to it either at the time. Though as things turned out, it's just as well . . ."

He looked at me and nodded abstractedly. I almost felt I was boring him, till I caught the glitter of interest behind his spectacles. "It would have been less than ideal to have a child by a criminal. Heredity—you would have been worried, in case the child took after his father."

"That would have been a consideration, certainly, though at the time, I had no idea that my husband was a criminal."

"You married this man against the wishes of your family, I believe?"

For a moment I wavered over my answer. Was I Rose, or Rosalie? The decision made itself. I heard myself say, "I have no family. My mother died when I was very young, and my father died a year ago. I was raised by our housekeeper, Miss Williams. She approved of the match."

Dr. Lattimer filled his pipe, slowly tamping in tobacco. When he was finished, he cast a mischievous smile up at me. "A young lady doesn't marry

160

to please the housekeeper, eh? Nowadays she doesn't marry to please her family either, but only herself—even at the risk of hurting others. When we assume authority for our own life, then we must accept the responsibility along with it."

"I am not blaming Miss Williams. You suggested I acted against the wishes of my family. I was merely pointing out that I had not."

"Ah, then your behavior was blameless. Mr. Audry's other wife—she is more culpable, don't you agree?"

"I'm not ready to judge her. Mr. Audry was attractive to women. I married him."

"Why?"

The doctor was easy to talk to. The fact that he was a perfect stranger whom I wouldn't have to see again made it easier to open myself to him. I wanted someone to talk to and answered without reluctance.

"I thought he loved me, as I loved him. We met in Paris, you know, in the spring. It was romantic. He was from a different world than I, a much more interesting world. He was wealthy and generous— or so I thought at the time."

"Miss Comstock, of course, had no such excuse. She too was from that world of privilege."

"And engaged to Mr. Harlow! That is what I find so hard to understand. How she could—"

A blink of interest flashed behind the curls of smoke that came from his pipe. The tobacco was sweet-smelling. "Mr. Harlow—you find him also attractive?"

"Yes, very attractive."

"You are familiar with both gentlemen. Why do

you think Miss Comstock forsook him?"

I pondered over this puzzle. "He was her guardian. I daresay she chafed under that. I understand she was rather headstrong. Her family probably encouraged the match a little more than was wise. Then too, if she grew up next door to him, there wouldn't be that excitement that comes from meeting a gentleman for the first time, getting to know his ways."

"Familiarity breeds contempt, as the old cliché goes."

"I shouldn't think she felt contempt for him."

"Was there some argument between them? Was this headstrong young lady teaching him a lesson?"

"If that is the case, Mr. Harlow never mentioned it. I wouldn't know."

He frowned thoughtfully. "What would those two have found to argue about, I wonder."

"He was her guardian. Perhaps he placed some constraint on her."

"The guardianship was to terminate on her twenty-first birthday. That, I understand, was to be the date of their wedding."

"He didn't tell me that. Why would he want to wait so long?"

"Do you find two years too long to wait?" he asked.

"When two people are in love, it is much too long. He should have married her sooner, and saved Rose from—from making that dreadful mistake."

Dr. Lattimer nodded as though agreeing. "Sometimes gentlemen are too scrupulous. With her fortune a little larger than his own, perhaps he feared the world would think he took undue advantage, marrying her when she was young, before she had other opportunities, so to speak. If Rose felt as you, perhaps his insisting on the delay was the cause of their argument. What do you think she would say if she could be here with us now, Mrs. Audry?"

I considered this strange question a moment before answering. Wrapped up in my own problem, I had thought of Rose Comstock as a mere shadow in the background. Dr. Lattimer's close questioning had made her come alive. What would she say if she were here to explain her thinking to us?

"I'm sure she would say she's sorry. She wouldn't like to do it—she was proud. Mr. Harlow said she was proud but never cowardly, so I believe she'd admit she was wrong."

"That is very difficult for proud people to do, admit to a serious error, particularly when it has had disastrous consequences. Proud people don't like to hear 'I told you so.' I don't believe Mr. Harlow is the sort of gentleman who would say 'I told you so.' He would say 'I understand, Rose. I forgive you.' Don't you agree, Mrs. Audry?"

"Yes, I know he would. He's very kind."

"And he is very much in love. Rose would be foolish to lose him only for want of saying 'I made a mistake.'"

"Yes."

"Then why don't you say it?"

"I? But I'm not Rose!"

Dr. Lattimer peered through the blue cloud. He wasn't condemning me, but he was persistent. "I wish I had weeks to talk to you, Mrs. Audry," he said. "Yours is a very interesting case. Mr. Harlow has asked me to go to Sussex and treat you, but alas,

I have to attend a conference in Paris. It is unfortunate so few medical men are following this new line of treatment or I would recommend someone for you."

"What new treatment? Are you saying I'm insane?" I demanded. I spoke fiercely, but inside I was shaking. Was I mad?

"Insane? That is old wives' talk, Mrs. Audry. The mind is so much more subtle than we have believed in the past. You are not insane. You have been subjected to heavy doses of drugs, and the delirium they induced has become more real to you than reality—and more acceptable. Deep in your heart, you feel guilty for an impetuous young girl's mistakes. You have hurt yourself—but that you could forgive. What you cannot forgive is having hurt the others, your family and Mr. Harlow.

"Forgive Rose. She wasn't a monster, you know, just a little spoiled. She's paid for her mistake. See if you can't learn to pity her. Once that is done, we shall see. I shall only be in Paris for a week. I'll be in touch with you when I return. I hope I shall have the pleasure of speaking to the first Mrs. Audry," he finished playfully.

Could it possibly be that simple? I felt guilty for my actions, and decided to blame them on some other woman? She had to be a woman very much like myself, so I had invented an alter ego named Rosalie. Every atom and fiber of my being rejected this facile explanation. Yet how else to explain the inexplicable? The close resemblance between Rose and Rosalie, and what seemed even more important to me, the fact that my house was gone.

I felt that this laughing-eyed little doctor could

unravel the tangle if only he would stay. "Must you go to Paris?" I asked.

"I must. Dr. Breuer is giving a paper of the utmost importance on asphasia and cerebral paralysis in children. Perhaps I shall learn something there to help you. But what will be better than my guidance is for you to go home, where you see that everyone else has forgiven Rose. Then perhaps you too will have pity on her. For myself, I like Rose very much," he said archly.

"Adieu, Mrs. Audry. We shall meet again soon."

He left, and I sat on alone with the pot of coffee growing cold as I thought about what he had said. With one item I agreed: going to Rose's home. Mine was no longer there, perhaps it never had been. And if I didn't live on 28 Watling Street, then my home was surely the Manor, neighboring Thornbridge. With Aunt Sophie and Gertrude there, forgiving me, loving me, who knows what I might remember.

Aunt Sophie might even be Miss Williams. But if she wasn't . . . I shook the troublesome thought away.

CHAPTER FOURTEEN

'HOME' WAS LESS THAN A DAY'S JOURNEY AWAY. AS I felt much stouter, we dispensed with Miss Piggott. She returned to King's Lynn to astonish her neighbors with stories of London, which she had seen mainly from the window of our rooms at the Savoy. While she packed the evening before our departure, I had privacy to ask Mycroft what he had learned about Fraser.

"He hasn't been picked up," he told me. "The police are on the lookout for him. He checked out of his hotel four days ago. That would be while we were at King's Lynn."

"He must have gone back to Longbeach. He couldn't know I'm gone."

"The police know about Longbeach," Mycroft said.

His worry was very obvious. Of course he was

eager to have Fraser captured, but he seemed more worried than before, and soon the reason came out.

"He's cashed in all your stocks and bonds, Rose. He had Hibbard sell everything. He closed his account at the bank and took out the jewelry collection. It looks as though he's gone off to Italy without you. It will be hard to find him once he gets to the continent with a fortune to aid his escape."

"He was only going to Italy to kill me there, where no one knew us. He's gone back to Longbeach. They'll capture him there," I said.

The loss of Rose's fortune, its recovery, and Dr. Lattimer's visit made up the main part of our conversation as we drove to West Sussex. The gray clouds had blown away, giving us a fine day for our trip. The scenery was a feast for my jaded, city eyes. Tree followed tree over hill and hollow of the chalk downs, till teaming London was only a memory. From the crest of a hill we looked down on prosperous farms nestled cozily in valleys, edged here and there with hedgerows. Forests in the distance looked black against the azure sky and yellow fields of stubble till we drew closer and could distinguish the fir trees. The sun was beginning to sink toward the horizon as we passed over the South Downs to the coastal area.

"Look familiar?" Mycroft asked with a smile that told me we were nearly home.

Ahead lay a village. The spire of an old church rose above rooftops. As we drew closer, I noticed the tower was square, the spire an ungainly octagonal shape, topped by a white rooster that looked out of place on a church. I was sure I had never seen it before. Such an oddity must have jogged my memory.

I examined everything closely as we entered the high street of Paget. The village green was totally unfamiliar. Wrought-iron benches with wooden seats were placed around the edges of the grass. The green had been turned into a playing field, with nets at the end. Mycroft drew the checkstring, and the carriage pulled to a stop in front of an apothecary shop.

"Do you feel well enough for a short turn up and down the high street?" he asked.

I nodded, understanding his reasoning. He hoped the street would stir me to remembrance. I hoped so too. We strode in state up one side of the main thoroughfare and down the other. The only thought that Milady's Fine Millinery Shop stirred was of a similar shop in Holborn, called Miss Filmore's Millinery Fashions. Paget Drapery Store meant nothing to me, except as a stage on which to place Rose Comstock. I envisaged her in the shop, mulling over silks and crepes.

As I stood, imagining, a gray head appeared at the window. An elderly woman stood a moment, looking. Her eyes grew wide with shock, then she smiled. In an instant, she was at the door.

"Mrs. Audry! How nice to see you again. You haven't been to the village in years."

Surprise robbed me of my manners. While I stood gaping, Mycroft said, "Good afternoon, Mrs. Hansom," and made a few comments on the weather. With the good woman's name in my possession, I added my greetings to her. I didn't want her to think Rose had forgotten her.

We made a hasty escape, but before we got back to the carriage two other ladies greeted me by name, in that same shocked way Mrs. Hansom had done. With no more than a glimpse of my face, the people of Paget were convinced Rose had come home. Such a monumental piece of news probably set the village buzzing.

The carriage continued a mile west of Paget. The road now was along the coast, but it was a coast unlike the fens of Norfolk that petered gradually to the water. Here the chalk cliffs fell stark to the sea below. No sense of familiarity gripped me. It was a pretty place, but a totally new place to me.

Ahead, a curved line of poplars marked a private road north off the main thoroughfare. The carriage turned into this opening and continued through a well-tended park. The spreading beech trees looked polite. They were prosperous and flourishing, not straggly and windblown like the trees of Longbeach, which had to compete for nourishment in the poor soil. Everything about the property spoke of wealth and care.

The carriage drew to a stop, and I looked out the nearest window. On my right, a stately stone mansion stood four-square, basking in the glow of the setting sun. It had no battlements, no towers or turrets, nor even a very elegant doorway. The sheer size of the house lent it dignity without such frivolities, and the proportions bestowed a sort of austere charm to the facade.

I turned and saw Mycroft studying me. "Is it the Manor?" I asked.

He tried to conceal his dismay when he answered. "That's Thornbridge, Rose. The Manor is to the left. You'll see a fork in the road just ahead."

"I'd like to see the Manor from a distance before you take me—home." I hesitated over the word.

He opened the door and we descended to the fork in the road. Beyond a stand of fir trees, I espied the Manor. It was a gothic building, with all the frills and furbelows that Thornbridge lacked. There were soaring lancet windows, crenellations along the roof, and a turret guarding the left front. Only flying buttresses were lacking. It was an admirable house, but, alas, one I had never seen before in my life.

"Well?" Mycroft said in that hearty way that betrayed his anxiety.

"It's very nice. Shall we go back to the carriage? The wind is growing chilly." We climbed back in.

"Aunt Sophie will be astonished to see me land in on her unannounced," I mentioned. "It seems a nasty trick to play on an old lady."

"She'll be delighted to see you have come home. As for a 'nasty trick,' you forget the house is yours."

"I wonder why Fraser didn't want to live here."

"I suspect it was the proximity to Thornbridge that deterred him," Mycroft replied stiffly. "You should have insisted."

Such a troublesome topic was not the optimum one to discuss as we approached the very door of Rose's home. Instead, Mycroft pointed out some garden beds that would no doubt look handsome in spring and summer, but were dreary in autumn. As we descended in front of the house, Mycroft offered me his arm, and with my heart pounding in my throat, we walked the last yards to the door. If it opened to Miss Williams' thin face and tart tongue, I would know I was home.

But of course a mansion door is opened by a butler. The butler who opened the house to us was called "Scraggs" by Mycroft. He didn't look like a butler, but a groom. He was a short, stout man with a rough face and grizzled hair. He stared at me a moment, then his face broke into a smile of welcome.

"It's the mistress!" he exclaimed. In his shock, he behaved as a butler shouldn't and shook my hand. "Welcome home, Miss Com—that is, Mrs.—Ma'am. Coo, won't Miss Sophie be knocked off her pins."

"Perhaps you would be kind enough to tell her we're here," Mycroft suggested.

I hadn't said a word. I was busy looking around the elegant entrance hall. It looked more like a church than anything else. It rose two stories high. The wood paneling was carved in trefoils, like a church pew. The stained oak tended to wreath the hall in shadows, but by gaslight I could see a table holding flowers and brass candlesticks. I looked and looked, hoping to feel a sense of recognition. Everything was strange to me, and I drew a deep sigh of regret.

Mycroft touched my elbow gently. "I'll take your wrap. We'll wait for Aunt Sophie in her parlor. She'll have the fire lit there."

He removed my wrap and bonnet and led me off to the right. On the left, I caught a glimpse of a grander chamber—that would be the formal drawing room. Without lights burning, it looked forbidding, but Aunt Sophie's parlor was a cozy, friendly room, not unlike our living room on Watling Street. It had yellow wall coverings like mine, and the grate was similarly situated to the right as we entered. But I don't mean there was any sense of complete familiarity. The sofa was different, the tables, all the furnishings and accessories were strange.

I was too nervous to sit down. Mycroft's dark eyes studying me did nothing to alleviate the tension. There was a sound of busy footfalls in the hall, and suddenly an elderly lady came bustling in. It was cruel to play such a stunt on an old lady. She looked on the edge of hysterics.

Her hazel eyes were staring, and her lean cheeks were blanched white. We stood a moment, taking each other's measure. She was not Miss Williams. It was strange she should be gray-haired, thin-faced, and wear a tart expression, yet bear no resemblance whatsoever to Miss Williams. Paltry language had led me astray. Miss Sophie was an elegant creature, with her hair arranged in fantastic coils. She carried herself proudly, with an air of nobility. My Miss Williams, a servant, was much less prepossessing. Miss Sophie was dressed for dinner in a dark green gown, with a paisley shawl around her shoulders.

But really all these details were hardly noticed at the time. It was her hazel eyes that held me spellbound. I looked as amazement turned to delight. Tears of pure joy gathered in her eyes, and she rushed forward to enfold me in her arms.

"Rose. Rose, you're home. My dear, we've missed you so. I always knew you'd come back. Didn't I tell you, Mycroft?"

I stood, writhing in embarrassment at her gushing welcome. Her arms bound me to her thin body, and from a sense of what was proper, I returned a slight pressure.

"How are you, Rose?" she asked, holding me back to study me. "Pale! We'll get that color back again. It was the miscarriage—but we shan't speak of that now. Where is—where is Mr. Audry?" she asked, looking out the door to see if he was awaiting entrance.

"He's not with me," I said briefly. Interest flashed on her proud little face. Interest and hope. She turned her gaze to Mycroft.

"That's a long story, Miss Sophie. I'll fill you in later, but now I think Rose would like to go to her room to freshen up. We've driven all the way from London."

"Of course. I'll send for Nevins. Scraggs!" she hollered into the hall. Scraggs couldn't have been more than a foot away. His face appeared at the door within half a second of her summons.

So strange to think of this whole grand household being put at sixes and sevens over me, a total stranger. It was wanton cruelty to mislead them so. I must make Aunt Sophie believe the truth, at once. I should really call Miss Sophie by her more formal name too. She was no aunt of mine.

Nevins proved to be a young servant in a blue dress and white apron. She wore her brown hair skimmed back from her face like Miss Williams. Large brown eyes were the most striking feature of an otherwise extremely plain face. Her complexion was pasty. Like Miss Sophie, her jaw fell open when she saw me. An awkward curtsey was performed.

"Welcome home, Miss Comstock," she said nervously.

"Mrs. Audry now, Nevins," Miss Sophie reminded her. "Please show Mrs. Audry to her room, and see that she has what she requires. Hot water, I daresay. Make yourself available to dress her hair and help her change for dinner. Your things are all as you left them, Rose. We'll dine as soon as you're ready," she added to me.

She looked at me hungrily, greedily, as though she wanted to hold on to me and never let me out of her sight again. There was fear in her expression too. No doubt she was worried about what had brought Rose home—and what might suddenly carry her off again.

While I made my toilette, I knew Mycroft would be filling Miss Sophie in on his version of the whole story. She would know, when I returned below, that I didn't remember her. That would make our relationship easier. She wouldn't expect me to treat her as my beloved aunt, who had raised me as her own daughter. I knew I was incapable of carrying off such a charade as that.

Nevins was as nervous as a bride as she attended me. "Which gown would you like to wear, Miss— Mrs. Audry? Miss Sophie kept them all ready to be used. Do you want your favorite blue?"

"Let me see what is here," I answered, and went to Rose's clothespress.

These would be the outfits Rose Comstock wore before her marriage, when she was nineteen. They were the gowns of a country belle, not the high fashions Fraser had chosen for me in Europe. The 'favorite blue' that Nevins lifted from the closet was charming. It wasn't satin, but it had a sheen to it. Lutestring, I thought Miss Williams had called this stuff. The color was a deep, rich blue. The style was

simple but elegant, with a modest décolletage edged
in Belgian lace. The gown had long sleeves and
fitted tightly around the waist.

"Yes, I'll wear the blue," I told Nevins.

"I'll just help you wash up, ma'am. It'll be like
old times."

I had no intention of being washed by anyone.
"I'll take care of it myself, Nevins. You set out
accessories for the gown, if you please. Whatever
she—whatever I used to wear with it. I can't
recall."

"Wash yourself?" Nevins asked, eyes goggling.

"I would prefer to." To keep her busy I added,
"And you can set out my night things for later."

"Yes, ma'am." Nevins was easily intimidated.
Was she used to a haughty mistress? There was a
cringing quality in the servant that suggested it.

The gown fit perfectly. Fraser had often urged me
to put on a little weight, but this extra weight must
have come after the marriage. I knew Mycroft had
seen Rose occasionally in London, and that she
hadn't visited home since her marriage. Of course
Fraser never dreamed I would ever come here. It
was only Mycroft he had been trying to convince I
was Rose Comstock.

When the gown was on, Nevins came forward
with a pair of dainty blue kid slippers with silver
buckles on the front. Rose was fashion-conscious,
and accustomed to the best. The slippers were well
made. They too fit like a glove. The very shape of
Rose's toes in the soft leather was correct for me.
When such unlikely things as this occurred, I remembered Dr. Lattimer's explanation. 'The mind

is so much more subtle than we have believed in the past.' 'The delirium has become more real to you than reality.'

As I stood gazing at myself in the mirror, I was struck with the plainness of the outfit. Some ornament was required. Fraser had Rose's jewelry, but a young lady would have trinkets. I walked to the vanity and sat down. A white leather jewelry box was there. I lifted the lid and looked at such an assortment of beads and knickknacks as I possessed myself, in that house on Watling Street that didn't exist.

A pair of glass beads the same shade as the gown drew my eye. I lifted them and fastened them around my neck. In the flickering gaslight, they looked well. Nevins appeared behind my shoulder in the mirror. She was nodding and smiling.

"They always looked well with that gown, ma'am," she smiled.

"Thank you, Nevins."

Her smile faded and she looked at me askance. She wasn't accustomed to so much politeness, it seemed. "I'll dress your hair, ma'am," she said, and took up a plain horn-backed brush. I frowned at it, remembering a chased silver dresser set.

"Miss Sophie put your old things out when you took your new silver set with you," she explained. "Will your things be coming back to the Manor, Miss?"

"*Mrs.*, Nevins. Mrs. Audry."

She looked abashed. "Sorry, ma'am. It's that hard to remember—me always calling you Miss Comstock. I'll get on to it. Shall I dress your hair the old way, the way you used to wear it with this gown?"

Curious to see what this style might be, I said yes. Nevins deftly brushed my hair back from my face and gathered it into a simple basket of curls with a round comb. The elegance of Rose Comstock was brushed away that easily. The soft waves around my face, the coquettish curl over the shoulder were gone, leaving a frightened-looking girl staring into the mirror.

"That'll please your aunt," Nevins informed me.

It pleased me too. Without the trappings of society, I more closely resembled Rosalie Cummings.

"I'll go downstairs now," I said, and went to the door.

The blue kid slippers made no sound as I glided down the curving staircase and into the paneled hallway that looked like a church. I walked toward Miss Sophie's parlor and heard her talking to Mycroft.

"The poor thing!" I heard her exclaim. "That beast of an Audry! It was a black day when he laid his eyes on her."

Mycroft was facing the door. He looked up and saw me, and froze in an attitude of surprise. Sophie's gaze followed his. I felt dreadfully self-conscious with them both staring at me, but entered as though I didn't notice.

If I had thought Miss Sophie loved me before, I would have to use some such word as 'adore' now. A softer look was on her face, and there was moisture in her eyes. This was how she would remember Rose, not as the stylish creature she had become but as the young country belle. I smiled shyly in response to her pleasure, then looked to Mycroft.

He looked as though he had seen a ghost. His affection for Rose was always evident, but I discovered that he, too, much preferred the old Rose, before she ran off with Fraser and became a fashion plate. Something glowed in his eyes. I watched, mesmerized, as he gulped. His body made a convulsive jerk toward me before he pulled himself back to attention.

"Very nice, Rose," he said in a hoarse voice that betrayed more than he knew.

A blush suffused my cheeks. It was embarrassing to be the object of so much love, and so many misguided hopes. Yet it seemed unfair that Rose Comstock should have all this affection, when she was a spoiled, selfish girl. Anger lent a harsh edge to my speech. I lifted my chin and said, "Did you tell Miss Sophie, Mycroft?"

"Your Aunt Sophie is aware of your—mental confusion," he answered gently. "Shall we ask her to determine whether you are her niece? She knows you better than anyone else in the world. What do you say, Aunt Sophie?"

"Ah, Rose, poor child," she said, shaking her head at me. "It is all that beast's doing, confusing you with opium. Try to forget him. Just imagine that Fraser Audry never happened, and soon you will realize you're home, where we all love you. At least he couldn't diddle you out of the Manor and your own income. It is only the money and Alvin's jewelry he made off with. It's worth it to be rid of him."

"We'll get it all back," Mycroft added. "And now shall we eat, ladies? I don't know about you, but I'm ready for fork work."

"It's roast beef and Yorkshire pudding, Rose."

"My favorite!" I said. Mycroft and Miss Simson exchanged a knowing, satisfied smile. Rose and I even had the same taste in food, it seemed.

Miss Sophie set an excellent table. Candlelight gleamed on silver and china and a damask cloth. We were served by footmen, who poured wine into the crystal glasses. I stared, remembering hotels in Paris and Karlsbad, but not a single memory of ever having sat at this table before came to me.

The names discussed over dinner were all strange. Mycroft had been away for some days, and Miss Sophie filled him on the doings of the community. "Elmer Dugan's bought a fine new carriage. About time—that old black wreck was on its last legs. You remember the Dugans, Rose. It's a pity Melissa moved to Hampshire when she got married. You would like to visit her as you used to. She married Leonard Ault after all."

That was the sort of thing they discussed, and I listened in confusion. Mycroft had been told by Dr. Lattimer not to upset me by harping on recent events. Peace and quiet were the prescription, and though I sensed that Miss Sophie was extremely eager to discuss more important things, she did as Mycroft had ordered and confined her talk to chitchat.

After dinner we returned to Miss Sophie's cozy

parlor. The heat of the fire made me sleepy. At my first stifled yawn, Mycroft jumped to his feet.

"Thoughtless of us, Miss Sophie. We're tiring Rose. She's had a long, hard day. She needs her sleep."

"We'll soon get the roses back in her cheeks. Bring Belle over tomorrow, Mycroft, and take Rose for a ride. You will like that, Rose," she said, with the air of conferring a treat.

"I don't have a riding habit." Thus far I had tried to avoid using any name when speaking to Miss Sophie. To call her my aunt seemed an imposition, yet I knew she would wince at a cold 'Miss Sophie.'

"Why, your scarlet habit is as good as new! You only wore it twice."

"Scarlet?" I was surprised at this garish color. Rose and I favored quieter shades.

"Now you're ready to admit it was a mistake. I told you it didn't suit, but you must always have your own way."

This skirted too close to a rebuke for Miss Sophie's comfort. "Not that it didn't look well," she added hastily.

Mycroft stood hesitating. I sensed that he wanted a private word with me and said I would accompany him to the door. Miss Sophie nodded contentedly. Before many days, she would be trying to put the idea of a match with Mycroft into my head.

In the privacy of the hall, we stopped a moment. My nerves were on edge from the uncomfortable evening. It is extremely enervating to be watched constantly, eyes waiting to see your reaction to everything, ears cocked to hear what telling words you let out. Worst of all was that they still believed I was Rose, and I became more certain by the moment that I was not.

"I told you I don't know how to ride," I said petulantly.

Mycroft just smiled at my mood. I think he was very accustomed to seeing Rose in pouts. "Tomorrow I shall prove you're wrong," he said confidently. "It will all come back to you. Such uninteresting creatures as Aunt Sophie and myself may have failed to restore memory, but Belle will do it. Once she has learned, a person never forgets how to ride."

"You said the same about piquet. That didn't work either."

Mycroft reached out and took my chin in his fingers. He wagged my chin a moment, smiling. "You haven't changed as much as you think, missie. Still determined to have your own way. I give you fair warning, this time I shall carry the day. Good night, Rose. Sleep tight."

A kiss as light as gossamer brushed my lips. His cheek lingered a moment against mine, and he was gone.

I said good night to Miss Sophie at the door and went upstairs. Nevins was waiting to undress me. I dismissed her and changed into Rose's lawn nightie, embroidered with rosebuds around the bib. Whose loving fingers had worked such delicate blooms for Rose? Miss Sophie's, very likely.

I took a last look around the room before getting into bed and extinguishing the lamp. It was the sort of room any young lady would covet. The furnishings were French, white with gold trim. The cream wall covering was sprinkled with a shower of rosebuds. There were books and a few dolls in a cabinet at the end of the room. The dresser and desk might provide some insight into the lady who looked like me. Tomorrow I would investigate them thoroughly, but tonight I wanted only to lie down and close my eyes.

A lively parade of images kept me awake for hours. The lovely chalk downs, so surprisingly lush and rich. The words 'chalk downs' had always conjured up bleak and barren wastes to me. New faces—Miss Piggott, Dr. Dahl, Dr. Lattimer, Nevins, Aunt Sophie, Mycroft.

Mycroft . . . It was his harsh face and gentle eyes that were with me as I finally dozed off.

CHAPTER FIFTEEN

I DON'T KNOW AT WHAT HOUR ROSE COMSTOCK WAS IN the habit of rising, but I was always an early riser. At seven-thirty I was at the window, drawing the drapes to read the sky. I half hoped for clouds to delay my maiden ride on Belle. Once Mycroft saw my clumsy hands and ungainly seat, he'd be convinced I wasn't Rose. One never forgets how to ride, he said, but if one has never learned, then she would make an egregious ass of herself. She would have to leave the Manor in disgrace. And where would I go? Where was home?

The sky was pale blue, painted with lacy clouds that moved along briskly in the breeze. I went to the clothespress to see what gowns Rose had for autumn day wear. Nevins had removed my traveling suit for pressing. I chose the dullest thing there, to match my mood. It was a dove gray sarsenet with a white collar and cuffs. Brisk, efficient, it looked like something a governess might wear. What had possessed Rose to choose it? Its snug fit told me it was not one of her later acquisitions.

I dressed my hair simply to match the gown. Pulled severely back in a knot, it lent me an air of dignity. While I had privacy, I decided to examine Rose's room. The dressers revealed a quantity of good but not elaborate lingerie. The desk held those items customarily found in a young lady's bureau. There were pens and ink pot, printed stationery, little used. A letter was still in the box, addressed to a lady's magazine, asking for a subscription. The handwriting was familiar. The tall, slanting R of the Rose was exactly as Fraser had trained me to sign my name. I wasn't imagining that. As if to assure myself, I wrote Rosalie Cummings in the old, crabbed way, and sat staring at it.

Had the delirium become more real than reality? The black kid slippers I wore were more comfortable than those Mycroft had bought me at King's Lynn. By day's end I would have literally walked a mile in Rose Comstock's shoes—perhaps I would have learned something about her, or myself. Perhaps even that we were one and the same? No, it was hopes and dreams that were becoming stronger than reality. I must be firm with myself. Becoming Rose Comstock would be fatally easy, and I didn't want to lose my real self.

The bookshelf was the last item I studied. Rose liked the same sort of literature as I. Besides a few books from the schoolroom, there were popular ladies' novels, including a well-thumbed copy of *Wuthering Heights*. What wild dreams had she dreamed as she read about the engrossing, enigmatic Heathcliff? She had some collections of poetry from the early part of the century. Shelley, Keats, Lord Byron. I wasn't an enthusiast of any of them.

There was nothing much to be discovered here. Rose would have carried off with her the few items she truly cherished. Her ivory and jade carvings, for instance, were in the attic at Longbeach. What remained behind was what she was forsaking, what she no longer wanted. I went downstairs to the breakfast parlor.

Miss Sophie was already there, sitting alone and musing over a pot of tea. A black sheep dog was resting at her feet. It rose and growled when I came in.

"Fiona!" Miss Sophie scolded. "Silly dog. It is Rose. Run and make her welcome." The dog rose and growled.

"How odd! She's forgotten you!" Miss Sophie exclaimed.

My look was all the answer she needed. She looked discomfited. "Good morning, Miss Sophie," I said. A shadow passed over her face at my way of addressing her, but the charade couldn't continue. She silenced the dog and made a few polite enquiries about my sleep.

"I'll call for a fresh pot of tea," she told me.

"I'd prefer coffee, if it's not too much trouble."

"Oh, you drink coffee now," she said, surprised.

"I have always taken coffee in the morning, Miss Sophie," I replied firmly.

"I daresay it is the fashion in London." It was a gentle insistence that I had changed my taste since going there with Fraser. The mulish set of her jaw

185

told me so. She wouldn't argue, but she would treat me as Rose. Equally mulish, I would fight her every inch of the way. She rang the bell and ordered coffee.

"I'm surprised you can still get into that gray gown," was her next speech.

"It's a trifle snug, but it fits."

"I thought you would wear your riding habit, Rose, as Mycroft is bringing Belle over. You're up early this morning. I didn't look for you before eight-thirty or nine."

"I usually rise at seven-thirty."

There was another of those teeth-grinding looks, but she still held her tongue. "Was Nevins up to tend you?" she asked.

"No, I dressed myself, as I have always done."

That was enough to break her patience. "You have never dressed yourself in your life, missie! Since you were able to stand up and toddle, Nevins has taken care of you." Her anger vented, she fell into apologies. "I'm sorry, Rose, but it is extremely exacerbating to get you back, only to find you changed so. Calling me Miss Sophie, as though we were strangers!" A tear gathered in her eyes and she raised the serviette to daub at it.

"I'm sorry, but if I ever knew you, Miss Sophie, I don't remember. I will call you Aunt Sophie if it pleases you, but I don't feel you are my aunt."

"You could *try* to feel it, Rose," she answered, with less patience than I expected. "But you always were a heedless girl. Oh, I love you as a mother, but now that you are here, I will tell you how badly you hurt me—and Mycroft when you ran off with that hedgebird of an Audry."

186

"How did it happen?" I asked coolly. My strategy was to learn every scrap possible about Rose and see if anything was familiar to me. This particular matter had never come up when I was with Mycroft.

"God only knows. I should never have let you go up to London to visit Cousin Elfreda. You would insist on going. If you weren't having a Season, you must at least have a visit, you said. And I, like a ninnyhammer, let you."

"But where did I meet him?"

"How the devil should I know? Cousin Elfreda swore black and blue she didn't know the man, had never met him. She knew all the East India Company crowd. They were her friends, and Audry's set as well. You must have met him at some party or other. But to run off with him! It was unconscionable!"

I refused to take blame for Rose's monstrous indiscretion. "Did she ever come back here after the elopement? How did she get her things—the silver dresser set and the collection of carvings—"

"Of course you came home when Mycroft found you at that hotel in Brighton. After two days Cousin Elfreda *finally* decided she ought to inform me. Mycroft went dashing off at once. He questioned Elfreda's friends and came up with the name of Audry. Finally he traced you to Brighton. You had been there, registered as man and wife for two nights. He arranged the wedding before your return, to keep your shame from our neighbors. You would have been ruined otherwise. He insisted on the visit, for the looks of it. Not one sou of your income would he give till you either left Audry, or married him. At the time we had no idea how wretched the man was, and there was no point thinking anyone else would take Audry's leavings. One visit, of one day, and not another sign of you in two years."

I listened, hating Rose more with every word. "Did she write?" I asked.

"If you can call a postcard a month writing. And of course nothing once Audry took you to Longbeach. We didn't even know you were increasing till after you had left London. You should have come home for the delivery. Dr. Chambers would have looked after you properly."

I listened, and could think of nothing to say. Rose was a monster of selfishness. She certainly owed humble apologies, but what had that to do with me? Miss Sophie jiggled in her chair and began to settle down. She couldn't remain angry with Rose for long. "Was it very bad, the miscarriage?" she asked.

"I don't know. I didn't have a miscarriage, but Longbeach was horrible."

A sad, defeated look took possession of her eyes. "Here is your coffee," she said when a servant brought it in.

The servants were curious too. Nothing but curiosity could account for the number of trips they found it necessary to make past the morning parlor, peeking in at me. I felt like a bearded lady at the old Bartholomew Fair.

"Help yourself from the sideboard," Miss Sophie suggested.

There was a board of food under hot covers. My appetite wasn't affected by the bizarre circumstances. I was hungry, and filled my plate.

Miss Sophie examined it and said, "Your smoked herring is there, Rose. I ordered it especially for you. You know I never take fish for breakfast."

"Neither do I," I told her, and began to eat my gammon and eggs.

After breakfast, I asked Miss Sophie if I might have a tour of the house. The wish was part curiosity and part a hope that something would trigger a memory. She stared in consternation. "It's *your* house, Rose. Naturally you must do exactly as you wish."

I wasn't accepting responsibility for Rose's folly, and I wouldn't accept her perquisites either. "Thank you," I said, to show she did me a favor.

Rose Comstock had been reared in the lap of luxury. I prowled the upstairs corridors till I discovered the nursery, in order to begin my search at her beginning. It was a fairytale room, with a cradle swathed in white and pink. There was her childhood bed as well. Every toy and trinket to amuse a child was there, ranged neatly on shelves. Some of the toys were well-worn, obviously her favorites.

I lifted a shabby stuffed doll with yellow wool curls and held it, as though I could absorb from its ragged limbs some essence of Rose. I felt sure it wouldn't have been my favorite. Grander dolls on the shelf looked untouched. As I stood, clutching the rag doll, a servant scuttled by and peeped in. I saw her give a significant look at the doll in my hands. No doubt she'd dart down to report that 'Rose' had gone unerringly to her old favorite toy. I hastily set the thing down.

In the corner a miniature table was set up with miniature dishes. The toy cups and teapot were of fine bone china. They were meant as ornaments, but they were all cracked and chipped. Rose had been given them to play with. It occurred to me that if Rose Comstock was spoiled, it wasn't entirely her own fault. From the cradle she had been treated like a queen. How could they expect her to be anything but spoiled and selfish?

I walked down the corridor, looking in at other fine bedrooms. Servants passed me in the hallway with a deferential bob, and always those curious, gleaming eyes. When I went back to my own room, Nevins was tidying the bed.

She looked at me, frightened. "Oh, ma'am, you should have wakened me. I didn't expect you up before eight-thirty." She looked at the gray dress. "What will Miss Sophie think, me letting you wear that old frock?"

"I decided to dress myself, but you can put out the scarlet riding habit, Nevins."

"Will you change now, ma'am?"

"No, just leave it on the bed and have your breakfast."

She babbled out another round of apologies before darting for the riding habit. This scurrying servility grated on my nerves. Rose must have shown them the rough side of her tongue. Having a personal servant at all was more of an annoyance than anything else.

After Nevins left, I walked to the window and looked out on the estate. Rose's window was in the southeast corner. From the front I could see the park, with the road and cliffs to the sea beyond. From the east window I saw more park that petered out to meadow after some yards. A mounted gentleman was coming toward the house. As he drew closer, I recognized Mycroft Harlow, and he was leading the bay mare behind him.

He was mounted on a sleek black horse that suited his proud bearing. His head was erect, his shoulders square. He looked completely at ease in the saddle. The very thought of riding filled me with apprehension, but he was bringing Belle, and I scrambled into the scarlet riding habit. The elegant outfit transformed me again into a fashion plate. With the stylish black hat tilted over my eye, I looked as fine as any lady when I went downstairs to greet Mycroft as Scraggs showed him in.

Mycroft's cheeks were colored from the brisk weather. His close-fitting jacket displayed broad shoulders and a wide chest tapering to a trim waist. Health, wealth, and authority hung about him like magic, but it was his eyes that held me. They were warm with approval as they studied me.

"Good morning, Rose," he said and bowed. "I didn't expect to see you dressed and waiting for me."

"Good morning, Mycroft," I replied, flushing under his steady gaze. "I saw you coming from the upstairs window. I didn't want to keep you waiting."

Surprise was added to the other emotions playing over his mobile face. He was accustomed to waiting for Rose, then. That she was spoiled by her family was regrettable but understandable. She was the only child, the darling of a doting father and aunt, surrounded by myriads of servants. It didn't explain why this highly eligible and handsome gentleman allowed her to bearlead him.

"Eager to put Belle through her paces, I see," he said, smiling. "I know you better than to take your eagerness as a personal compliment. Shall we go?"

"I'll just tell Aunt Sophie I'm leaving."

This ordinary courtesy also surprised him. Again a look of approval was in his dark eyes. I told Miss Sophie we were leaving and she said, "That's nice, dear. Have a good ride. Oh, and would you like to order dinner before you leave?"

Miss Williams had been in charge of our kitchen at home. I hadn't the slightest notion what would be suitable here. "Why don't you do it, Aunt Sophie? You would have a better idea than I."

"But what would you like?" she persisted.

"Anything," I said comprehensively, and fled back to Mycroft.

He led me out to where the mounts were tethered to a tree. At close range, Belle looked as big as a mountain. There was a mischievous glint in her eyes that upset me.

"I—I don't believe I'll ride after all," I said.

"Afraid, Rose?" he taunted.

"Yes."

Mycroft put his head back and laughed. "You're not going to let a dumb animal get the better of you?" he teased.

"No, I refuse to have my head split open just because a dumb gentleman insists I can ride, when I know I cannot."

He lifted an arrogant brow at my insult, but there was no sign of offense. He took my hand. "Come, this is foolishness. You'll enjoy it thoroughly once you're mounted."

"I take leave to differ, sir. I know how I feel."

"And I know you are an accomplished rider. Are you afraid you'll be proven wrong?" he asked. The flaring of his nostrils was close to a sneer. Very well, if he wished to be proven wrong, I was the one who could do it. And it wouldn't take long.

It seemed impossible even to get up on Belle's back without a ladder. I took the reins he handed me and just stood, immobile. The mare was moving her head restively, which made me nervous.

Mycroft looked doubtful. "Aren't you going to say hello to Belle?" he asked.

"I didn't know she spoke English. Hello, Belle," I said, laughing.

Mycroft smiled, but I knew I had done something out of character for Rose. "I'll give you a leg up," he said, and formed a foot support by interlocking the fingers of his two hands. I lifted my right leg, which was closest to him.

"You'll end up facing her tail if you do it that way," he pointed out.

A second's consideration showed me he was right, and I changed feet. The mounting of Belle was a comedy of errors. Interlocked fingers were an inadequate footsupport when the mounting took as long as mine did. And what did one do with one's hands? The welter of leather straps Mycroft tossed at me seemed more than I could handle. My skirts were very much in the way, and to cap it, I was frightened out of my wits. After much clumsy struggling, I was sitting aloft a moving mountain, holding the reins all wrong.

Mycroft gave me a long, uncertain look. "We'd best start with a walk till you get the feel of it again," he decided. "I'll let Thunder lead the way."

His mount immediately began a sedate walk. Mine stood rooted to the ground.

"Walk," I told Belle. She lowered her head and began chomping the grass. The lowering of her head made my seat even less secure than before.

"Mycroft!" I called fearfully.

He looked back. I raised a hand to indicate that Belle was eating, and the mare immediately lifted her head and began to walk. To see ladies walking their mounts in the park in London, it had seemed the easiest thing in the world. All you had to do was sit and hold on to the reins. In reality, it was an entirely unpleasant experience. Every step caused me to bounce in the saddle.

Mycroft rode alongside me, often glancing at my progress. "Don't play with her mouth!" he called when Belle took it into her head to pick up the speed.

"I couldn't reach it if I wanted to!"

"You're jobbing the reins. Keep your hands quiet, and down close to her withers."

"Where are her withers?" I asked.

He thought I was joking, but apparently my hands wandered astray and he answered, "That bulge at the bottom of her neck."

I placed my hands there and tried to keep them quiet. Belle proceeded nicely for some yards. Just as I was beginning to think this might be a possible means of locomotion after all, Mycroft said, "Shall we pick up the pace?" He didn't wait for an answer but touched his mount's sides with his heels and clattered off.

I was horrified when he disappeared into a spinney behind the house, leaving me alone. My first fear that Belle would speed up proved unfounded, however. She continued walking gently. My wish was to keep her out of the spinney, on even, flat ground that offered easy falling. But how was I to let Belle in on the secret? She was following the path into the spinney and paid no heed to verbal commands. I pulled at the reins and she came to a dead stop.

Again her head lowered and she began chomping the grass. After a moment I became annoyed with the nag and flapped the reins to urge her into motion. It proved to be a disastrous move. She lifted her head, let out a whinny of joy, and took to her heels at a wild pace that set me bouncing precariously in the saddle. Hooves thundered over the earth, and the low-lying branches of trees ripped my hat from my head.

I hollered "Mycroft" at the top of my lungs. When I saw him ahead of me on the path, however, he presented a new danger. The path wasn't wide enough for us both, and Belle took no notice of this rather important fact. There were three options open to her: she would either have to leap over Mycroft and his horse, go crashing against them, or turn off and hit a tree. I didn't care for any of them. One further course was open to me, and I took it. As we flew past a slight widening of the path, I pitched myself from Belle's back on to the ground.

From flat on my back I uttered a prayer of thanks for my escape. Had I remained aloft, I might have been hurt. Belle came to a screeching stop just an inch from Mycroft by rearing up on her hind legs. Thunder stopped and reared up too, whinnying like a maniac. I might have been caught under their hooves and trampled to death had I not leapt off.

In a flash Mycroft dismounted and came pelting back to me. His face was white and strained with anxiety as he leaned over me in the spinney. "Rose! Are you all right?" The harsh timbre of his voice was raw with fear. It turned his eyes to black glittering diamonds. It etched furrows from his nose to his lips, which were slightly open as he hung over me, staring.

This awful concern for a mere tumble in the dust surprised me, till I discerned the real fear—that he had caused a single hair of Rose's head to be hurt. In that instant, I hated Rose Comstock. She didn't deserve all this love. She was a spoiled, vain, heedless girl.

I made a motion to sit up, but Mycroft's hands were on my shoulders now, unwittingly holding me down. He gazed at me, realizing that I was fully conscious and not in pain. Then a new expression captured his features. A conscious feeling of electrically charged intimacy hovered in the air, blocking my lungs. It sparked between us with the force of lightning. I couldn't go on gazing into his eyes. They were too demanding, and too knowing.

I looked past his head to the lacy pattern of leaves against blue sky, etched with black branches. Ancient evergreens towered behind, pointing like spears. The pungent aroma of pine resin perfumed the air. The fallen needles formed a slippery, silken sheet below me. There were other nature scents too, that indefinable odor of pollen and moss and the last wildflowers on the verge of decay. The grass rustled as a mouse or squirrel nearby ran for cover. It was the loudest sound, louder than the whisper of leaves and our rapid, shallow breaths.

Mycroft's head moved, blocking out the sky and trees. It descended slowly, inevitably, to mine. I tried to see his face, but already it was too close to make out more than a dazzle of dark eyes and the line of black hair as his lips came closer. The first touch was a soft, tentative brushing. It might have been a spontaneous gesture of relief that I was safe, but I knew it wasn't that innocent.

I knew the taste of passion, and it was on Mycroft's lips as they seized mine. His arms went around me to protect me from the damp earth beneath. His closeness was much more treacherous. The weight of his body pressing mine wasn't the familiar weight of Fraser, but a more dangerous presence. His arms tightened till the breath swelled in my lungs, suffocating me.

Every atom of my body knew it was wrong. I was married—to a faithless, wretched man, but I was married. It wasn't even me that Mycroft wanted. I pulled my head aside; his lips traced a kindling trail along the taut column of my neck, chasing swiftly to seize my lips. Then there was no stopping it. He thought he wanted me, and I knew I wanted him. Every pressure of his lips increased the need. My arms went around his neck, pulling him to me in desperate longing. My fingers reveled in the crisp texture of his black hair, so different from Fraser's silky softness.

I knew what would come next. There was no surprise but only a thrill of victory when his moist tongue nudged my lips open and possessed my mouth. How it had shocked me the first time Fraser did it. 'I want to explore every inch of you,' he had said. But Fraser soon fell from my thoughts. A quivering started at the vital core of my being. It trembled along my arms and legs, and let loose a shudder in Mycroft.

His lips were at my ear, whispering fierce words of love. "Rose, why did you do it? You knew how much I loved you. I only delayed the wedding for propriety's sake—you were my ward. My God, did you think I didn't want you? The waiting was hell for me."

"Mycroft!" It was a moan wrenched from my throat. "Stop! Please stop!" I didn't want to hear his outpouring to her.

His head rose swiftly, and anger flared in his eyes. "You didn't tell *him* to stop, did you, Rose? You didn't hesitate to run off to a hotel with *him*, without even being married!"

"I'm not her!" I shrieked. My fingers raked the ground, pulling up fistfuls of dry pine needles that pricked my palms.

"You're you, all right!" he said through clenched teeth, fire blazing in his eyes. "What other woman ever showed such overweaning stubbornness, such blind insistence on having her own way? Dr. Lattimer was right. You know you've behaved reprehensibly, and refuse to acknowledge it. Face it, Rose, you're not magic. God wouldn't be cruel enough to let two of you loose on the world. The opium may have caused some confusion, but that's had time to wear off. Till you admit to yourself that you made a gross error, you won't recover."

His hands not only released me, they pushed me aside roughly. I sat up, trying to recapture some shred of dignity. Mycroft rose too and offered me one stiff arm to help me up.

"Thank you," I said briskly.

The horses began wandering back to us. "I should think my performance on that demented mare would show you I'm not Rose, if nothing else I've said convinced you."

"You're playing your role well," he said through stiff lips. "You never were one to do things by halves."

Thunder wandered close, and Mycroft took her rein. "I'll give you a lift up," he said.

"I shall walk back to the Manor."

"You're being perfectly ridiculous!" he shouted, all efforts at politeness abandoned.

"You're right. It is ridiculous of me to stay here and take everyone's abuse for something I didn't do."

"And where will you go? Back to the stationery store where you used to live?" he asked ironically.

"That's a good place to start. I'll go back to Watling Street. Someone there must know what happened to Miss Williams."

"What happened is that she became Miss Sophie. Where's your bonnet?" he asked.

"It got pulled off along the path. I'll find it."

Mycroft gave in to walking home by using the pretext of looking for my bonnet. The subject of my leaving didn't arise again. When we reached the Manor, I went upstairs to change and Mycroft visited with Miss Sophie. I knew what the subject of their talk would be. My amazing stubbornness. I hoped Miss Sophie would remember to tell him that Fiona hadn't recognized me, and that I didn't take fish for breakfast.

I knew it would be for me to bring up the matter of my leaving. I couldn't very well get back to London and Watling Street without their help. And I knew too that they'd fight my going.

CHAPTER SIXTEEN

"PREPOSTEROUS!" WAS MISS SOPHIE'S OPINION WHEN I broached the idea of my return to London.

Mycroft supported her to the top of his bent.

"I am not a child," I reminded them. "I'm free. I can go, and I shall."

"How do you plan to get there?" Mycroft demanded. His bristling facade didn't deceive me. I was beginning to understand that he hid his fear behind a veneer of anger, and he was afraid of losing Rose again.

"As you all insist I am Rose Comstock, I shall take her carriage. And I shall need some money, Miss Sophie. Naturally I'll repay it—"

"Oh, Rose," she said in disgust. "Repay it to whom? Yourself? Speak to Mycroft. He is in charge—"

"My charge ceased when Rose attained her

twenty-first birthday," he pointed out. "The principal is in trust, in Audry's name. He won't dare to go after it, but he'll have taken this quarter's income. The rest will be tied up in a legal fight for months," he announced, not without satisfaction. The situation gave him power.

It also left me at the mercy of these two. Miss Sophie was deeply disturbed at the very idea of my leaving, but when Mycroft left, I went out with him to wait for Thunder's delivery from the stable.

"I'm serious about leaving," I told him.

Frustration lent a livid hue to his complexion and pursed his lips in a thin line. "I can't stop you, but I'll be damned if I'll help. Are you forgetting that Fraser hasn't been captured yet? I reported the matter to the police, but you're still his wife. The law doesn't much care for interfering in domestic matters. If he manages to capture you and spirit you off to Italy . . ."

"I thought of that. I believe Fraser is at Longbeach."

"I expect he went there, but when he learns his parents are locked up, do you really think he's the sort of dutiful son who will stick around to help them?"

"I think he's the sort who would sell them to Satan for a guinea. He'll hop the first freighter out of the country. He has plenty of money now."

"He also has you making it impossible for him to return to England. He's a thorough, painstaking scoundrel. It would tie up the loose ends if he could be rid of you once for all. It would also put your fortune permanently in his hands. I wouldn't count on Fraser's having left England," he cautioned.

A ripple of apprehension ran through me. I had managed to shove Fraser to the bottom of my mind. That ordeal was too painful to think of yet, but Mycroft was right. It wasn't over. While I was still mistaken for Rose, he had Alvin Simson's fortune in his control and the income from Rose's. If I convinced people I wasn't Rose, that she had died—or been killed—before she reached her majority, then he'd lose everything. The surest way to keep his secret would be to kill me. That was what he had intended all along, and it hadn't changed.

"Well?" Mycroft said when I stood silent, thinking.

"I don't like to go alone," I admitted. Who else was there I could turn to but him? I cast an imploring look at Mycroft.

He refused to meet my gaze. I think he knew his own weakness, and feared I would convince him. "What is it you want to investigate in London?" he asked. "We've already been to Watling Street."

I had thought about that visit a good deal, and had a few ideas. "We were only there at night, and we didn't even get out of the carriage."

"We could see without dismounting that there was no gray frame house," he reminded me. "You were wrong about Watling Street."

"No, I was right! The house was gone, but I remembered the rest of it. There was time for the house to have been razed and another building put up," I said boldly. I had to speak boldly to keep from blushing at this outrageous idea. "I left early last spring, you know."

"Why would anyone raze a perfectly good house?"

"I don't know. Maybe it burned down and the printing place was built over it. Maybe Fraser wanted to make sure I never went back there and was recognized. Or maybe he just wanted to get Miss Williams out of the neighborhood."

"You're suggesting he had it burned down?" he asked, staring in disbelief.

"Yes—no. I don't know. I just know that's where I lived, Mycroft. The neighbors would be bound to recognize me. Please take me back."

His locked jaws gradually eased to submission. "It might be worth it to get this bee out of your bonnet. I'll make a bargain with you, Rose. You stay here till Dr. Lattimer returns from Paris. It will only be a few more days. Try to suspend your disbelief. Pretend you're Rose, if you can't believe it. Act as though you were her, and if I discover there was a fire at your house on Watling Street, or that it's been torn down and a new building put up, I'll believe all you've been telling me. When—if—I come back and tell you that printing company is twenty or thirty years old, then you'll put yourself in Lattimer's hands to be cured."

It was a fair bargain. "All right," I said.

Mycroft drew a deep breath and put his hat on. He looked down at me and smiled. "You always could wind us around your thumb. I had begun to hope—"

"What?"

He frowned into the distance. "I thought you had become—softer. More thoughtful. Nevins told Miss Sophie you weren't your old demanding self. I've noticed a few things as well. I thought your marriage to Fraser might have had one good result.

He had trimmed you into line." The one good result, however, brought an angry scowl to his face.

"You all spoiled Rose. How could she be anything but selfish, treated as she was?"

Mycroft gave me a knowing, half-hopeful look. "Are you learning to forgive her?" he asked. "That is the first step toward your cure, you know. Are you sure this trip to London is necessary?"

"Yes."

"I have to go anyway. There'll be no end of legal work with Hibbard tying up the estate, and of course I'll see the police."

"Thank you, Mycroft."

My humble tone surprised him. How would Rose have thanked him for performing a service for her? Would she have bothered thanking him? He found me 'softer,' he said. The admiration was still there, glowing in his eyes. It would be interesting to see how he treated me when he came back and had to acknowledge that I wasn't his beloved Rose.

"I'll leave this afternoon and be home probably late tomorrow. Take care of yourself, Rose."

Mycroft made a jerky, spontaneous motion toward me. Some fit of shyness overcame me and I pulled away awkwardly. For a moment our eyes met in one of those uneasy, questioning looks. Thunder began to paw the ground, and before any new embarrassments arose, I said, "Goodbye." Mycroft didn't even say that. He just nodded, dissatisfied.

I watched as he mounted Thunder and cantered across the meadow to Thornbridge. My hopes rode with him. He looked competent and powerful enough to extricate me from all my problems. And if he did discover the truth and catch Fraser, I would have no further hold on him. I sighed wearily and returned to the house.

The bargain was struck. I would pretend I was Rose, since I couldn't believe it. How would Rose behave toward Miss Sophie? She wouldn't give the old lady a thought. She would only do what she wanted to do. What did I want to do? It would be amusing to go for a drive in the family carriage in the afternoon while Mycroft was away.

"Aunt Sophie, I have an idea," I said, when I joined her for lunch. "What do you say you and I go for a drive this afternoon?"

She looked pleased with the idea, or my friendly manner. "Is Mycroft not coming over? I thought he might take you to visit Thornbridge."

"He's gone to London on business," I said vaguely.

"Then we shall go for a drive, if it would please you," she agreed readily.

"I expect it's a trip into Paget you have in mind?" Miss Sophie suggested when we were ensconced in the carriage.

I didn't want the prying eyes of the villagers following my every move. "No, let us go into the countryside, if you don't mind, Aunt Sophie." I had surprised her again.

We drove west along the sea, then turned north, circling home over the South Downs. In the few days since my arrival at the Manor, a subtle change had come over the downs. They were less green now; a dun color was coming over the trees and the grass was yellowing. This new sad beauty just suited my mood.

Miss Sophie's conversation was largely incomprehensible to me, featuring as it did so many unrecognized names. But I was interested, and pretended to understand. Miss Sophie was a good talker. All that was required was to nod and smile. As we neared home, Thornbridge and the Manor loomed in the distance, towering over the country landscape.

"It's unusual to see two grand houses so close together," I mused.

"The Manor has been here much longer, of course," she stated proudly. "Mycroft's house is only forty years old. You can tell by the style of it, or the lack of style. They don't build as they did in the old days."

"I like its austere grandeur. One of his ancestors built it, I expect?"

"Well, of course!" she exclaimed, with a look that told me Rose knew it perfectly well and was just being difficult. "When his papa came home from India loaded with money, he set himself up as a country squire. His elder brother got the family home, so George, Mycroft's papa, built Thornbridge."

"Mycroft's family were in India too!"

"Only his papa. It was before Mycroft was born. And his Aunt Gertrude, George's sister, was there as well. When George returned, he married Alice Comstock—some cousin of your papa. It was her idea that he build here, alongside the Manor. She had grown up in Paget and didn't want to leave the area."

"And Gertrude is still at Thornbridge. She must be quite old."

Miss Sophie looked startled. "Oh, no! She is only

fifty-five. It was the harsh Indian climate that destroyed her looks. One would think from her complexion she was a decade older. She remained in India after George left. She married an officer, but when he died fifteen years ago, she came home and lived with her brother. She and Alice seemed to get along, and she had really nowhere else to go."

I had heard the name 'Gertrude' often enough. It was she who had sent me the ivory Buddha for my birthday. I had noticed at the time that it was of Indian make. As Miss Sophie spoke of Mycroft's parents in the past tense, I assumed they were dead, and didn't wish to annoy her by asking. It must be just Gertrude and Mycroft living at Thornbridge, then. It seemed such a waste, these two grand homes, each with only two people and the servants living in them. Such houses should be filled with children.

"Why don't we drop in for a visit with— Mycroft's aunt," I said. The hesitation was due to my ignorance of Gertrude's married name. What would I call her when we met? Mycroft referred to her as Gertrude or Aunt Gertrude—perhaps Rose had called her that as well?

"It would please her," Aunt Sophie said, and pulled the checkstring to direct the carriage there.

Every intimate acquaintance of Rose's that I met was a new ordeal. I always looked sharply to see if they sensed the difference between us. Miss Sophie and Mycroft were so determined I should be Rose that they really didn't look. It occurred to me that Gertrude might be more discerning. She couldn't have been delighted with the idea of Mycroft marrying Rose. It would mean a new mistress at Thornbridge, where she now ruled the roost, and a headstrong, spoiled mistress to boot. And if that wasn't enough to disgust her, Rose's elopement with Fraser would surely have turned the trick.

We descended from the carriage at the front door. The more recent age of Thornbridge was very evident at this closer range. The stone wasn't darkened with moss and time as the Manor was. The double doorway was less ornately carved. When we were shown in, the interior was also more modern. In the cheerful entrance hall there were no dim portraits of ancestors on the walls but pretty paintings of the local countryside.

The saloon we were shown into held some relics of George Harlow's sojourn in India. The decor was traditional English, but the bibelots were similar to some Papa had at home—ornate brassware, an Indian shawl on the sofa, and several small Indian carvings. Before long a sallow-faced woman appeared at the doorway, and Miss Sophie exclaimed, "Well, Gertrude, I've brought the black sheep to see you."

I found myself being examined by a hawk-faced lady who did indeed look more than her fifty-five years. Her hair was still black for the most part, but her eyes were badly pouched and her features sagging. She was lean and stringy, but elegantly outfitted in a black worsted suit with a lace fichu at the throat.

"So, Rose, you're home with your tail between your legs, eh?" was Gertrude's greeting.

"Devil a bit of it," Miss Sophie defended. "She's

as saucy as ever. Don't harp at the child, Gertrude, she has had a perfectly wretched ordeal at Audry's hands."

Gertrude continued glaring. If there wasn't hatred in those black eyes, there was at least satisfaction that Rose had got her comeuppance. She didn't embrace me, or even offer her hand.

"As you sow, so shall you reap!" she said, and strode slowly into the room. She took up a seat on the chair closest to me and stared so hard I felt a tremble. "Mycroft told me how he found you," she stated severely. "I can't condone your behavior, Rose, but not even you deserved that. I hope they hang Audry from a gibbet."

"They have to catch him first," Miss Sophie said.

"Mycroft means to goad the police into action," Gertrude said with satisfaction.

Her next speech was entirely unexpected. I soon deduced that Mycroft had warned her from discussing my recent ordeal. "I hear you took a tumble from Belle yesterday," she said archly.

"Rose! You didn't tell me!" Miss Sophie exclaimed.

"It was nothing, Aunt Sophie. My hat is all that suffered."

"Your pride felt the sting, I warrant," Gertrude said.

She may have been forbidden from asking questions, but if staring could tell her anything, she would soon know all my secrets. I was never examined so thoroughly in my life. I felt as if those black eyes were piercing my flesh and reading my heart.

"Have you been to see the vicar yet?" was her next question.

Sophie leapt to my defense. "She's only been home less than a day! Give the poor child time to collect her wits."

"You've had time to go gallivanting into Paget, I daresay?"

"We drove in the country, Gertrude," Sophie answered loftily. "At Rose's request. She didn't want to be the subject of talk in the village."

"Hah! When did that ever bother Rose? She's just waiting till she get new gowns made up, that she may go in the highest kick of fashion and astound the commoners." She raked my plain gray gown as she spoke.

My eyes flashed and I felt a flush of annoyance stain my cheeks, but I held my tongue. These slurs were not directed at me, and I would not retaliate. I would, however, try to change the subject. "I didn't thank you for the birthday present, ma'am," I said. The 'ma'am' sat uncomfortably on the air, but I didn't know what else to call the lady.

She dismissed it with a wave of her hand. "What did you do with the engagement ring Mycroft gave you? That is what I would like to know."

I was stymied. This was the first word I had heard of any engagement ring. I knew it must be valuable or she wouldn't have mentioned it. "I don't know," I said. My throat felt dry, as though I were guilty of having stolen the thing.

"Rose's memory is uncertain," Aunt Sophie in a cautioning way. "I was sure Mycroft must have told you."

"Aye, he's told me a deal of skimble-skamble stuff. In India I've seen men who ate opium like bonbons, but I never heard of it making them think they're someone else."

Tea was served, but it brought no lightening of the conversation, or of Gertrude's mood. I spoke only when spoken to, and often not even then, for Miss Sophie was always swift to defend me. It was a vast relief when we rose to leave.

While Miss Sophie was having a word with the butler at the door, Gertrude turned a dark eye on me. "You seem to have lost your spunk, Rose," she taunted.

"As well as Mycroft's ring," I replied stiffly.

She gave a snort of amusement, but her expression soon firmed to seriousness. "Mycroft tells me Fiona didn't recognize you," she said.

"The black sheep dog? She growled and stiffened her legs when I first saw her."

"That is odd," she said, frowning. "Fiona was a great admirer of yours."

"Of Rose Comstock, you mean," I countered.

"That was my meaning, of course. I would be interested to hear more of this Cummings lady who lived in a printing shop on Watling Street."

All the while her black eyes studied me. What was she looking for? What was she seeing? The question in her eyes deepened. It seemed to me I had at last found someone who was willing to share my feelings.

"I am more than willing to tell you anything about her you care to know, ma'am."

"I would like to know everything." She cast a furtive glance to the door, where Miss Sophie had finished her talk and turned to us. "But not in front of her. Can you come back soon — say tomorrow morning?"

"Yes."

"Your papa—was he Norman Cummings?" she asked.

My face blanched, and I stared at her. "Yes."

"Married to a whey-faced lady with mousy brown hair?"

This wasn't the way I would describe Mama. "My mother's name was Augusta Morrison," I answered stiffly.

"Augusta, yes, that was the name. I didn't know the Cummingses well, of course. He was only a clerk. Come back tomorrow morning and we'll talk."

I left in a daze. My wildest hope was that Gertrude would be willing to consider my story. That she had actually known my parents was incredible. Yet she had been at Madras when I was born. Had I been less upset, I would have canvassed the possibility. Miss Sophie gave vent to a host of slurs against Gertrude Mallory as we drove home, but I hardly listened. I now knew Gertrude's last name, and could address her properly when we met the next morning.

We passed a quiet evening and retired early. As Gertrude had seemed to want privacy for our meeting, I said after breakfast the next morning that I was going for a little walk. My walk took me directly across the meadows to Thornbridge, where Mrs. Mallory was peeking out the window, awaiting my arrival.

CHAPTER SEVENTEEN

GERTRUDE WAS AT THE SIDE DOOR WAITING FOR ME when I reached Thornbridge. She admitted me with a frightened look all around, as though she didn't want even the servants to know I was here. We hustled into a small parlor, not unlike Miss Sophie's parlor at the Manor, and she closed the door. There was a fire glowing in the grate and a decanter of wine on the table before it.

"Sit close to me so I can see you," Mrs. Mallory directed. Her dark eyes still examined me in that disconcerting way. Her whole manner was bossy. Rose would have disliked this woman, but at the moment I wasn't following Mycroft's decree of pretending I was Rose.

"We'll have a glass of loll shrub to take the chill off," she said, pouring two glasses of red wine.

"My father used to call red wine that sometimes," I said. It sounded strange to hear the words again.

"It's drunk like water in India. Three, four bottles a day—and that's the ladies I'm speaking about. But we have more important matters to discuss, Rose."

"You knew my parents?" I asked eagerly.

"I couldn't say I knew the Cummingses well. I knew *of* them—recognized them, you know, and said good evening at the larger parties, but they were—"

"Untouchables?" I snipped.

She gave a satisfied smile. "Our English caste system is not quite that formidable. What do you know of your parents, Rose?"

"I remember everything about my father. He died only a year ago."

"And your mother?"

"I don't remember her at all. I had a little ivory miniature . . ." It had been left at Longbeach with my things. My heart ached when I thought of losing it.

"Did you imagine some resemblance to yourself?" she asked.

"There was a resemblance around the eyes, I thought."

She shook her head. "You are imagining it. Augusta Cummings wasn't your natural mother. You didn't know you were adopted?"

She dropped this earth-shattering news as calmly as any idle bit of gossip. I felt as though I were in another nightmare. But I believed her. That's the strangest thing about it. I didn't for an instant question her authority.

She calmly sipped her wine and continued. "I felt obliged to tell you. Your mother never had any children," she said, and frowned at this piece of paralogy. "What I mean to say is, I remember very well Augusta Cummings lamenting her lack of fertility. She was so desperate for a child that in the end she even had her old ayah prescribing local cures. Something to do with snakes, I believe was the magic formula."

"Who were my real parents?" I asked. As soon as the words were out, I felt glimmerings of knowledge. I was some actual blood kin to Rose Comstock, obviously.

"I have been canvassing that very question ever since Mycroft told me this incredible tale of yours," she said. "It was no secret who the Cummingses adopted. A Mrs. Ford from Madras died in childbirth. Her husband was one of those Englishmen who went to seed in the tropics. A drinker, gambler—a very bad lot. His wife was a pretty little thing, though. Unfortunately, she died giving birth, and the Cumminges adopted the girl. It is odd your papa never told you."

"Yes, he should have told me," I agreed sadly. Why had he not? He was a solemn, quiet man. Did he think I would love him less? I wouldn't have thought that would bother him unduly. He wasn't that affectionate toward me. Perhaps he loved me more than I knew, but didn't know how to show it. Or perhaps he kept the secret for some other reason.

"However," she continued pensively, "it still doesn't explain your uncanny resemblance to Rose Comstock. Rose, you see, was *not* adopted. I begin to fear that Mycroft is correct. He wouldn't listen to anything I tried to tell him about the Cummingses. You *are* Rose. But where did you get this tale of Rosalie Cummings, eh? Tell me the truth now, missie. Is this some stunt you're pulling off to diddle Fraser out of your fortune?"

"No! I don't have any fortune." I was too overcome to try a logical explanation. A terrible confusion gripped me. "We were born the same day, October thirty-first," I said at random.

"Yes, the season of the retreating monsoon in Madras. I remember the day well. Our Madras weather differs from the rest of India, you know. We get the monsoons later. October was a wretched month. Ten inches of rain. It seemed the sky was gray forever. Sukey, your mama (she meant Rose Comstock's mother), was as big as a tent. How I pitied her, waddling around like a duck, unable to go out for a breath of air. You were late in coming. The doctor expected you a week earlier. Sukey went into labor in the late afternoon. She had Dr. Stack in to attend her. A good enough man."

"Were you there?" I asked, eager to cull any details she might remember.

"I? Good gracious, no. My brother George had a large dinner party that evening. We were all so fed up with the weather that we decided to have a party, and damn the rain. Everyone attended—except the Comstocks, of course. Well, for that matter, Sukey's husband did come. Arnold dropped in around midnight to announce Sukey had given birth to a girl. He tried to hide his disappointment, for of course he wanted a son. But he was relieved it was over and Sukey had survived. 'We are calling her Rose Isabel,' he announced. We all drank a bumper to the child. George didn't feel champagne was necessary for a daughter."

"Mrs. Comstock had only the one child?" I asked. "She didn't have twins?"

"No, just the one. That is what I cannot understand. Mrs. Ford was delivered of a girl the same night—again just the one girl, which the Cummingses adopted." She lifted her shoulders and made a questioning face.

"That can't be true," I said. "Rose *must* be my sister. What else could account for the similarity?"

"A common father could account for *some* resemblance," she said sagely. "Not that I mean to infer Sukey was one to fool around with the gentlemen. And even if she had, the two girls would not be close enough for them to be mistaken one for the other. If you are not Rose Comstock, you are her double. One does occasionally encounter twins so identical in every detail that they may pass for the same person."

"Am I really that much like her?" I asked.

She studied me closely for a long time. "Yes," she admitted with regret. "I would swear on a Bible you are Rose."

"Didn't she have any birthmarks or scars—something that could differentiate between us?"

She thought for a while and shook her head. "No birthmarks, so far as I know. She was never hurt badly enough to leave a lasting scar."

"I have a scar on my ankle," I remembered, and even pulled down my stocking to show her. It was a white cycle, where I had been caught on a nail when I was young. "You can see it's an old scar," I pointed out.

218

"You've been gone for two years, Rose. The scar could be two years old, or twenty."

"I'm not Rose!"

"I am inclined to believe you. Not only because I don't like to see Mycroft falling under your spell again, but because nothing else makes any sense. Why would you claim *not* to be Rose if you were? This Dr. Lattimer Mycroft mentioned—it sounds like idiocy to me, deliriums being more real than the truth. Rubbish. Where did you meet Fraser Audry?"

For half an hour we talked about my early life, and my association with Fraser. Mrs. Mallory was consumed with curiosity, asking a million questions. She was very much impressed with his efforts to change me into an approximation of Rose.

"The scoundrel killed Rose before she reached her majority, then realized he had lost out on her fortune. No, he wouldn't have murdered her, though, for he knew when her money come to her. She must have died while giving birth. That would put the fear of God into him. That's why he rushed her off to Longbeach, because the doctors warned him the delivery would be dangerous to Rose. He concealed that she had died till he hatched this scheme of replacing her. But how did he know about your existence?"

"He had family in India—in Madras," I said. "He might have known I was adopted. He knows more than we do, Mrs. Mallory. He knows how it comes that Rose and I are so much alike."

"I don't recall any Audrys being at Madras at that time," she countered. "The story Audry told when he married Rose was that he had an uncle in India.

219

There was a Mr. Warner who came after both the Cummingses and Comstocks had left. That's who he claimed to be kin to. A no-good lout if ever there was one."

"Warner—that's the name his parents used at Longbeach. It could be his mother's maiden name," I said pensively.

She nodded, seeming to agree. "He might have heard the story from this Warner uncle. It's clear he knew about you all along. He even knew you had gone to Paris for that holiday, as he followed you there. It suited his purpose very well to keep you away till he had transformed you into a fine lady."

"Did Rose have a sable cape?"

"Oh my, yes. A lovely dark sable she got for her visit to London. She used to wear violets on it."

"Fraser gave me the coat for my twenty-first birthday," I told her. "He had me wear it to sign the papers at Hibbard's office that day. He said it was new."

"The man ought to be drawn and quartered," she said with disgust.

"He got Rose's jewelry collection out too, and had me wear one piece. No wonder Hibbard and Mycroft thought I truly was Rose. I looked like her, I was dressed in her things, wearing my hair like her. We didn't stay a minute—just signed the papers and left."

"He must have been laughing up his sleeve when he walked out that door with Rose's money in his hands. He fooled even Mycroft, and a man in love isn't likely to make a mistake like that."

"Mycroft cared very much for Rose, I think?"

"From the day she put up her hair and let down her skirts, there was never anyone but Rose for him. She was very pretty—vain and spoilt, of course, but then she was an heiress. Everyone petted her out of all reason. It would have been a good match. I hadn't a word to say against it when he gave her the ring. She wanted to rush ahead with the wedding at once. Mycroft felt it more proper to wait till he was no longer her guardian. She only went to London to teach him a lesson. If he had ever known she would meet Fraser Audry—"

"No one could have foreseen that."

"Audry must have something to have attracted the both of you."

"He had charm. He was handsome too. A young girl could easily be conned by him."

She made a sound of disgust at such a paltry excuse. "Whatever about yourself, *Rose* was engaged to Mycroft at the time. There is no excuse for *her*."

"Perhaps Rose's engagement ring from Mycroft is with the collection. You asked about it. What was it like?"

I couldn't remember a band of baguette diamonds being in the case. I stayed for an hour. It was such a relief to have someone willing to listen to me and not think me mad. My dislike for Mrs. Mallory receded as we talked. I shared many of her feelings about Rose. Her attitude to me softened as well.

When I rose at last to leave, she said, "This hasn't been a very good time for you either, has it, Miss Cummings?"

"Mrs. Audry," I reminded her. "It has been a

nightmare. Sometimes I awake at night and can't believe the things that are happening to me. I wish it were over."

"When Mycroft returns from London, perhaps we will see the light at the end of the tunnel. I must put on my thinking cap and try to remember who else was at Madras at that time. Perhaps someone has more information about the Cummingses than I. Fraser Audry must have stumbled across the truth somewhere. Your papa wouldn't have had any friends . . ."

"He didn't keep up any association with his old friends. My governess, Miss Williams, might know something. She wasn't in India, but—"

"Then she will know even less than I. Who might be able to tell us something is the doctor who delivered Rose and the Ford baby. Dr. Stack. I wonder if he is still alive, and if he ever returned to England. He'd be an old man now. I should have told Mycroft to begin a search for him."

"Mycroft knows about me—that I was adopted?" I asked.

"I had the devil of a time convincing him. Of course he doesn't want to believe his beloved Rose is dead. 'You haven't seen her, Gertrude,' he kept saying. He wouldn't listen to a word I said till you talked him into going back to Watling Street. The first trip there convinced him you were Rose. We shall soon know what he discovered. He returns tonight."

"I hope he'll come to the Manor."

"No doubt you'll hear his story before I do— unless I am invited to join you for dinner," she added archly.

"Please come. We would be happy to have you."

"I'll be there. And, Mrs. Audry," she added hesitantly, "whatever we learn about you—you must not feel you are adrift alone in the world. Mycroft told me about Audry's stunt in stealing your little patrimony. Between us, we shall see you are reimbursed for it. We can't turn you out on the world without friends or money."

My pride was stung at this assessment of my situation. "I may not have money, but I have friends, Mrs. Mallory. I shall go to my old governess till we decide what is to be done about my future."

"It is news to me if a governess is able to support her charge."

"I can support myself," I said tartly, and left.

After this proud boast, I began to worry about the future. It lay in ruins before me. I could only support myself in some such menial way as Miss Williams did. After the recent taste of luxury, becoming a servant would be doubly hard. But at least I would be me. The shadow of uncertainty that came over me at times would be pushed aside. Better a poor, sane woman than a wealthy lady, troubled and anxious for her very sanity.

CHAPTER EIGHTEEN

Miss Sophie was worried about my lengthy absence from the Manor. There was no point trying to hide my activity when I had invited Mrs. Mallory to dinner. Miss Sophie relaxed into a smile at the news.

"That was well done, Rose," she said. "It is wise to ingratiate her a little. She was out of reason cross with you after—that business." Rose's elopement had shrunk to 'that business.' She was back, and all was forgiven. The wisdom of ingratiating Mrs. Mallory wasn't hard to figure out. Miss Sophie assumed, or hoped, that the planned wedding might take place yet.

As we were having company to dinner, I decided to choose my gown with care. It might be the last time I would be wearing Rose's clothes. What hung in the clothespress were all at least two years old.

They had been virtually abandoned, yet as I sorted through them, I saw there was plenty to choose from. Like me, Rose favored various shades of blue. The softer pastels of summer muslins deepened to sapphire in her winter gowns.

I chose a deep blue silk with rustling skirts and a maidenly décolletage. Nevins came in when she heard me and put herself at my disposal. I wished she would leave, but she appeared to know what accessories went with the gown. A lovely Indian shawl fashioned in blue and white arabesques and boasting a three-inch fringe was laid out. Lace-edged petticoats, high-heeled slippers, silk stockings—all the paraphernalia of a lady awaited me.

Nevins' assistance was needed for doing up the row of tiny buttons that marched down the back of the gown. When she had fastened them, the gown nipped in tightly at my waist, showing an alluringly feminine curve. As before, the gown and slippers felt perfectly at home on me. Nevins dressed my hair up for the occasion and suggested a pearl comb, which proved to be missing. Rose had apparently taken this favorite with her.

I felt an air of excitement as I stood examining myself in the mirror. Behind me, the elegant appointments of Rose's dressing room were reflected in the mirror, providing a suitable background for the fashionable lady I resembled. Soon all this would be replaced by a dreary servant's room in some household that required a governess. The sapphire silk would fade to gray serge. In short, Cinderella would return to her ashes.

Ever since Mycroft had rescued me, I had been

trying to convince him I wasn't Rose. Tonight I regretted that I wasn't her. But for a hapless twist of fate, I might have been the one who was born to all this. It would have been me that Mycroft loved with such a passionate intensity. Was that why I had chosen this provocative gown? To show him I was as pretty as his Rose? He already knew I looked like her. I had dressed up from instinct, to make myself attractive to a handsome man. Once he knew for certain Rose was dead, might he learn to love me instead, since we looked alike? And would I be satisfied with that sort of vicarious love?

During the afternoon, my mind had often harped on the mystery that had produced two identical girl babies born on the same night in the same place. It was inconceivable that Rose and I weren't twin sisters. Some chicanery had put Rose in Sukey Comstock's cradle, me in the Cummingses'. The obvious conclusion was that Mrs. Ford had had twins, and had it not been that Sukey Comstock's child was born at her home, I would have concluded that some careless nurse had mixed up the babies. It must have happened the night we were born, for by the next day the switch would have been detected. A new mother would recognize her own child. Mrs. Mallory had mentioned Dr. Stack. How I hoped he was alive and could help us.

All these troubles combined to heighten my nervous condition. My chest was heavy with agitation, but the outward effects were an attractive flush and a sparkling eye.

When I went to the drawing room, Mrs. Mallory had already arrived. I saw by Miss Sophie's distracted appearance that she had been hearing about our afternoon meeting. I wished Mrs. Mallory had waited, but perhaps it was better for Sophie to have some warning.

"You can see for yourself that she is Rose!" Miss Sophie exclaimed angrily when I entered. She jumped up and grabbed my hand, as though afraid I would be snatched from her.

"Mrs. Audry certainly bears a startling resemblance, but you must begin to entertain the notion that Rose is dead, Sophie," Mrs. Mallory said sternly. "In any case, we shall know as soon as Mycroft comes. Meanwhile, Sophie, we might as well have dinner."

"How anyone can think of eating at such a time!"

"Rubbish. We must be well fortified to withstand the shock," Mrs. Mallory replied. But it would come as no shock to her. She had made up her mind, and was only waiting for confirmation. Nor would it require any special fortitude on her part to withstand the blow of Rose's death. Of all Rose's family and intimate acquaintances, it was only Gertrude—Mrs. Mallory—who judged her severely. She would know better than Sophie how Mycroft had suffered.

Two quick glasses of sherry took the edge off Miss Sophie's temper, and she made a hearty dinner. For myself, I couldn't eat a bite. I felt as though my throat had closed. I moved my fork around on my plate to give the illusion of eating, but my dinner consisted of two glasses of wine, and later a cup of tea when the tray was brought to the drawing room.

At nine-thirty we were all on thorns waiting for the sound of Mycroft's carriage. The older ladies' bickering began to grate on my nerves, and I wandered off to the music room for a little peace and quiet. There was a magnificent pianoforte there. It sat by a window that gave me a view of the road, and I went there for that reason. But as I sat waiting, I began to idly play a few pieces I knew without the assistance of the printed sheet. Chopin was a great favorite of both Miss Williams and myself. His concertos were beyond us, but some of his simpler études had been studied.

I played softly to avoid disturbing the ladies. The hauntingly sad minor chords suited my mood. I was inundated with memories of our little parlor on Watling Street, where the pianoforte was our proudest possession. Miss Williams had insisted that Papa buy it and give me lessons. 'A home is not genteel without a pianoforte,' she had insisted. So the instrument, much too large for the room, had been installed. It had to be brought up on ropes and pulleys through the window, since the men couldn't get it around the bend in the stairs. How had I ever conned myself into believing for even a second that I wasn't Rosalie Cummings? One does not manufacture such details as that, even in a delirium.

It is easy to get carried away by the magic of Chopin. I didn't notice when the ladies came to the door. I expect they had been there a moment. They stood perfectly still, as though they had been listening awhile. When I looked up and saw them, I stopped. They exchanged a glance that obviously had some significance I didn't grasp. Sophie looked bereft.

"What is it, Miss Sophie?" I asked, jumping up. I feared I had inadvertently played Rose's favorite piece.

"If this doesn't prove it, I don't know what does," Mrs. Mallory declared.

"She could have learned! She's been gone two years," Miss Sophie replied, but her heart wasn't in it.

"You don't learn to play the piano without practicing. When did Rose ever have the fortitude to study? Not when she was home with nothing to do, and surely not when she was a married lady, with all society at her beck and call."

So Rose didn't play the pianoforte. Another little piece of the puzzle fell into place. That was why Fraser hadn't encouraged my one genteel accomplishment, because Rose hadn't played. By my playing, done idly to pass the time, I had finally convinced Sophie I wasn't Rose. There was knowledge in her eyes as she gazed at me, and grief. And fear.

"My God, where is Rose? What has happened to her?" she breathed.

Sophie was so overcome we had to support her to get her to a sofa. Mrs. Mallory called for wine, and while this melodrama was going forth, Mycroft arrived. I turned at the sound of his voice and felt a pronounced desire to rush into his arms. He wasn't even looking at me.

"What's happened?" he demanded sharply.

It was Mrs. Mallory who answered. "Mrs. Audry sat down and played the piano. It has finally convinced Sophie of the truth."

"Good Lord!" he exclaimed, and finally turned to look at me.

I knew at once that he had already discovered the truth. Curiosity was the dominant expression on his face. Curiosity, not surprise. The love that used to glow when he thought me Rose was dissipated. I looked the same as before, rather better if anything, but I wasn't Rose, and the magic aura had deserted me. When we had Sophie settled down, I asked what he had learned in London.

"You were right all along. There was a fire at 28 Watling Street last spring. The place burned to the ground one night. A few weeks later the printing company bought the land and put up that brick building. Going there at night, we didn't realize it was a new building. It's perfectly obvious by daylight. The top flat of the gray frame house had been leased to a family named Cummings. I made enquiries of the neighbors. They all remember Miss Cummings very well. A pretty young lady, blonde, blue-eyed. Miss Williams told them of your wedding in Paris to a wealthy gentleman."

"What caused the fire?" Mrs. Mallory demanded.

"Arson was suspected but never proven. There didn't seem to be any point to it. The landlord was making a clean profit on the house. It was in good repair—he could have sold easily enough if he wanted his money out of it."

"Audry did it," Mrs. Mallory decided.

"I expect so," Mycroft agreed.

"He was in Europe with me," I pointed out. "He couldn't have done it. And why would he anyway?"

"He could have arranged to have it done," Mycroft thought.

I didn't think Fraser had set the fire, but the older ladies wished to discuss other matters. Sophie's main concern, quite naturally, was to discover what had happened to Rose.

"Where can she be?" she asked, dazed.

"Where is she buried, you mean," Mrs. Mallory corrected.

Mycroft explained more gently but insistently that Rose must indeed be dead, or why would Fraser have married me? The admission took its toll on him. Though he had now had several hours to assimilate the fact, his grief was barely held in check as he spoke with Sophie.

"As they were at Longbeach at the time, it's logical to assume Rose is buried there, in some unmarked grave," he explained. His jaws clenched with the effort to remain calm. I thought I knew where that unmarked grave was.

"Oh, my poor baby, lying in the cold ground without even a coffin to keep the elements away." I saw Mycroft's fingers clench to fists, and wished Sophie hadn't spoken.

Sophie set up such a wail that Mrs. Mallory sent off for a doctor to give her a paregoric draught. She took Sophie up to bed. The long-awaited moment alone with Mycroft had come, but it had turned to ashes. The alluring gown was forgotten, the hope of eliciting his interest, of detaching him from a ghost. All I wanted to do was hold him in my arms and tell him how sorry I was. I wanted to ease the bleak anguish from his eyes and tell him it would be all right.

"I'm sorry, Mycroft," I said in a tight voice.

He swallowed convulsively without even looking at me. After a moment's agonizing silence, he finally lifted his eyes, which were coldly curious.

"I ought to be apologizing to you as well, Mrs. Audry. It occurs to me I've caused you no end of problems with my mulishness. You told me from the start you weren't Rose, and I wouldn't believe you. I couldn't. The likeness was perfect in every detail."

"You didn't want to believe it," I said.

"That's true, but I'm left with no choice now."

"What will you do? Was there any word on Fraser?"

He shook his head. "No, he's disappeared. I'll go to Longbeach and look for—for Rose's remains," he said, tightening his jaws to hold them steady. "Sophie will want them interred here."

"There's a spinney a few hundred yards behind the house. Fraser didn't want me going into it. She must be buried there. You'll find her things in the attic. I shouldn't think Fraser would have taken time to dispose of them."

"I don't know if it's a good idea to bring them home, laden with memories to haunt Sophie. I should like to have the Corot portrait, though. I saw it at an exhibition in London last year."

Mycroft looked like death, and I felt like it. "I'll get us a glass of wine," I said.

We both had wine and sat on the sofa, staring into the fire. I couldn't bear to look at him in his grief. The uncertainty of my own future would have to wait for later discussion. This moment belonged to Rose. I could almost imagine her face there, in the leaping flames, smiling at us. It was a shock when I felt Mycroft's fingers close over mine. I stared at him, wondering what he would say.

"Mrs. Audry, I have something to tell you," he said softly.

Ever a romantic, it immediately darted into my head that he was going to ask me to stay here. That he thought with time he could forget Rose. My heart hammered with excitement as I waited with bated breath.

"It's about your Miss Williams," he said, shattering my foolish dream. "I'm afraid she didn't survive the fire. Her body was recovered the next morning—the family downstairs escaped, but she was apparently asleep and was asphyxiated. Her sister arranged the burial."

"No! Not Miss Williams! It can't be true. She's all I have left. I was going to go to her."

Tears sprang to my eyes, and Mycroft comforted me in his arms, as one might a sobbing child. Poor Miss Williams. I never realized I loved her till after she had left. I had been wanting to tell her, to indicate in some way that I appreciated her life of dedication to me and my father. The realization only came after I was married.

When I had settled down, Mycroft removed his arms and drew farther away on the sofa. With a discreet foot between us, conversation resumed.

"I wonder if Audry did set fire to the house," he mused.

"He might have done it to get rid of Miss Williams. She could prove that I wasn't Rose Comstock. I remember she wanted to put a wedding announcement in the papers, and he asked her to wait till he had notified his family. Yes, he was afraid of her spreading the word."

He nodded in agreement. "There might even have been some proof in your father's effects that

233

you were adopted. Did you speak to Gertrude about that? She meant to talk to you during my absence. I thought it a bag of moonshine when she told me, but now . . ."

"Now we know she was correct. There was no point to my pretending I was Rose, as you insisted. And it won't be necessary for Dr. Lattimer to treat me."

"Of course we shall repay the money Fraser stole from you."

"I don't see any reason why you should repay Fraser's debts."

"However it came about, you are obviously some close kin to Rose—a twin sister, apparently. We would like to help you, for her sake. It's the last thing we can do for her." His voice petered out to a sigh.

Mrs. Mallory came down and joined us when the doctor arrived. "Poor Sophie, she's taking this very hard. She never had any fortitude," she said and poured herself a glass of wine.

"God knows this quagmire is enough to sink even you, Gertrude," Mycroft said.

"Devil a bit of it. What is needed here is some clear thinking. Mrs. Audry and I had a good cose this afternoon. I'm happy to tell you, Mycroft, she is a rational lady. And I'm sure she agrees with me that this situation could only have arisen by one means. Her mother, Mrs. Ford, must have had twins. Sukey's daughter died at or shortly after birth, and someone took the notion of giving her Mrs. Ford's other daughter. No doubt it was meant as a kindness. Who could ever have foreseen the results?"

"Wouldn't there have been official records kept?" Mycroft asked.

"India isn't England," Mrs. Mallory said blandly. "The Raj did pretty well what it wanted in the matter of records, and if Sukey's husband didn't want her to know Rose was adopted . . . Then too during the monsoon everything was at sixes and sevens."

"The substitution must have been made the night the babies were born, or Sukey would have noticed the switch," I said.

"Her husband wasn't aware of the death when he came to my ball. I'd swear it on a Bible. He was chirping merry. 'Only a girl,' he said, 'but Sukey is well, and has promised me a boy next time.' He wasn't clever enough to have acted the part of a happy father. And as it was only a girl, he would have told us if the child died. If he knew, he didn't tell Sukey. He just had Dr. Stack slip the other child in the cradle and let her believe it was her own. It's the sort of muddle-headed, well-intentioned nonsense one would expect from him."

"We should try to find out if Dr. Stack is still alive," I mentioned.

"What strikes me as curious," Mycroft said, "is why no one knew this Mrs. Ford had twins. What would have been the point of hiding it? Who was born first, Gertrude, the Ford woman's baby or Sukey Comstock's?"

"Now there you have me," she replied. "Mrs. Ford's accouchement was of little interest to my set. I only remember hearing the next day that she had had a girl, and died in the delivery. Norman Cummings and his wife adopted the child."

"Even as babies, the girls must have been identical," Mycroft said, frowning. "You would think someone would have noticed."

"I rather think the likeness was commented on. Two darling little roses, both so pretty. I didn't remember what the Cummingses had called their girl, but it must have been Rosalie. So long ago, it's hard to be certain. The Ford's and Cummingses' set didn't socialize with our set, you know. There wouldn't have been much chance for comparing. Sukey's daughter was considered a marvel of beauty. She looked so sweet in her little bonnet and gowns, lying in that great crib Sukey had shipped from England. Like a little princess, she was."

I had a mental picture of the other child, much less lavishly outfitted. From the cradle, fate had favored Rose.

"And the other child?" Mycroft asked.

She couldn't remember. The Cummingses had left India very shortly after the adoption. The two families had gone their separate ways, never meeting, and if they knew the whole truth, never telling.

"Fraser Audry knew the whole truth," Mycroft declared. His chin firmed in determination. Mrs. Mallory explained about his uncle, Mr. Warner.

"I'll ask around for this Dr. Stack and Mr. Ford, but I still mean to find Audry. I'll beat the truth out of the bastard," Mycroft growled.

"Language, Mycroft. There are ladies present," his aunt said, and lifted her glass.

We talked till the doctor left. He told us Miss Sophie was sleeping, and he would come back tomorrow to tend her. Soon after, they rose to leave.

"Miss Sophie is a strange bird," Mrs. Mallory mentioned as she drew on her gloves. "If she turns unpleasant toward you, Mrs. Audry, you may come to stay with us till we decide what is to be done with you."

This condescending speech got my hackles up. "I shall take care of myself, Mrs. Mallory. I assure you I have no intention of battening myself on Miss Sophie or anyone, now that you are all convinced I am who I said I was all along."

"Be sensible, Mrs. Audry," Mycroft said, scowling. "You can't leave alone, with no money. Where could you go? We'll discuss this tomorrow."

He bowed, Mrs. Mallory nodded, and they left. I sat on alone, considering what I could do with the rest of my life.

CHAPTER NINETEEN

WHEN I WENT DOWN TO BREAKFAST THE NEXT MORN-
ing, the butler handed me a note from Mycroft. I
read with dismay that he had gone to Longbeach to
find Rose's grave and have the remains brought
home for burial. I knew he loved her, even if she
was dead, but it struck me that a live victim's needs
might have come first. Rose had already been
buried for months. Surely a few more days could do
no harm. It left my fate up in the air. Necessity
forced me to remain at the Manor as an uninvited
guest.

Miss Sophie didn't come downstairs, and didn't
send for me. I feared my presence would be painful
to her and spent the morning alone, trying to plan
my future. I would have to find some genteel
position, probably that of governess. I was decently
educated, but of course had neither experience nor

anyone to vouch for me save Miss Sophie or Mrs. Mallory. Ladies with such flamboyant pasts as mine wouldn't be welcome in a polite home. Marriage to a fortune-hunting murderer would hardly endear me to polite parents.

I thought of Miss Williams too. As a change, but not improvement, of occupation in the afternoon, I wrote her sister a letter expressing my grief. I was just sealing it when Mrs. Mallory was announced.

"Miss Sophie hasn't been down all day," I told her. "Would you like to go up, Mrs. Mallory?"

"I'll say good day to her, but it is really you I came to see, Mrs. Audry. We'll have a word when I come down."

She remained upstairs for only fifteen minutes. "How is Miss Sophie?" I asked when she returned.

"She's in a very bad way. Rose was her whole life," she told me. "You'll have to try to cheer her up when she comes down tomorrow. You could read to her, or make her play cards. I have been thinking about your position, Mrs. Audry. There is no saying how Sophie will take to you—she might take it into her head to blame you for Rose's death. What we must do is find you a position."

"I have been thinking the same thing, but I fear no decent family will want me."

"That is true. Any irregularity in a lady's past, even if it is not her own fault, is bound to put parents off. I think it will be best if we find you a position as companion to some elderly lady. I have friends here and there I can write to and make enquiries."

"That's kind of you, ma'am. I would appreciate

it. Mycroft left very early this morning, did he not?"

She gave me rather a cool look. "Mr. Harlow was most eager to regularize Rose's interment," she said in a way that hinted I ought not to make free with Mr. Harlow's Christian name. "How did you come to know he was gone, Mrs. Audry?"

"He left word here on his way," I replied stiffly.

"I see."

Mrs. Mallory was not a lady to hold her tongue or to mince words. When she assumed a somewhat nervous expression, I knew she was going to push beyond the bounds of politeness.

"Mr. Harlow, as you know, was very fond of Rose," she began. "Mistaking you for her, he may have been a little warmer in his manner than he ought. You realize, of course, that any sort of alliance between you and him is quite impossible."

I felt my spine stiffen. "You forget, Mrs. Mallory, that I already have a husband. Any other sort of 'alliance' is quite out of the question," I snipped.

"It is marriage that is out of the question, Mrs. Audry!"

"That pretty well covers all ground, I believe. Could I offer you a glass of wine before you leave, ma'am?"

I expected to have some abuse hurled at my head for sniping at her, but received none. A reluctant smile pulled at her lips. "I am happy to see you know how to stand up for yourself. You have that in common with your sister. Mrs. Ford was an arrogant miss, now I come to think of it. I have nothing personal against you, Mrs. Audry. It is only Mr. Harlow I am thinking of. He has suffered quite enough over Rose Comstock. Let him bury her and forget the woman. That will best be done if you are out of sight. About the wine—I should prefer tea, thank you."

"Mr. Harlow is not more eager to forget Rose Comstock than I am, ma'am. She has brought me nothing but grief as well," I replied, and sent for tea.

"As soon as we have sorted out the cradle mixup, you can leave. I'll send out those letters making enquiries on your behalf today. Mr. Harlow feels you may be in some danger from Audry till he is caught, but I don't see he would have any reason to do you harm."

It was true he had no reason to kill me now that we knew the truth, but I still shivered to know he was on the loose.

"Mr. Harlow will be talking to the police in London while he is away," she added.

The tea came and we enjoyed a chat. Once she was assured I didn't intend to fling my bonnet at Mycroft, she was willing to assess me at my own worth. She asked a great many questions about my past life.

"It sounds very tedious, Mrs. Audry," she decided.

"It was, till I convinced Miss Williams to go to Paris."

"I rather think I would have done the same thing. You enjoy travel, do you?"

"I adored it."

"I shall write a letter to Lady Bricklin—an old friend of my youth. She is a widow who travels about a good deal. She likes to imagine she has weak lungs to have an excuse to visit Italy every winter. She may already have a traveling companion, but one meets so many people when traveling about that she could probably put us on to someone. It would be the best thing for you to get out of the country. A change of scene will put all this unpleasantness out of your mind."

"Thank you. You're very kind."

There was a sly look in her eyes. It was only defense of Mycroft that brought about this particular kindness. The farther away she could get me, the better. She wouldn't have been so concerned had she seen the chilly way he treated me last night. After two cups of tea, she left.

Miss Sophie didn't come down for dinner—she didn't leave her room all day. There were no callers, so I spent the long evening alone. The next morning Miss Sophie, swathed in blankets and looking haggard, came downstairs. As Mrs. Mallory had warned, she seemed to blame me in some manner for her troubles. She wore a rebukeful face every time she looked at me. I felt sorry for the old dame, and tried to pamper her a little. I read to her in the morning and sat by her side all afternoon while she reminisced.

Mrs. Mallory found us together when she called late in the afternoon.

"I have been just telling Mrs. Audry about the time Rose got into the carrot brandy, Gertrude," she said smiling wanly. "I remember it as if it were yesterday. Ah, it is a great pity it couldn't have been Mrs. Audry who was taken, and Rose spared."

Mrs. Mallory cast a sapient eye at me. "Mrs.

Audry might have something to say about that," she replied.

"Oh dear, not that I wish you ill, Mrs. Audry!" Miss Sophie exclaimed. "I'm sure she has been a perfect ministering angel all day."

The visit proceeded without further insults. The next day, Miss Sophie asked if she might call me Rosalie, as she hated to utter the name 'Audry.' I agreed with enthusiasm. She felt stout enough to drive to the graveyard and show me where Rose would be buried, beside her parents. Mrs. Mallory had a meeting of some volunteer committee that day and didn't come to call.

We were all eager to learn what Mycroft had discovered, but as he had at least four or five days' travel ahead of him, and a few days to find Rose's grave and arrange the transport home, we knew we wouldn't see him for some time. The next day, Mrs. Mallory came with a letter sent from London.

"The mystery is solved!" she exclaimed, holding it in the air. "Old Dr. Stack is dead, but Mycroft tracked Mr. Ford down in Slough. Imagine the old stump still being alive after all these years. I fear Mycroft went out of his way—Slough is not en route to Longbeach, but as it is so close to London, I daresay he decided to go there first."

"What does he say?" I asked eagerly.

"It is just as we thought. What else could it be? Mrs. Ford had twin girls. It seems Dr. Slack no sooner delivered Sukey's baby than he got called off to attend Mrs. Ford, who had twins. Sukey's infant seemed stout enough at first, but during the night she lost the ability to breathe. She was found in her

243

cradle with a blue face. When Dr. Slack was called for he mentioned to Comstock that he had had a wretched night, losing two patients. Mrs. Ford never recovered from the delivery.

"He told Comstock about the twin girls, with Norman Cummings adopting one and suggested that Comstock adopt the other child. Arnold knew Sukey would be heartbroken and hatched the idea of not telling her her baby had died. In all the terrible confusion of the night, word hadn't gotten about that Mrs. Ford had twins. The only ones who knew were Mr. Ford and the doctor, and of course a few Indian servants, but they were easily hushed up.

"Word never leaked out. Sukey accepted the child as hers. There was no formal adoption. She was simply registered as the daughter of Arnold Comstock. Good God, *I* never suspected the truth all these years, and I was *there*. They ought to have told someone."

"Apparently they did," I said. "Fraser Audry knew."

"Ford stayed on at Madras for eons. He was a drinker, like Warner. No doubt Fraser's uncle heard the story from Ford one night when they were in their cups. There is nothing more natural than that Fraser's uncle should pass it along to his nephew when he learned who Fraser was marrying. And when Rose died so inconveniently on him, Fraser would have set about finding you, Rosalie."

It was the first time Mrs. Mallory had used my Christian name. I didn't think she even noticed she had done it.

"He wouldn't have had much trouble. He used to have rooms close to where I lived. Mr. Harlow pointed out the house when we went to Watling Street. He may even have seen me in the street."

"If that is true," Mrs. Mallory said, "it made his job easier, but he would have found you if he had to go to the ends of the earth. It was the only way he could hold on to Rose's money." This set Miss Sophie sniffling quietly into her handkerchief.

"You wouldn't have heard from any of your friends yet about finding a place for me?" I asked, to give Miss Sophie time to recover.

Miss Sophie heard and turned like a fury on Mrs. Mallory. "Eh, what is this? A place for Rosalie? She is staying here with me. I can't do without Rosalie. Why should she leave? The poor child has nowhere to go. Mr. Audry is skulking about in the world, waiting to leap on her and finish her off with opium. Of course she will stay here. I won't hear of anything else."

"Rosalie wishes to go abroad," Mrs. Mallory told her firmly.

"Rosalie!" Miss Sophie turned a tearful face toward me. "You cannot leave me! There is Rose's room and all her things going to waste. You are her sister—who else should have them but you? She would want it. Why, it is almost like having Rose back."

She was clutching my hands and looking so distraught that I didn't wish to upset her further, but I didn't want to become her replacement for Rose either. I had my own life, and wanted to get on with it. I could see by Mrs. Mallory's narrowed eyes that she was highly displeased with this turn of events. When she left, she asked me to accompany her to the door.

"You are more clever than I have been giving you credit for," she declared angrily. "Winding Sophie around your thumb."

"You're the one who suggested I be kind to her!"

"Aye, and I was a fool to do it. The Manor and Rose's fortune will revert to her once we prove Rose's will leaving it to Audry is forged. Till Rose's twenty-first birthday, they were held in trust to prevent some fortune-hunter taking advantage of her. Arnold Comstock was a fool, but he had wise legal counsel. He didn't foresee the possibility that Sophie might hand it all over to a stranger!"

My temper broke and I laced into her. "Mrs. Mallory, if it had been my intention to steal the Manor and Rose's fortune, I had every opportunity to do it. All I had to do was keep quiet and I could have had the lot. I could have pretended to be her when I came here. I don't want to be Rose Comstock. I don't want her house or her life or her money. And I don't want her rejected fiancé either. That is what really worries you."

"Then you'd best leave, Mrs. Audry. The longer you stay here, the more you manage to complicate things. As soon as Mr. Harlow returns, we shall decide what is to be done with you."

She flounced out and slammed the door. I went back to Miss Sophie, writhing under her attack. What business was it of hers if I stayed with Sophie or left? What was it to her if Miss Sophie left me the house in her will, for that matter? It was none of

Mrs. Mallory's affair, and I wished I had told her so.

I was pulled two ways in the matter. My anger urged me to play up to Miss Sophie. I hadn't been trying to wind her round my thumb, but in her present mood I could do it with no trouble. My better nature told me this was unconscionable—to prey on the loss of a foolish old lady. I meant it when I said I didn't want to be Rose Comstock, and that is what would happen if I stayed here.

What stung most of all was that Mrs. Mallory really thought I was running after her nephew. My guilt was the grain of truth in it. I wasn't chasing Mycroft, but I was interested in him. And as she was so worried, she obviously feared that he would develop some interest in me.

I began to think I must take the money if Mrs. Mallory offered it. That would enable me to get away immediately, and support myself till I found a position. In all this tangled web of mystery and deceit and money, I was owed that much. My peace and happiness had been snatched away because of Rose. Let Rose's friends and relatives provide me a start on a new life. They could well afford it.

CHAPTER TWENTY

During the next few days I trod a narrow line in my dealing with Miss Sophie, trying to keep my distance while still being kind to her. Human compassion demanded kindness. She was so very lonesome and bereft over the loss of Rose. Mrs. Mallory only came to call once, and to show my annoyance with her charges I excused myself till she was leaving.

I went to meet her in the hall then and asked stiffly, "Have you had any word from Mr. Harlow, Mrs. Mallory?"

"He'll be home Monday. I have just been telling Sophie she must contact the vicar and arrange the funeral. Mycroft found the grave. He didn't give any details."

"Is there any word of Fraser?"

"Not directly. Mycroft spoke to his parents—

they are incarcerated at Longbeach, you know. They confirmed what we had already learned. They feel he has escaped to Italy. I daresay it's true. He wouldn't risk his neck by lingering in England. It will dump a wretched mess in Hibbard's lap. I should be hearing from Lady Bricklin soon," she added, watching me closely.

"Excellent. I look forward to it."

She nodded, satisfied, and left.

Miss Sophie asked me to send off for the vicar. Discussions for the funeral occupied the next few hours. We asked the undertaker to come as well to discuss coffins. It is no wonder my head was splitting by the time dinner was announced.

When Mycroft came to the Manor that Monday evening, he was accompanied by Mrs. Mallory. She was like a guard dog at his elbow, watching me with angry, jealous eyes. Her vigilance wasn't necessary. After saying good evening and enquiring for my well-being, Mycroft hardly looked at me. He spoke gently to Miss Sophie, mitigating as much as possible the horror of Rose's last days, and her burial.

"Fraser's parents assured me she had every assistance in her confinement," he explained. "It's true Fraser buried her without benefit of clergy, but not without proper respect in other ways."

I assumed this meant he had somehow procured a coffin, and had her laid out and so on. That must have been a singularly unpleasant chore for his mother. Questions were in my head, but they could not be asked in front of Sophie. After half an hour had elapsed, Mrs. Mallory seemed satisfied that Mycroft wasn't in love with me and relaxed her vigilance. I managed a few private words with him then, still in the same room but on the far side from the others.

"If Rose had medical attention during her confinement, why didn't the doctor report her death?" I asked.

"She had only the assistance of a midwife. I would prefer that you not tell her aunt so, however. Fraser's mother says the midwife knew her business. The child was stillborn, but Rose was still living when the midwife left. She died later in the night. Fraser wanted to keep it quiet so her income would continue coming to him. He forged her name on the checks and had no trouble cashing them."

"Where was she buried—was it in the copse behind the house?"

"Yes, in an unmarked grave."

"At least she had a decent coffin," I said pensively. It was a pretty spot, the little copse behind the house.

"She was buried in a blanket," Mycroft said through clenched teeth. "Naturally I don't want to disturb Miss Sophie with these details. She has suffered enough, poor woman. We'll give Rose a proper burial now. That will lay her to rest in all our minds. The uncertainty was worse than anything else."

The funeral arrangements were made privately. It was a small funeral, but a decent one. On a bleak afternoon in late autumn, with the sky a leaden blanket above us and the branches denuded of leaves, Rose was laid beside her parents in the graveyard in a pretty mahogany coffin. Mycroft said the child had been buried in her arms at Longbeach, and the same arrangement prevailed at home. I felt as though a part of myself were interred with this sister I had never met, yet whose life was intimately entwined with my own. It was infinitely sad, but as Mycroft said, it laid Rose to rest at last, in her own body as well as the minds of the survivors.

This survivor was eager to get on with her life. I could not broach the subject of my departure the very day of the funeral, but the next afternoon Mycroft came to call, and I meant to discuss it with him before he left. Mrs. Mallory didn't accompany him. He sat with Sophie and me in her little parlor.

"I brought home some of Rose's effects, Sophie," he said hesitantly. "Is there anything in particular you would like to keep, or shall I have Gertrude prepare a box for charity?"

"What effects are those?" she asked.

"The Corot portrait—I would like to buy that from you."

"Oh, I shall want that myself, Mycroft!" she exclaimed. "What else did you bring?"

"Her collection of carvings from India, her silver dresser set, her sable coat."

Sophie examined me in the most peculiar way. "Give her personal things to Rosalie," she said. "Rosalie will need a warm fur coat with winter coming on. I have noticed her dresser looks bare without its silver ornaments. We always kept the collection of carvings on the set of small shelves in the corner, Rosalie. Now you must remember to keep it dusted, and not let it turn gray as you did before."

Sophie occasionally let her mind wander in this way. I don't mean to say she was deranged—she knew I was not Rose—but she liked to imagine I was, and sometimes made a verbal slip. Mycroft, not having heard her do this before, looked alarmed.

"I'm quite sure Mrs. Audry wouldn't let dust accumulate," he said firmly. "You're thinking of Rose, Sophie."

"Yes, I have been thinking of Rose a great deal lately. How could I not? That was a strange story you wrote us about Dr. Stack and Mrs. Ford's twins."

"It was strange, and poorly done not to let the girls know they were adopted."

"If Sukey had known there were two little girls, she would have taken both of them, I expect. That's what she ought to have done. Rose and Rosalie should have been reared together, here at the Manor. It was unfair for one to have so much and the other to have nothing."

I felt my hackles rise at this speech. "I had plenty, Miss Sophie. I had a father, a home, a life of my own."

"Oh, my dear child," she said, frowning sadly at me. "That was no life, but now we shall make up for it. You will have all Rose's things. It looks like the hand of God, sending you along just when I lost Rose. I want to adopt Rosalie, Mycroft. Speak to Hibbard next time you are in London." She didn't even ask my opinion of this ordering of my life! In her own quiet way, Sophie was a tyrant.

"Rosalie is a little old for adoption," he pointed out. I knew from the questioning look on his face that Gertrude had been telling him her fears. "What have you to say to all this, Mrs. Audry?"

I gave my answer to Miss Sophie. "It is very kind

of you to offer, ma'am. I hope we shall remain friends, but I am not a child, to be adopted. I have my own life to live. I can't become Rose and take up where she left off."

"But why not? You have nowhere to go," she said bluntly.

"I'll find somewhere."

"Actually, Mrs. Audry does have somewhere she must go," Mycroft said. "Now that we know her mind is not—disordered," he said, embarrassed, "the police would like to speak to her—about Fraser. She will have to give statements regarding her unwitting part in the masquerade—the signing of the will and so on. This has to be done in London."

"That will only take a day," Sophie pointed out.

"A few days," he countered. "When will it be convenient for you to go, Mrs. Audry?"

"I can leave tomorrow." A few days away from the Manor sounded like a very good idea. If Mrs. Mallory received an offer from any of her friends in the meanwhile, I might never have to return.

When Mycroft rose to leave, I once again went with him to the door. There were dozens of things I wanted to discuss with him, and preferred not to do it in front of Sophie.

"Did you learn from Fraser's parents how he managed to find me?"

"Why don't you put on your wrap and walk outside with me?" he suggested.

I did this, and we walked through the park, with the cold wind pulling at us. "It seems Fraser's uncle, Mr. Warner, was a friend of your natural father, Mr. Ford. Ford mentioned one night the strange story about his twin girls, one adopted by a wealthy family, the other by a clerk. Fraser's curiosity was aroused by the wealthy one," he said, "for what reason you may easily imagine. When he read of Rose's London visit in the papers, he arranged to meet her at a party given by one of the old crowd from India. They get together occasionally in London to discuss the old days. He went after Rose hammer and tong and charmed her into eloping with him."

"Then he knew her strange history even before he married her."

"He knew she was an heiress—that's all that interested him. He also knew that Rose's money didn't go to her outright till her twenty-first birthday. The doctor warned him her accouchement might be dangerous, and he knew if she died without producing a live child, he'd lose out on her money. I believe that's why he took her to Longbeach. A death would be easier to conceal there. I imagine you were in his mind even before her death. How he traced you I don't know, but he knew your father's name, and it wouldn't have been very difficult."

"He once lived near Watling Street. You remember you showed me the place."

"Perhaps he knew you by sight even before he married Rose. In any case, it suited him perfectly when you went abroad. It must have been a harrowing day when he had to produce you at Hibbard's office, but once that was done, he had what he wanted—the money."

"Unfortunately he had me as well. He planned all along to do away with me." I shivered to recall his act of loving husband. How had I not sensed the monster behind the charming man?

"The man is a viper. I don't mean to let it stop here. Recovering Rose's body and straightening out exactly who you are were more exigent, but now I mean to trace Fraser Audry and bring him to justice."

"It won't be easy."

"No, but it must be done."

We had walked to the edge of the park and turned back. The Manor rose before us in the distance. Rose's home—it must evoke a thousand memories in Mycroft.

"Sophie has certainly taken a great liking to you," he mentioned diffidently.

I heard the echo of Gertrude in the speech and felt my temper rise. "You needn't worry I plan to exploit her!"

His brows rose in surprise. "That's a strange word to use—exploit. You would be doing her a favor to remain; whether you wish to devote so much time to pleasing an old lady is, of course, your own affair. As you said, you have your own life to live. Gertrude mentioned your wish to go abroad."

This was true, without giving the true nature of my remark. "I must work, Mr. Harlow. It's doubtful that I could get work as a governess with my history. Mrs. Mallory thinks she might help me get a position as traveling companion to some elderly lady."

"If lady's companion is what you aspire to, you couldn't find a more obliging elderly lady than Sophie. Why do you not stay?" he asked, and looked very interested to hear my answer.

"She wants to turn me into Rose."

We stopped walking and he studied me closely. "You are very like her," he said. "Very much like her in appearance, though I'm bound to say Rose was not so selfless. She would not be blind to the opportunity that Sophie's offer represents. Rose liked her luxuries," he added thoughtfully.

"She was born to them."

"No, she was adopted into them," he corrected. "It seems fitting, almost providential, that you, her sister, should fill her shoes. But that is mere selfishness speaking," he added.

I felt a quivering tremble through me at this telling speech. Was I imagining he referred to another role of Rose's—that of his fiancée? When I continued walking, his hand was on my elbow.

"In any case," he continued, "you must remain till something else is found for you. Let us hope Gertrude's friends are dilatory in answering her letters." There was a small smile in his eyes at this remark.

I increased the pace, mentioning the cold as my excuse. Before I went inside, he said, "So you will be ready to leave for London tomorrow morning, Mrs.—damme, this is nonsense. May I not call you Rosalie?"

"Certainly, if you wish. But please do *not* call me Rose."

"I'm not likely to make that mistake!" he said angrily. "I haven't called you by her name since we learned the truth. I haven't tried to—" He came to a conscious stop that set us both to blushing.

I lifted my chin imperiously. "I've noticed Rosalie Cummings is less desirable than Rose Comstock, heiress," I said loftily.

"By God, there isn't a hair's difference between the pair of you at times. Leaping to unfounded conclusions, rushing off on scatterbrained, freakish starts. Why did you have to come here, if you only mean to desert us?" His wild-eyed anger acted on my nerves like a goad. I felt in my bones that this lecture was being delivered posthumously to Rose. Mycroft was turning me into her too.

"I didn't come here voluntarily, as you very well know. I was all but suborned."

He made a sound of disgust and then settled down.

Harking back to my trip to London, I wondered about that 'you will be ready to leave,' which hinted at his accompanying me or at least lending his carriage. "About London—shall I use Sophie's carriage or—"

"She may want hers. We'll take mine."

"You've had a great many trips recently, Mr.—" He stopped me with an angry look. "Mycroft. I can go alone. I'm sure you have matters to attend to about the estate."

"I have things to do in London too. I'll call for you early, about eight-thirty. Gertrude will be happy to act as chaperone. I don't think a married lady and a respectable gentleman require one, but if you consider it more proper, then she will be happy to come."

It would be much more proper to have Gertrude along, but I dreaded her company. "Whatever Mrs. Mallory thinks is suitable," I answered evasively.

We left it at that. Mycroft departed with a stiff bow, to which I returned a stiff nod.

As I prepared for the trip that evening, I found myself hoping Gertrude would stay at home, but felt she would come. Especially she would come if she knew Mycroft was urging me to stay on at the Manor. Should I do it? It offered a life of ease. There was some poetic justice in Rose's sister taking over in her place, but Rosalie Cummings didn't want to be swallowed up holus-bolus.

Most of all, I didn't want Mycroft to kiss me and imagine I was Rose. He must learn to love me for myself, or not at all.

Chapter Twenty-one

When Mycroft called for me in the morning, he was alone. "Gertrude has an earache," he explained. With Miss Sophie in the room, it was necessary for me to feign sorrow, but my heart lifted to hear it. I noticed that Mycroft was in good spirits too.

"It's very chilly. You'd best wear your sable cape, Rosalie," Sophie suggested.

"My blue wool will do well enough," I answered firmly. It wasn't as fine, but the sable cape was imbued with so many horrid memories that I never wanted to see it again.

Sophie walked us to the door, warning us to drive carefully and watch out for a hundred menaces she imagined lurking in London, ready to besiege the unwary.

After the coach door was closed and the carriage

lurched forth, I said primly, "I'm sorry to hear Mrs. Mallory is unwell."

"I fancy she's much better by now," Mycroft replied with a smile. "The earache was caused by my jawing at her. You didn't tell me Gertrude had been interfering in your affairs. I read through the fumes of her harangue that she had. I hope you haven't let her decide your course, Rosalie. These elderly aunts have a way of monopolizing our lives if we let them."

"It's only natural she should want to look out for the family interests. She's afraid Sophie will make me her heir."

"There's no reason that should concern her. She has no hope of inheriting anything. No, I believe her interest lies in another direction."

I didn't ask which direction, but he must have read the knowledge in my eyes, for he continued speaking quite frankly.

"When Rose jilted me, Gertrude took her in great dislike. Even though Gertrude is the one who believed you, she's been imputing Rose's wrongs to you. She admitted you were behaving much better than Rose ever did in her life."

"I'm surprised to hear you utter a word against Rose!"

"I hope I'm not maligning her. I loved Rose, warts and all. She was spoilt and selfish—she was what life had made her. If you had been raised as she was, you too might have developed a flaw."

"I don't claim to be flawless."

He gazed at me with an intense look. "No one is. No doubt flaws will appear in the fullness of time. I don't know you well enough yet to have discovered your secrets. I'm beginning to suspect you have your share of temper, and perhaps your determination may soon be called stubbornness. I hope I shall have the opportunity to learn more secrets. In any case, I know you have courage and fortitude. You must have your share of recklessness as well, to have married Fraser so precipitously. A romantic, are you, Rosalie?"

"I was," I admitted.

He reached for my fingers and squeezed them. "Don't let one bad experience sour you. The young should be romantic—so long as their romance is leavened with a dram of caution."

We wiled away the long trip by talking about my past, and Mycroft's. He told me many things about Rose too.

"We seem to be always harping on her waywardness and folly. She really was a charming girl," he said. "Fun-loving, generous, clever. Whatever folly she committed, she paid for it dearly."

The last item was something else Rose and I had in common.

"As Rose's guardian, I was used to looking out for her interests. I knew she had made a wretched match, and went on worrying after the matter was out of my hands. I felt culpable, to a certain extent. If I had agreed to marry her before her twenty-first birthday, this wouldn't have happened. A man tries to do the right thing . . ."

I could see it still gnawed at his conscience. "You didn't do anything wrong, Mycroft. That must be some consolation to you."

"I'm coming to accept that, and learning to live with it."

We arrived in London late in the afternoon. Our first stop was the police station, where I gave my statement regarding Fraser.

"You haven't seen anything of him?" Mycroft asked the officer.

"Not a smell. Could the young lady give us the name of any friends or associates?"

The only name I could give was the Ramplings, who had gone to the masquerade ball with us. "I believe they were close friends. They knew who I really was—that I wasn't Rose Comstock, I mean."

"Mr. Harlow already gave us that name," the officer said. "They're still in London. We have a man watching them, but Audry hasn't showed up on their doorstep. He hasn't left the country, however, unless he did it on a forged or stolen passport. We checked all the ports. There's no record of his having gone abroad legally."

"He might have slipped out from Scotland," Mycroft suggested. "Or on a private yacht, for that matter."

"More likely he's still here—we've made very close enquiries," the officer said. I must have looked alarmed, as he tried to reassure me. "You have nothing to worry about, ma'am. There'd be no point to his going after you. We know his trick now. What would he have to gain by hurting you? Mr. Audry has no conscience, but he isn't a man who involves himself in senseless crimes."

Common sense told me he was right, but a feeling of uneasiness still hung about me.

We stayed at the Dorchester Hotel and took dinner downstairs.

"Tomorrow I'll have to spend some time with

Hibbard," Mycroft mentioned. "There's no necessity for you to waste your day there. Do you have some friends you might be in touch with? I don't like to think of you being alone on the streets."

"I'd like to visit Watling Street. I have plenty of old friends there."

"Take the carriage," Mycroft offered. "I can walk to Hibbard's place. You should be perfectly safe at Watling Street. If Audry's still in London, he wouldn't have any reason to go there."

I was looking forward to the visit. I'd call on our next door neighbors and drop in on a few other friends as well. After dinner, Mycroft surprised me by asking if I'd like to dance. A small orchestra was playing in the dining room, and some diners were dancing in the middle of the room.

Excitement curled in me, but I wasn't sure it was proper. "Do you think we should?" I asked.

"Yes, I very much think you and I have earned a little pleasure, Rosalie. It wouldn't do back home, but no one will recognize us here, and this isn't a conventional mourning. Rose would be the last one to begrudge us a waltz. Come," he said, offering his hand. "I want to waltz with you again. I shall behave better than the last time."

Memories came flooding back. How long ago it seemed since I had waltzed with Mycroft, and kissed him behind the door. I felt a hundred years older now, but when he put his arms around me, the magic was still there. A bud of pleasure blossomed to fullness inside me when he lowered his head and smiled softly, his lips just inches from mine. I saw the involuntary quiver of his lips, and knew what he was thinking. My own lips tingled. We wheeled and spun to the heady music till I was dizzy. Then we had some wine and danced again, till nearly midnight. He held me closer than before. I could feel the pressure of his body along the length of mine, and when we moved, our legs brushed intimately. It was good to put all our troubles aside for a few hours and pretend that life was a ball.

We didn't talk about Rose or Fraser or Mr. Hibbard or the police or anything troublesome. Like two strangers becoming acquainted, we discussed music and plays and books—what we found to laugh about escapes me, but we laughed. It sounded strange to hear laughter again. Mycroft enjoyed the theater in particular, while I was a better authority on books.

"Perhaps we can go to the theater tomorrow evening," he suggested.

"Will we not be going home tomorrow?"

"It's a long drive. I won't be finished with Hibbard in time to make it home that day. London offers a better evening's amusement than Crawley or Horsham, where we'd have to stay. Besides," he added with a daring smile, "it may be possible for a lady and gentleman to share an hotel in London. Such carrying-on would raise eyebrows in the provinces, madam."

It made me aware that our behavior verged on the fast, but it didn't rob the evening of its pleasure. I enjoyed every second of it, and when Mycroft accompanied me to my room, I thanked him heartily.

"I had forgotten that some people live like this. It was wonderful. Thank you, Mycroft."

He took my hand and lifted it to his lips. "We

shall enjoy many such evenings, if I can convince you to stay at the Manor. I wish you will think about it, Rosalie."

I could hardly think of anything else when I closed the door and was alone with my thoughts. Why shouldn't I stay? Sophie wanted it; Mycroft wanted it—and I was coming to want it very much. It was only Gertrude Mallory who objected. What did I care for Gertrude Mallory? If I stayed, I would have to make Sophie understand that I was going there as her companion, not her long-lost niece. Certain ground rules were vital.

We breakfasted together downstairs in the morning. Mycroft had a ten-o'clock appointment with Hibbard, and left at a quarter to. My plan was to go to Watling Street after luncheon. In my old neighborhood, the ladies oversaw their household duties in the morning and did their visiting later in the day. I did a little shopping with a few guineas Sophie had given me, and enjoyed a pleasant morning.

At two o'clock, I called for the carriage and was driven to Watling Street. I descended at the spot where a gray frame house used to stand and gazed a long moment at the printing shop. It was a very ordinary sort of building; three-story, brick, square, with a discreet hanging sign. The floor where I had lived most of my life appeared to be a storage area now. There were no curtains on the windows, but only white blinds.

My heart pinched to see what little impression I had made on the world. A few bricks and some mortar eradicated any trace that Father and Miss Williams and I had occupied this spot for twenty years, more or less. Father and Miss Williams were dead and gone. Only I, of that tight little circle, remained. How short life was, and how tenuous. What was I going to do with the rest of my brief span?

While I stood staring, Mrs. Fletcher spotted me from behind her lace curtains and came out. She invited me to join her for tea. She had been our closest friend on Watling Street, and all she wanted to do was quiz me about my marriage and discuss the fire. She didn't know anything about Rose Comstock or Fraser's true character. Her questions were mere prying to discover whether it was true my husband was 'a very highly placed gentleman,' and where did I live, and had I met the queen. I made an excuse to leave as soon as I could. I didn't want to drag out all the tragedy of my recent past for her to cluck over, and couldn't go on smiling and pretending I was a happy bride.

I went straight back to the hotel. At four-thirty Mycroft returned, and over tea he told me about his visit with Hibbard. There was no doubt Rose's estate would be kept from Fraser, but there would be some lengthy legal work involved. We studied the entertainment guide and selected our play for the evening. Afterwards, we were going to have a late supper. We went to our separate rooms to dress for the evening. I had brought Rose's sapphire blue silk gown with me to London and wore it.

I was so eager for the evening that I was dressed and ready to go half an hour before Mycroft was to come for me. To pass the time, I scanned the evening journal the hotel had sent up. I nearly missed the most interesting item. Mr. Ford wasn't famous enough to be on the first page. His death was buried several pages back. He had been murdered in his home in Slough. The story suggested he had caught a robber in the house and been shot while trying to defend his property. It was too convenient a death to be mere coincidence. Fraser! He had gone to Mr. Ford and shot him to prevent him from telling anyone about his twin daughters.

I must tell Mycroft at once! Just as I hastened to the door, someone knocked. I assumed that Mycroft had come a little early. I opened the door and found myself staring at Fraser Audry.

CHAPTER TWENTY-TWO

MY BLOOD TURNED TO WAX. I COULDN'T EVEN SCREAM, but just stood gaping with disbelief as he barged in and closed the door behind him. With Mr. Ford's murder fresh in my mind, I glanced surreptitiously to see if Fraser was carrying a gun. There was none in his hand, but his jacket had a suspicious bulge.

How could I ever have loved this man? He looked the same—he wasn't unshaven or unkempt in any way. His curls still waved on his noble forehead. His jacket was of the latest cut and his shirt immaculate. But, as I knew his true nature, my only emotions were terror and revulsion.

"So, my dear, I see you landed on your pretty little feet," he said in a quiet, insinuating voice. His blue eyes examined me from head to toe. "What, not wearing any of the fashionable gowns I bought you? This one looks a decade old."

I backed off from him. "What do you want?" I asked in a shaking voice.

"I have come to claim my bride," he said. His ominous laugh sent a chill up my spine. "You've run me a merry chase, my dear. It is time you and I continued with our wedding trip. I think you'll like Italy."

"You can't leave England. The police are looking for you."

"What nonsense have you and Harlow been tattling to the police?" he asked. "I see you've been hard at work, figuring out the secrets discovered in the attic. From talking to Harlow, you must know the truth." He tried for an air of ease, but I could see the wary light in his eyes.

As I couldn't hope to overpower a man, I wanted to keep him talking till Mycroft came. "They know everything, Fraser."

"Everything?" he asked, and laughed. "I think not, Rose. I was at considerable pains to follow your trail after Harlow abducted you. I have made discreet enquiries at King's Lynn. A Miss Piggott was very helpful. Her poor patient having delusions she was not who I can prove she is. Oh yes, I can prove you are Rose Comstock. Your very face proves it. Harlow himself believes it—and I promise you, you'll never convince anyone otherwise. How could two identical ladies roam the earth?"

I swallowed and tried to convince him he must flee. "It's too late, Fraser. We know all about the twins born at Madras."

His eyes narrowed to slits as he rapidly considered how this must change his plans. Perhaps I shouldn't have said it. I wouldn't acknowledge knowing about Mr. Ford's murder in any case.

"Shocking bad records they kept at Madras," he said. "Rose didn't know she was adopted. You didn't know you were. Where did you hear this story?"

My mouth was so dry I couldn't move my tongue without pain. And what story could I tell him? "Gertrude Mallory remembered it," I said, and watched to see if he believed me.

"Gertrude didn't know," he said, but a frown pleated his brow.

While he pondered this, I tried to see the matter from his point of view. He thought people still believed I was Rose. He had no way of knowing all that had happened since my rescue. That's why he had come after me. If he could spirit me away while her family still believed that, he would have no trouble holding on to her fortune. Now that Rose was twenty-one, he had control of Alvin Simson's money during her life—and her own fortune was his. I would be much less troublesome dead than alive . . .

"They'll never prove a thing," he said cockily, but cracks were beginning to appear in his confidence. That the truth had come out worried him. "What was Harlow doing at Hibbard's?" he demanded. "Don't bother lying to me. I've been watching Hibbard's office. I knew if Harlow tried to make any mischief, he'd use Hibbard. Not man enough to tackle me himself."

"Something to do with Rose's business," I said vaguely. When Fraser didn't question me further, I realized he didn't know I had been at the Manor. He had followed me to King's Lynn, perhaps on to

London, but he didn't know I had been staying with Miss Sophie. His next question confirmed it.

"You've made yourself scarce. Where have you been hiding yourself, Rose? Don't say with Miss Williams' sister—I've been there looking for you."

"Harlow gave me money. I've hired a flat till—"

"Till I caught up with you," he said, laughing. "It gave me quite a shock to see you step down from Harlow's fancy carriage this afternoon. He sent for you to join him here, did he?" He took my silence for confirmation. "You want to watch out for Harlow. He might take a fancy to you himself. God knows he was always after Rose."

"What do you think you're going to do, Fraser? You can't escape. The police are looking for you."

"Oh, I haven't done anything wrong," he said. "It's not my fault if my wife took a little too much opium and had delusions."

Fraser hadn't been back to Longbeach, where the police were looking for him, so he didn't know Rose's body had been found. He still thought he could go free. *I* was the only impediment to his life of ease. If I lived, I might eventually convince people of the truth. He had come to kill me. Not here, not right away, but he meant to get me away to some private spot and kill me, as he'd killed Miss Williams and Mr. Ford. A third victim would come easy after two murders. What could I tell him to change his mind? To announce that we already knew he was a murderer might only hasten my death. A man can only hang once, and Fraser was spiteful enough to want to take me with him.

I didn't know what would be safe to say, but I wanted to keep him talking till Mycroft came.

"How did you find out about me in the first place?" I asked.

His pride lured him on to do a little boasting. "My mother's brother was at Madras. He told me the story, and we read in the journals that Rose Comstock was visiting cousins in London. 'There's a dainty fortune on the hoof,' he said. I was curious about *you* as well, of course, and ferreted out where you lived. The resemblance was not startling at that time," he added maliciously.

"I thought I might tell Rose one day to amuse her. Then when we learned her pregnancy was going astray, I remembered you. You had gone to Paris when I called at Watling Street. I really feared the masquerade was impossible—you were so provincial, so thin and gauche and timid. But still, the seed was there. I cultivated it, and watched the Rose bloom."

How cleverly he glossed over all the ugliness of Rose's death, and his burying his wife in a blanket.

"It's really your own fault," he continued. "If you were a more clever sort of girl, I could have taken you into my confidence. We might have had a merry life, but I knew what I was dealing with," he added contemptuously. "I liked Rose, you know. I would never have killed her. Her death was an unpleasant ordeal for me."

Fraser drew out his watch and glanced at it. "I see you're dressed up. Is Harlow taking you out to dinner?"

I wanted to deny it, but why else would I be dressed for the evening? If only I could delay him. "Of course he is," Fraser answered himself. "And very soon, I expect. We had best be on our way,

Mrs. Audry. Get your cape." He looked around the room. "Missing your sable, I expect," he laughed, and picked up the blue wool.

I lifted my chin in the air and said, "I have no intention of going with you. You can hardly force me to, in a busy hotel."

"Why must you always make things difficult?" he complained, and pulled out the gun. Waving it at me, he said, "I won't hesitate to use it, Rosalie."

Desperation goaded me. It wasn't another murder that would deter him, but the probability of being caught in this public spot. I was safer here. "I think you will," I replied. "You were probably seen entering the hotel."

He lifted my blue cape and hung it over his arm, concealing all of the gun except the black circle of the muzzle. "We'll leave by the fire stairs," he announced.

"You were seen coming in, Fraser. If another dead body turns up—"

He leapt on it. "Another?" he asked.

"Miss Williams . . ."

"Poor old Willie. I didn't want to have her killed. But she would persist in that foolish notion of putting a wedding notice in the newspapers. And though she wasn't likely to talk to anyone who mattered, word does get about. Then too there was the possibility that your father might have some documents regarding the adoption. Burning the lot seemed the best idea."

"Who did it for you, the Ramplings?"

"Margot was instrumental. We go back a long way, the lady and I. Her husband would sell his soul for money," he added, with no awareness of irony.

"The police know it was arson," I told him. My hope was to convince him he couldn't kill me without bringing the police down on his head.

"I told them not to use coal oil," he said with a frown. "With one thing and another, I begin to think . . ."

I listened with bated breath to hear what new plan he might come up with. I could almost hear the cogs of his mind turning as he stared into space. "Harlow was desolate when I married Rose," he said, as if to himself. "Heartbroken and guilty. Such a burden can unhinge a man's mind. There's no telling what such a pitiful man might do."

How did he plan to involve Harlow in this business? He knew he was coming here for me.

"When he comes, just call for him to enter, Rosalie. Don't go to the door. You sit on that chair, and let him walk toward you." He examined the chair and looked toward the door, as though mentally arranging the meeting.

I knew by his scheming face that he meant to kill Harlow. But what advantage did he hope to gain from that senseless slaughter? The rest of it fell into place without too much trouble. Harlow, heartbroken and guilty about Rose's marriage, brings her to London, ostensibly on business, but with the ulterior motive of killing her and himself. A murder-suicide. Fraser meant to shoot Harlow, then me. He'd throw the gun on the floor and dart out before the police arrived. He would accomplish two aims in one stroke. Rose and the man most likely to make trouble both dead, with no suspicion pointing at himself.

"No!" I said firmly.

His face clenched into an ugly mask and he reached for my arm. Twisting it behind my back, he forced me into the chair.

"I'll shout the minute he comes to the door. I won't let him come in," I warned.

His hand came up and swatted my cheek. My head was wrenched aside, but I didn't care. All my pent-up hatred for Fraser Audry boiled up in me. I wanted to attack him, to scratch out his eyes and pummel him. The frustration nearly drove me mad. But this was no time for madness. I must be cold and calculating. I must outwit my treacherous husband. Leveling the gun at my chest, he walked to the table and extinguished the lamp.

Now why had he done that? We glared at each other in the gathering shadows of twilight. He didn't want Harlow to see too clearly when he entered. Where did Fraser plan to station himself? No matter, wherever he hid, I'd shout as soon as I heard Mycroft at the door. Fraser walked behind my chair. I turned my head, following his movements, but lost track when he was directly behind me.

The next thing I knew, I felt a rope pulled over my head. He had even brought a rope with him, prepared for any contingency. I heard Fraser panting at my ear, felt the rope tighten, and could only make a strangled sound in my throat. He held it tight with one hand and rudely yanked my head back by my hair with the other while I flailed my arms about, trying to loosen the rope. My lungs were blocked. The room began to move in dark waves. My flailing arms fell, and I grasped his plan with my last moment of consciousness. He was going to kill me before Mycroft came. It was a corpse propped up in a chair in the shadows that Mycroft would see. When Mycroft came to see why I didn't move, Fraser would shoot him. The room grew dark.

When I stopped struggling, Fraser must have loosened his hold on the rope. A little sliver of air was drawn painfully into my aching lungs. The room wavered back to shadowy light. I mustn't move a muscle. I must make him think I was dead, or unconscious. I must retain one atom of energy to call when Mycroft came to the door. I must listen. Another breath of air was quietly drawn in. Not enough. Every instinct urged me to reach up and loosen the rope. It took a nearly superhuman effort to restrain the instinct. I thought I might have the energy for one warning call. Perhaps if I let my head loll to one side, he'd think I was dead and loosen the rope. My head fell, and I felt one last tightening of the rope.

Just when I feared I had outwitted myself, Fraser dropped the rope and jerked to attention. He must have heard Mycroft's approach before I did. He darted to the door and stationed himself behind it. I couldn't see him. My vision was blurred, but in my mind's eye I knew he must be raising his gun, cocking it. Was that the faint click of metal on metal I heard? He'd let Mycroft open the door, while he hid behind it. When Mycroft came to me, he'd shoot. No, he couldn't shoot him in the back if he wanted it to look like suicide. He'd creep up behind him and call his name to make him turn around.

Mycroft knocked on the door, softly at first, all unsuspecting, thinking I was waiting for him. I opened my mouth to call, and nothing came out but a strangled whimper. I tried to rise, and found my legs had turned to water. The next knock was louder. I managed a sound, but not loud enough to be heard through the door.

"Rosalie! Are you there? Are you all right?" Mycroft sounded beautifully worried.

It was that worry that saved us both. In his concern for me, Mycroft threw the door open so forcefully that it knocked the gun out of Fraser's hand. I heard it fall on the floor with a loud thump. At the first sight of Mycroft rushing toward me, I managed to whisper, "Fraser!" and pointed to the door.

Mycroft turned, and I watched with horror as Fraser leapt out and reached for the gun. Mycroft moved as swiftly to stop him. He kicked the gun into the middle of the room. In the shaft of brighter light from the hall, I watched as they struggled, the gun momentarily forgotten. It was man against man as they released their long enmity in savage blows.

I think they had been wanting this chance for a personal struggle for years. Nothing else could account for the ferocity of that battle. When I was able, I got up and retrieved the gun, but I knew it was beyond human power to stop them. A man passing in the hallway glanced in and stared in disbelief, then very sensibly ran off to get help.

By the time the manager came, Fraser was lying on the floor unconscious and Mycroft held me in his arms. He didn't ask if I was all right. He could see I was not, and I knew he was in a worse state than myself. But we were alive. We had survived Fraser's last onslaught.

CHAPTER
TWENTY-THREE

IT WAS THE TWENTY-FOURTH OF MAY, QUEEN
Victoria's birthday. As I sat on a rock, gazing across
the Channel toward France, I was carried in my
mind back to last spring when I was in Paris, staring
across the Seine at Notre Dame. I had lived a
lifetime in the intervening months. I had married, I
had traveled abroad in a style beyond my highest
expectations. I had known love, and loss. Miss
Williams, friend of my whole life, was gone forever.
My husband too was gone. I had been close to death
on two occasions, but I had survived, and with a
keener lust for life than before. I now found more
beauty in the tame nature of Sussex than in all of
teaming Europe.

Aunt Gertrude—she finally asked me to call
her Gertrude, with the honorary title of 'Aunt' to

avoid sounding brash—put it in her usual blunt way when Fraser hanged himself in his cell to avoid trial. "Good! It will save the country the expense of executing him, and the family the notoriety of being hauled through the courts and newspapers." The newspapers had something to say about it, but it was a nine days' wonder, soon forgotten. I read that his parents got a three-year sentence for their part in the affair, but the Ramplings got off scot-free, due to lack of evidence.

Rose was, and is, harder to forget. I wish I had known my sister. To know all is to forgive all, they say. Sometimes I feel I do know her. Like me, she was impatient to marry Mycroft. Like me, she fell under the spell of Fraser's superficial charm and lived to regret it. But not for long—poor Rose. Fate, which favored her in the beginning, exacted a hard revenge. When I am in her room, surrounded by the luxury of her life, I sometimes imagine I hear her voice, coming to me, soft as a whisper on the wind. I imagine those conversations we would have had, had we ever met.

After Fraser's capture, I went back to the Manor to recover, and never left. When I look in the mirror at the spoiled creature I am fast becoming, I see a haughty lift to my chin and an imperious light in my eyes. I have twice snapped at Nevins, but both times pulled myself up short. It is her servility that grates on my nerves. But that is a poor excuse for bad manners.

The trouble is, you see, Sophie likes me to be Rose. She smiles fondly at any show of temper on my part. I know what she is thinking. Rose, to the very tip of her toes! It is well established in the family that I am a miracle, sent from heaven above to fill the gaping hole left by Rose. No less a tyrant than Aunt Gertrude calls it a miracle that I survived my strangulation and had the wits to warn Mycroft of Fraser's presence behind the door. I doubt that Mycroft even heard my whispered warning.

The greatest miracle in my own eyes is that Mycroft can stand the sight of me after what Rose put him through. But he at least always remembers that I am Rosalie, not Rose. The sadness is gradually fading from him when he uses her name. He has forgiven her; one day he may even forget her.

When he proposed to me, I had to broach the subject of my sister. "Don't marry *me* because you loved *her*," I charged.

He was shocked at the allegation. "The truth of the matter is, I had come to dislike Rose very thoroughly," he said. "She changed after her marriage. Fraser's way of carrying on influenced her for the worse, I fear. She hadn't developed that steadiness of character I find in you, darling. Oh, I was enchanted by her beauty, her charm when she was young. Egoism has a certain fascination in pretty women. She was a close neighbor and friend, and proximity led to love. It was considered a 'good match,' as folks say."

"You thought I was Rose the first time you kissed me, at the ball. You still loved her then."

"That kiss was born of frustration at her handing her fortune over to that rakehell husband. I never kissed Rose as I kissed you. She was still in her teens when she left the Manor. She had no experience of men then. The kiss was—I don't know—a punishment, perhaps. Curiosity to see how marriage had matured her. But from that moment on, I believe it was you I loved, Rosalie. There were enough differences that I sensed you had become a different woman—softer, more gentle. Rose wouldn't have cried.

"She never did cry when she complained of Fraser's indiscretions. I saw her from time to time in London after her marriage. She used to say she'd leave him, or kill him, but it was mere pique talking. I think she rather enjoyed the role of wronged wife. She didn't really care enough for him to be hurt—it was only anger. Then when she became pregnant, she seemed to settle down a little. We hoped the child might have a settling influence on Fraser as well."

"You were on thorns worrying about her after you rescued me, Mycroft," I reminded him.

"I felt responsible. As her guardian, I had botched the job, and as Sophie's nearest friend and neighbor, I had to do what I could to help her. Then too there was so much pity for Rose's plight, and pity is akin to love. Naturally there was some confusion in my mind—after all, you and Rose were identical twins. It is natural that if I loved one, I should love the other. But I love you more. Rose hadn't the fortitude and courage I came to love in you. You are what Rose could have been. You have her appearance, with all her aggravating tendencies burned away. Now that I have come to know you better, the similarities are blurred. It is the differences I love, Rosalie."

"I don't know if I am so different. If I had been the one adopted by the Comstocks—"

"But you weren't. An adult's character is forged in the crucible of life. Your life has made you a very different woman from Rose. Don't think me fool enough to marry a pretty face at my age, and after my experience."

"Not without a pretty fortune to match," I smiled pertly. "There is no saying Sophie will leave it all to me, you know. Rose's cousin already has Alvin Simson's fortune and the jewelry collection. It was kind of him to give me the sapphire peacock, was it not?"

Mycroft lifted a dissatisfied brow. "Give is hardly the correct word. He took the engagement ring I had given Rose in exchange, as you didn't want it."

The missing ring turned up in the bottom of one of Rose's trunks—a fine diamond ring tossed aside like a discarded trinket.

"But you were right," he admitted. "A new bride deserves a new ring."

He pulled me into his arms and kissed me. I had thought I truly loved Fraser, but I am convincing myself that was a mere fascination. Oh, there was the feverish excitement of first love, but it wasn't the solid, satisfying experience of kissing Mycroft. When I was with Fraser, I thought of moonbeams and champagne. With Mycroft, I think of a home and children and a life of love—but all of it sprinkled with stardust.

It will all come. I turned my gaze from the ocean

to the Manor, and saw Mycroft pacing across the field toward me. He comes before dark, because tonight Sophie has forbidden his presence in the house. It is bad luck to see the bride the night before the wedding, she says. It will be a small, family affair, performed in the garden at the Manor if the day is fine, and in the drawing room if not.

Mycroft is hurrying, running now. I hopped up and ran to meet my future.